SAVING
BONNIE

A ROB MADDEN NOVEL

The Hacienda of the Sola Mesa Cartel

Cynthia Croon

SAVING
BONNIE

THE THIRD ADVENTURE IN
THE AWARD-WINNING
ROB MADDEN SERIES

LT. COL. JOHN WITZEL
(USAF, RET.)

WILDCATTER
PUBLISHING
Omaha, Nebraska

Wildcatter Publishing books may be ordered from your favorite bookseller.
www.wildcatterpublishing.com

Omaha, Nebraska

Wildcatter Publishing
c/o CMI
4822 South 133rd Street, Suite 200
Omaha, NE 68137
wildcatter@conciergemarketing.com

Paperback ISBN: 978-0-9911029-6-9
Mobi ISBN: 978-0-9911029-7-6
EPUB ISBN: 978-0-9911029-8-3

Library of Congress Cataloging Number: 2021913439
Cataloging in Publication data on file with publisher.

Printed in the United States of America
10 9 8 7 6 5 4 3

"In my distress I called upon the Lord; to my God I called. From his temple he heard my voice, and my cry came to his ears."

2 SAMUEL 22:7 ESV

Dedicated to the unsung, courageous legions of undercover law enforcement officers who risk their lives daily while facing uncertain and dangerous situations to protect the communities they serve and love.

CHAPTER

1

"Oh God! Help me! Please, please, help me," Bonnie McCord screamed into the night as two Bolivian cartel members roughly manhandled her. They tied her arms to the metal frame of the now overused and bloodstained mattress.

"Carlos, your next," ordered Juan Castillo. "A little gift for you from this undercover DEA bitch we captured."

"No, No. Please no more." Hysterically crying out, McCord desperately tried to free herself from the ropes tying her down while Carlos dropped his worn blue jeans to the floor. His anticipation heightened as he got ready for his turn with the gringo DEA bitch.

"Hurry, Carlos. We have several others waiting their turn." Castillo left the room and closed the door. He paused to savor the pleasure of hearing the bitch's death-curdling screams of pain amid the obnoxious grunts of her drunken assailant.

As Castillo left the bedroom door and walked down the hall of the ranch house, he heard the definitive sound of violent slapping and returned to investigate.

"Carlos, I've warned you several times about slapping the bitch," Castillo yelled into the bedroom. "We have several other amigos waiting their turn and marks on her face and body could lose her appeal—and value."

"OK, jefe," a crazed and breathless Carlos responded before resuming his turn with the helpless McCord who was experiencing hell on earth.

Castillo just nodded and returned to his office down the hall from the bedroom where he made a quick phone call to the cartel's interrogation specialist and quasi doctor.

"Francis, this is Juan Castillo at the Ranch." He sat down in his brown leather chair. "We may have to administer more drugs to our patient here. Could you come over sometime today and take care of it?"

"Certainly, Juan Castillo," the doctor politely replied. "The same arrangements as before?"

"Yes, the sooner the better, our patient is looking at a long night ahead." Satisfied that the doctor was on his way, Castillo placed the phone down, opened a private desk drawer, and took out a premier Cuban cigar.

"Yes, another long night," he murmured to himself as he lit the Cuban. While enjoying his first puff of the cigar, he savored his luck in capturing a bona fide DEA agent from the United States. And more importantly, putting her to work. "I'll bet she never thought she would be working this hard in Bolivia." He laughed while rising from his chair and leaving the office. He made his way to the kitchen for his noon meal where he would await the arrival of the interrogator—Doctor Francis Valdez.

He reflected back to when the Sola Mesa Cartel had learned about the true identity of Patricia Turner, the local Georgia Fried Chicken franchise manager at the Santa Cruz Mall. Through their very reliable, well-paid sources, which included the US Embassy in Bolivia, they discovered that Patricia Turner was an undercover DEA Special Agent named Bonnie McCord.

Castillo called in his loyal office staff members to join him for lunch in his conference room. The staff arrived happily while he continued to enjoy his cigar.

Savoring its expensive qualities of smoke and aroma, he laughed and said to his staff, "the government of Bolivia has laws that DEA agents are prohibited from entering Bolivia. So, what do we do with her?"

"Should we arrest her?" A lieutenant smirked as Castillo pulled out the bottle of tequila, poured a shot, and passed the bottle around.

"Should we call the Federal Police and report a DEA agent in Bolivia?" another lieutenant piped up.

"Dios mío, we already have the off-duty local police guarding the hacienda here twenty-four hours a day." Laughing hysterically, another lieutenant poured himself a shot and put the cork back in the bottle.

"Stop the search...we have found her," Castillo mockingly cried out, laughing at their good fortune. He knew full well his hacienda was safe from any foreign intervention, both from the sky and the land. The gringos knew any type of rescue effort would result in a dead DEA agent and very bad relations with the government of Bolivia. "Too bad Uncle Sam...your bitch is safe here for now," he yelled. He raised his glass, and they all swallowed the light-yellow liquid. Drawing deeply, he then blew out the dense blue smoke. Castillo sat back, relishing his good luck and pondering if there were any other DEA agents roaming around Bolivia that could be of service to the cartel. His thoughts quickly were put on hold when he saw the security guard rush to the conference room door. Castillo came back to his senses and looked to see who the visitor was.

"Señor Castillo, I apologize for interrupting you, but you have a visitor at the door—Doctor Valdez," the on duty security guard announced to a now relaxed Castillo.

"Yes, yes, thank you, George." Castillo politely excused himself and made his way to the front door to greet his old friend and cartel associate.

"Mucho gusto, Doctor Valdez. Thank you for taking the time to help our little patient tonight," Castillo said while warmly shaking the doctor's hand.

"No es una gran cosa, amigo. What appears to be the problem, my old friend?" Valdez placed his large doctor's black professional case on the floor.

"Our little DEA bitch is more popular than I realized. Many of her new friends come at all hours to spend time with her and I believe it is truly wearing on her," Castillo sarcastically said. "Is there anything you can provide her to keep her going—for a while longer?"

"Escuchame, amigo, por favor." The doctor reverted to a medical professional caring for a patient. "Castillo, listen to me! I don't like the gringo bitch wandering around Bolivia, but if you want to keep her alive, you are going to have to let her have some rest and, for God's sake, feed her right.

"If you don't," the doctor warned, "she will be dead in a week. Do you understand me, my old friend?"

"OK," Castillo initially hesitated then nodded his head with approval. "As soon as Carlos gets through with her, I'll have you and Maria take care of her immediate needs. Yes, we'll give her some time to rest after Carlos." He knew she needed to be cared for if his friends were to continue taking advantage of this unexpected prize. "You are correct, Francis. She is a prize that needs to be ready for her duties here with the cartel.

"Maria! Maria, would you please come see me," Castillo yelled down the long hacienda hallway.

A few moments later, a well-kept, middle-aged Bolivian woman appeared wearing a brown utility dress and apron. She approached Castillo and bowed her head out of respect for her boss.

"Señor Castillo, at your orders," Maria obediently replied.

"Thank you, Maria, I would like you to accompany Doctor Valdez in looking after our gringo prisoner," Castillo ordered. "Please ensure she is properly fed and take care of her personal health needs—whatever you feel is required—OK, Maria?"

"Si, mi jefe, I understand," Maria answered in Spanish, knowing the time and place when appropriate to speak English of which she was fluent. She had proven herself a loyal housekeeper for many years and never questioned Castillo's orders or motives. She did what she was told and kept her mouth shut—no questions.

"Start preparing what you think you may need for this job and I'll call you in about thirty minutes. Understand?"

Maria nodded her head and began a slow walk down the main hallway to the kitchen's cabinets and supply room. Waiting until he saw her vanish down the hallway, Castillo sat back and picked up his cigar and clumsily poured himself another shot of tequila.

"You are blessed to have such a loyal and longtime housemaid looking after you and your family, my old friend." Valdez admired Maria for all that she probably had to put up with as a maid to a cartel boss.

"She is paid extremely well for her services," Castillo added with a devil's grin. "She also knows her family's safety depends on her loyalty."

Doctor Valdez knew only too well the price paid for extremely good services and the consequences to his family if he should stray. Those members who had "strayed" still gave him nightmares and pause for concern if he were ever to stray.

Castillo offered Francis a cigar. Minutes passed while they sat back smoking, savoring their glasses of tequila, and swapping stories from their glory days.

"Tell me, friend, how did you ever get your hands on this DEA agent?" Valdez only knew a few bits and pieces of rumors about her.

"Francis," Castillo suddenly rose from his chair and raised his hands in the air excitedly, "to tell you the absolute truth as unbelievable as it sounds—just an incredible amount of buena suerte—good luck.

"The top bosses at the various cartels really love this shit called Georgia Fried Chicken. So much so, that they literally will go to great lengths to get it. They even made a deal with the CEO of this chicken chain to get a restaurant here in Santa Cruz." Castillo tapped the ashes of his cigar into a gold-plated ashtray.

He continued, "And as you know, we looked at the whole organization to see if there was anything we could use against them to ensure they were in our pocket. Pablo discovered that

GFC was on the verge of bankruptcy and needed an influx of money fast, or it would go bankrupt and cease to exist."

Francis took another puff of his cigar, wanting to hear more.

"As you well know, our banks were overflowing with cash from the cartel's drug businesses and were actively trying to unload it anywhere legitimate. What is more legitimate than the All-American Georgia Fried Chicken?" Both men laughed while Castillo found another bottle of tequila and poured Valdez another glass.

"Please, please go on," Valdez almost begging to hear more of this intriguing mystery.

"Pablo traveled to their headquarters in Savannah, Georgia, and personally met with the CEO of Georgia Fried Chicken— some crazy, power hungry lesbian bitch named Doctor Elizabeth Alexander. It was obvious to Pablo that GFC was desperate to the point of making a deal with the devil to survive. Not only that, but the leaders of this chickenshit corporation were extremely well compensated and didn't want to let go of their lavish lifestyles— above all, the queen chicken bitch herself, Alexander."

"What the hell does this have to do with the DEA bitch you have staying with you?" asked Valdez anxious to hear more of the story.

"The deal was that the banks would keep GFC afloat and, in return, the chickenshits would open a new restaurant here in Bolivia at the Santa Cruz Mall—next to the Steel Rock Café. The sticking point was training and finding a gringo to come to Bolivia and run the joint while our cartel front men just showed up to make it look like it was being managed by Bolivians," Castillo explained. "You know the typical setup."

Valdez sat back intrigued by what he was hearing while blowing smoke and admiring his Cuban cigar. "OK, what does that have to do with the DEA agent you got locked up?"

"The stupid shits at GFC recruited and trained what appeared to be a very capable candidate to run the franchise here, except for one gigantic problem." Castillo poured himself another shot and offered Valdez another, but he refused as he needed to attend to a patient soon.

"What was the problem, old friend?" Valdez asked.

"The fuckin' management candidate we got was an undercover DEA agent," Castillo yelled. "A fuckin' DEA agent—Fuck, how does that happen?" A now drunk Castillo yelled down the hallway where the agent was being held and tortured, "Come on bitch, tell us how that happened?"

"How did it happen?" An amazed and stunned Valdez put his cigar down and quickly rose to his feet, shaking his head and staring at Castillo in disbelief.

"I understand that this queen of chicken Alexander had a sixth sense that something was not right with McCord and ordered more investigations into her past," Castillo now calmer continued. "According to Alexander, she received an anonymous call from someone in the Fed who revealed that McCord was working undercover on an assignment to Bolivia. Later, the GFC paid operative in the government found that McCord was indeed undercover in Bolivia."

"My God," a shocked Valdez responded, "probably a jilted lover ratted on her."

"If Alexander hadn't contacted us, we would have never known she was a DEA plant," Castillo admitted. "We believe Alexander panicked, thinking that if we took care of the problem here, it would never reach her in Savannah."

"What a stupid bitch," Valdez slapped his palm on the table. "If she would have kept her mouth shut, no one would have ever known."

"However, for her career and safety, it was important to keep good relations with the banks and the cartel. Otherwise, GFC was sure to go bankrupt," Castillo said. "There is no doubt she panicked."

"We have a team traveling up from Miami now to ensure Alexander never talks to anyone about the DEA, Bolivia banks, cartels—nothing." Castillo nodded his head as if it was a done deal already. "We're counting on our team to take care of business prior to the Feds getting wind that McCord's cover is blown.

"When we interrogated her a few days ago, thanks to the crazy drugs you gave her," Castillo nodded his approval at Valdez, "she provided us so much valuable information about the DEA operations here that we felt like we should have given her a medal. Instead, we are all going to fuck the little bitch for doing such a good job."

"She also provided us the special communications codes that agents use to relay their status in country." Castillo smiled. "And we have been relaying back that everything is just fine in Bolivia and everyone is having a good time frying chicken."

Loud laughter could be heard throughout the hacienda as both Castillo and Valdez reminisced on their good fortune. The final screams of torture and pain came from McCord's holding room as Carlos finished his turn with her.

"Francis, how about you and I make a house call on Special Agent Bonnie McCord and take care of her health needs," Castillo directed. The men rose and put out their cigars. The doctor grabbed his bag and they headed for McCord's room, passing a sweating and clumsily dressed Carlos just leaving the hacienda through the servant's entrance.

"Maria, please meet me in the guest bedroom with all of the supplies we discussed," ordered Castillo over a small intercom system. Maria acknowledged his call and hurriedly rolled the basket of supplies to the bedroom holding McCord.

Unlocking and entering the bedroom, both Castillo and Francis were taken aback by the foul smell and odor in the room. It resembled that of a soccer team's locker room after a tough game.

A small lamp faintly illuminated the room. A very thin woman clutched a blanket over her bare body. Crying hysterically, she thought the two men were more cartel members waiting their turn with her. "Please, please, no more, no more."

"Agent McCord, I'm Doctor Valdez. We met when you arrived here—do you remember me?" Valdez took a seat on the stained, overused mattress and opened his doctor's bag.

"Doctor, help me for God's sake." McCord grabbed his arm tightly, desperation in her eyes. "What do you want from me?"

Castillo stood in the corner of the room watching. He almost felt sorry for her plight, but knew full well, she was in Bolivia to cause problems for the cartel—life and death problems. Anyway, he had favors to pay back to his cartel friends and associates. McCord was his prize.

"Señor Castillo," Maria said while knocking a few times on the bedroom door.

"Yes, Maria, please come in," Castillo calmly said as he unlocked the door and helped her with the cart. It was full of assorted clothes and female necessities, including a tray of leftover food from the kitchen. Valdez turned away momentarily from administering various drugs to McCord and was somewhat relieved to see Maria's cart and what was in it. The supplies would definitely help McCord's quality of life and usefulness to the cartel until her end came.

"Maria, when Agent McCord is available and has no visitors scheduled, I want you to care for her as you see needed." Castillo turned his attention to the bed. "Doctor Valdez are you finished with your patient?"

Getting up from McCord's bedside, Valdez stared for a moment at the sad and ugly sight of what once was a very beautiful woman. While reorganizing his doctor's bag, he pulled out a couple of drug bottles and syringes and prepared additional injections for her overstressed state.

"Por favor, Castillo. I recommend you give her time to rest between sessions," the doctor again advised. "If you don't, she will be dead within a week regardless of what care you provide her now."

"Bien, bien!" Castillo replied. "Maria, please care for our DEA agent now and do whatever you feel necessary—showers, clothes—whatever!"

"Si, señor," Maria answered. "Would it be possible to remove the ropes tying her down on the bed so I can care for her?"

"Of course, Maria," Castillo smiled. "She'll have some busy days this week. Get her cleaned up and ready."

The ropes and cloth towels restraining McCord were gently removed. She had numerous bruises and bleeding blisters.

Showing no emotion, Maria methodically began cleaning the wounds with alcohol and warm soapy water. After caring for the bruises, she moved onto McCord's filthy body, which was covered with men's body fluids and blood. Maria had cared for several women and men that were "special guests" of the cartel here at the hacienda. Resembling a hospice nurse caring and cleaning a patient prior to their final passing, Maria, in a compassionate way, attempted to do what she could for this unfortunate gringo.

"Thank you, Maria, I am going to walk Doctor Valdez to the door." Castillo watched her dedication in caring for the unfortunate house guest. Turning to the doctor, he said, "We'll take your advice and take better care of McCord until her time and usefulness is no more. Thank you, my trusted friend, for all your exceptional service and skills to the cartel."

"We need to talk again, my old friend," Valdez said. "I am anxious to hear how the interrogation went with your DEA agent."

"On your next visit, we'll discuss it further." Castillo sighed and placed a wad of one-hundred-dollar bills in the doctor's hand. "She literally spilled her guts about everything we requested and then some. Those drugs you gave her opened her up like a songbird. Interestingly, she kept calling for some hombre named Rob Madden." Castillo paused to take a draw of his cigar. "Out of her mind, she screamed that Rob Madden would come soon to get her out of there."

"Who is Rob Madden?" Francis asked.

"Probably some stud she saw on one of those American soap operas," Castillo replied and stopped for a moment in thought. "Francis, just curious, see what you can find out about this gringo named Madden."

"Oh, by the way, your little gringo bitch was pregnant," Valdez indifferently mentioned.

CHAPTER

2

Metropolitan Gas service trucks drove through the private security entry gate at the private Highland Lake Estates in Savannah, Georgia, at 2:00 AM. Slowly driving up to a large, guarded estate at 2356 Country Club Drive, the lead truck identified the house belonging to Dr. Elizabeth Alexander.

The trucks stopped in her driveway and men wearing Metropolitan Gas overalls exited, looking as if they were on a routine call. They stopped at the front door to look at their work orders on a clipboard, ensuring they had the correct address. At the same time, another party of three men emerged from the truck in black military SWAT (Special Weapons and Tactics) clothing. They quickly made their way to the extensive back patio and pool area and immediately found their way to the back entrance.

Without a sound, the trio of black-clad easily opened the door and disabled all three of the state-of-the-art security locks. While the fake gas service men waited on the front entrance for the owner to come to the door, the SWAT members followed the floorplan of the house to the upstairs master bedroom.

Quietly and slowly, the SWAT team entered the spacious bedroom of Alexander. Their flashlights lit up the darkened room. Her female companion lay next to her in an opulent king-sized bed with a huge white canopy covering. For a moment, the men eyed the extravagant bedroom, knowing her days of extravagance were over. The lead SWAT member looked at his two partners and nodded. The two men immediately took their positions near the bedroom door.

"Doctor Alexander, good morning, ma'am," Special Agent Joe Dejka softly spoke, prepared to cover her mouth with a muzzle if she attempted to scream. The other team members went to the side of her companion and injected a strong drug that immediately left her unconscious.

Alexander was confused and dazed as the SWAT team chief firmly held his hand over her mouth and calmly and softly said, "Doctor Alexander, we are not here to hurt you or your companion."

She glanced furtively to the side where her companion lay. An anguished moan escaped.

"We gave her a very strong sedative and she is sleeping very comfortably."

Alexander didn't buy it, but her screams for help were quickly muffled with a warning. "Doctor Alexander, if you continue, we will also give you a sedative, or we can have a nice little chat right here." The team chief kept his voice level. "We are not here to rob or hurt you. We just need some information. Do you understand?"

Frightened and shocked, Alexander nodded her head in assent. The team chief uncovered her mouth while she continued her heavy breathing and crying. Again, Dejka assured her they were not there to harm her. They just wanted some information.

"Now, Doctor Alexander," the team chief calmly directed, "please put a bathrobe on and go down to the front door. Tell the gentlemen from the gas company that you smelled gas in the house and want them to check it out. Put on the front porch lights and ensure the neighbors see you at the door allowing them in. If you fail to follow my instructions, you and your companion will be hurt badly. Do you understand?"

The CEO nodded vigorously.

"If you panic and scream for help, you will only make matters worse for you, your friend, and Georgia Fried Chicken."

Regaining her composure, she put on a bathrobe and nervously lit a cigarette. "Does this have anything to do with Patricia Turner?"

The SWAT team leader said nothing as he escorted her to the front door. She disabled the locks, turned on the front porch lights, and opened the door to the service crew from the gas company.

"Doctor Alexander, it would not look well if you called the gas company for a possible gas leak while you smoked a cigarette," Agent Dejka commented. She immediately put the cigarette out with the sole of her slippers on what appeared to be an expensive polished, wooden floor.

"Good morning, Doctor Alexander. Sorry to bother you at this hour," the lead service man said. "We got a report from you about a suspected gas leak. May we can come in and check it out?"

"Of course, come in." A terrified Alexander attempted to act as calm as possible. She already regretted putting out her cigarette.

"I highly recommend you do not light anymore cigarettes until we find the cause of your gas leak," the lead service man ordered.

Lights began to come on in the nearby luxury mansions. Curious neighbors walked out to see what was going on. One curious and sleepy neighbor ventured out with a flashlight and head for the gas trucks. Approaching one, the man shined his flashlight at the two men in gas company overalls sitting inside. One man got out of the truck with an official-looking service clipboard.

"Hey, what's going on here?" the neighbor sleepily asked while pointing his flashlight at the man approaching him.

"Good morning, sir. Sorry about the disruption, but we got a call about a gas leak at this house," the gas man answered, agitated and annoyed for having a service call in the middle of the night. "We should be out of here soon. Here is my card in case you or any other neighbor of yours suspects a gas leak. We put service and safety first."

"OK," yawned the neighbor. He slipped the card in his pocket and headed back to his house.

The man got back into the truck. His companion smiled and said, "You should get some sort of acting award for that performance."

Satisfied it was a routine check, the neighbors' lights went out, one by one.

The men dressed in Metropolitan Gas Company uniforms immediately began thoroughly searching and collecting files, computers, and anything that might link Doctor Alexander and GFC to the Sola Mesa Cartel. Meanwhile, the SWAT team members escorted Alexander down the stairs to the basement. The game room and sports bar would rival a private, exclusive club. Strategically setting up video recording equipment, the team prepared for a quick initial interrogation of the CEO.

Alexander sunk into a chair at the opulent poker table. Her fingers shook as she tried to light a cigarette from a pack conveniently set before her. Tears streamed down her cheeks.

"Please, please hear me out," she begged, "I had nothing to do with the disappearance of Patricia Turner. I swear, I swear!" Placing her face in her hands, she sobbed loudly.

The team members ignored her pleas. Agent Dejka approached Alexander and slowly sat next to her, while the recording and video began.

"Doctor Alexander, we do not have much time so listen to me very carefully. Your life depends on it. Do you understand?" Dejka calmly advised her.

Inhaling the last drag from her cigarette, her hands shook violently while nodding her head that she understood.

"I would like to talk with my attorney before we go any further," Alexander demanded, slowly settling down and attempting to regain her composure.

"In less than four hours, an assassin team, contracted by the Sola Mesa Cartel, will be arriving here to kill you, your friend, and gather all of your files, computers, and any other documents in this house that link you to the cartel or the banks in Bolivia," he warned her. "So, I suspect you would rather work with us, or you can stay here and welcome the Sola Mesa team. There really are no other options for you."

Crying profusely, she pulled a cigarette out of the pack.

"You're more valuable to us alive than dead." Dejka helped light the cigarette for her, since her hands were shaking uncontrollably. He kept his voice calm. "We are going to move you to one of our safe houses outside the Savannah area where you will stay for an indefinite period of time. Other agents will interrogate you during your stay. You will need to explain your relationship with the banks in Bolivia and the Sola Mesa Cartel. You will provide contact information on all of your associates. Do you understand me, Doctor Alexander?"

Alexander closed her eyes in resignation.

Dejka nodded to the other federal agents monitoring the short, but required, interrogation. They shut off the lights and camera and began packing them in their carrying cases.

While the agents were preparing to take the equipment upstairs, a woman appeared at the bottom of the steps dressed in one of Alexander's nightgowns. No one paid any attention to the woman except Alexander.

"My God, who is that woman and why is she wearing my clothes?" a startled and terrified Alexander screamed.

"Roberta, would you like to meet Doctor Alexander?" Dejka asked the newly arrived woman.

Roberta just stared at the pathetic Georgia Fried Chicken CEO with a cold and frightening look. She had begun preparing herself for her assignment earlier that morning. It had been easy work rummaging through the CEO's oversized walk-in closet. Unlike the sobbing woman in front of her, Roberta had various weapons hidden under the nightgown.

"Roberta came along with the team this morning to imitate you for the benefit of your curious neighbors and the cartel assassination team. They are on their way here at this moment." Dejka checked his watch. "They should be here in a couple of hours."

"Assassination team? What assassination team?" Alexander begged to know while trying to find her cigarette case that had dropped to the floor.

Dejka realized that Alexander had forgotten about the cartel's team with everything else going on.

"In approximately two hours, a team of assassins from Miami are scheduled to be at this house with two objectives. First, they will collect all of your files, computers, and items in your safes. Then they will torture you to ensure you never have the opportunity to tell the Feds or DEA anything about your relationship with the Bolivian banks and cartels." Dejka pointed to Roberta. "However, Roberta will take your place here and the assassins will assume that she is actually you. What a surprise they will be in for." He chuckled softly.

Alexander looked at him incredulously.

"You see, Roberta is a special kind of contractor. Her specialty is appearing like criminals, like you. She will look and act like you, giving them a false sense that it will be an easy hit. Except, she will seek to capture and, if necessary, kill the hired guns.

"You are lookalikes…are you not?" Dejka said jokingly.

Roberta ignored the comments as she strapped on another 9mm Beretta pistol and secured the sharpened commando knife to her lower legs—all covered by the nightgown.

Alexander trembled with fear as she stared at Roberta, attempting to completely understand her purpose that morning, but the CEO did not need to know.

"When we depart here in a few minutes, Roberta will stay behind, like a welcoming committee for our friends from Miami." Dejka grinned.

"OK, Joe. I'm ready. You can take off now. I'll take care of the rest." Roberta completed her inventory of her personal armory and mentally catalogued her stash of weapons in the house.

"Roberta, our contract calls for one to remain alive," Dejka sternly reminded her, recalling a few operations where she had killed all the assassins in her zeal.

"Listen to me, you little prick. You don't have to remind me of shit. You'll get your live one," Roberta harshly replied. "Now, get the fuck out of here so I can earn some money."

"OK, OK, Roberta. We are out of here. See you at the safe house," Dejka said, attempting to please her.

"Hey, boss," one of the other agents called from the stairs. "We have everything we need in the truck. You about ready to go?"

"Thanks, Fred. Let's go ahead and get Doctor Alexander ready for her little trip to the house," Dejka said. "Go ahead and put her in her work overalls."

"Work overalls…you expect me to be seen in public in work overalls!" Alexander unexpectedly demanded, forgetting for a brief moment her precarious situation.

"You are to put them on now, or I'll leave you here for the assassination team." Dejka held out a Metropolitan Gas Company outfit.

Alexander looked at herself in the extravagant main entryway mirror for a moment and snapped back to the reality of the situation she was in. It was difficult for her to put aside the high-powered executive persona. Placing aside her nightgown on a coffee table, she reluctantly tugged on the overalls and put on the black baseball cap to hide her hair.

Dejka gathered his team inside the house, made a quick head count, and confirmed they had confiscated every file, document, and personal computer.

"Doctor Alexander, where are your safes?" Dejka asked politely. "We know you have a safe in this house, and we need to open it now."

"I don't know what you are…" Alexander could not finish her sentence.

Whack! Roberta slapped Alexander in the face with such force she fell on the floor.

On the ground sobbing and crying in a fetal position, she provided the locations to two vaulted safes in the house. Another confrontation with Roberta provided the combinations and security features.

Her face white, Alexander cringed as she realized the contents of her personal vaults definitely linked her to various criminal organizations. More damaging to her reputation and family were associations with many various unscrupulous activities that Georgia Fried Chicken had participated in with her as CEO.

"Agent Dejka, sir. We've bagged everything from the vault." An agent handed Dejka a clipboard. "Checklist complete, sir."

Grabbing the clipboard, Dejka scanned the list before leading his team out the lighted front door to the two waiting trucks. At the front door, Roberta stood in her borrowed nightgown and wig, waiving to the gas crew and thanking them for the early morning service call. Nosey neighbors watching the staged scene would assume Alexander was at the front door; however, they would never see the CEO again. Both gas company trucks drove silently down Country Club Drive heading out of the gated community.

Roberta watched the trucks depart before nonchalantly returning inside the house. There she began her preparation for the Miami visitors. With a sadistic grin, she tenderly sharpened her commando hand knife. She was getting excited about the assassin's arrival.

CHAPTER

3

"Head to the lot," Dejka ordered over the radio. The two vans headed southbound on the US 516 Loop where they entered the entry checkpoint for Hunter Army Airfield.

The military sergeant on duty viewed the suspicious vans approaching the well-lit and secure vehicle entry checkpoint. He immediately ran out of his small guard shack and frantically waved the vehicles to stop. Others on duty quickly followed the sergeants' actions and readied their weapons for a possible encounter with the strangers in the dark early morning.

"Halt!" shouted the sergeant as he positioned himself in front of the path of the vans.

Approaching the halted vans twenty yards from the entry checkpoint with a flashlight, the sergeant readied his M4 Carbine. His other team members were either on the telephone reporting a possible incident or at the gate kneeling in a firing position.

"You in the van, exit the vehicle and place your hands on the hood of the vehicle—NOW!" The sergeant readied his weapon for any possible reaction.

With numerous lights illuminating and pointing at the van, Dejka slowly got out of the van, placed his hands on the hood of the vehicle, and awaited further instructions. Being a seasoned FBI agent, he had been through this drill hundreds of times without incident.

"OK, mister, please slowly pull out your ID and hand it to me." The sergeant lowered his weapon to inspect the agent's badge and credentials. On guard and taking precautions, the sergeant followed his orders by asking what the nature of his business was on the post. Without going into detail, Dejka asked the sergeant to call his commanding officer, Lieutenant Colonel Erickson, for authorization to allow them access to the post.

"Please wait here, sir," the sergeant requested as the sound of radios crackled to life in the early morning. After a short conversation with his commanding officer, the sergeant returned and professionally thanked Dejka for his patience.

"Good job, sergeant. We are going to make our way to the government impoundment lot over by the transportation company—we are expected there." Thanking the sergeant, Dejka returned to the van where they proceeded to the post impoundment lot. The two vans were waved into the facility surrounded by barbwire, where they stopped. An Army officer came out of a small utility shed, walked up to the first van, and pointed a flashlight inside the open driver's side window.

"Are you Dejka with the FBI?" the officer asked while reviewing a paper on his clipboard and asking to see Dejka's badge and credentials.

"Yes, captain. I am Special Agent Dejka. Is everything ready?"

"Yes, sir. I have been ordered to supply you with two black SUVs with tinted windows and standard Georgia license plates—they are sitting over there with the keys in the ignition." The captain pointed to the parked vehicles and asked Dejka to sign various government release forms. He had been through this drill many times.

"Thanks, captain. We'll take it from here," Dejka said while the occupants of the two vans went to a nearby storage shed and took off their gas company overalls or black commando uniforms. Doctor Alexander put on a plain, cloth jumpsuit. All of their working clothes were stuffed in a military-style duffel bag and placed in the back cargo compartments of the first SUV.

"Agent Wright, please make sure Doctor Alexander is comfortable on your trip to the resort," Dejka sarcastically commented.

"Will do, boss," Wright replied. He allowed Alexander one last cigarette before she climbed into the SUV.

"Everyone ready?" Dejka asked over the radio with an affirmative reply from all vehicles. "Then let's go to the resort."

CHAPTER

4

While the two SUVs headed to the resort in Jesup, Georgia, Roberta Potter prepared to confront the three assassins contracted to kill Alexander. What made this job unique and challenging for Potter was that she had to take one of the assassins alive. In her mind, it was easier and quicker just to kill all three in the house and get the hell out of there, but now she'd be burdened with a lone survivor. She put her mind at ease by weighing the fact that a live assassin paid significantly more than a dead one. The CIA front company she worked as a contractor for literally paid for her services and had nothing to do with her taskings and assignments. The front company merely compensated her as directed by the CIA's case officers.

Ten minutes flashed on her smartphone in a text message from Dejka. Relieved to have received confirmation of the assassins impending arrival, Roberta double-checked the cache of weapons strapped to her body under a Neiman Marcus nightgown. She mentally reviewed the assassin's expected path of entrance, starting with disabling the alarm system that she had put back into operation after the team had left. The leader and another assassin would climb the long stairway up to the main bedroom and immediately gag her with duct tape. They'd torture her for the location of all her personal files, computers, and safes. Once they were convinced they had everything, they'd shoot Alexander in the back of the head with a semi-automatic 9mm pistol. The state-of-the art silencer would muffle the shots.

Usually, the third, and usually the most inexperienced member of the assassin team, stood watch at the bottom of the stairway to act as a lookout.

"Alright, so who is going to live?" Roberta mumbled to herself. She moved upstairs to one of the four guest bedrooms near the main bedroom and waited. The open door gave her a clear view of anyone coming or going. Reaching into her tool bag, she pulled out night-vision googles and adjusted them to her face. She was ready.

The sounds of the back door unlocking and the disabling of the house security system were unmistakable to Roberta. Their slow, nearly silent movements indicated their level of skill. No doubt they'd also be wearing bulletproof vests and night-vision goggles.

As the tense moments passed, adrenaline rushed through her veins. She took a couple of deep breaths and steadied her Heckler & Koch MP5 submachine gun with silencer.

Coming up the stairs, she could make out two individuals dressed in black overalls, black watch caps, and armed with what appeared to be standard M4 Carbines with extended silencers attached to the end of the barrel. They came at a quiet, leisurely pace with pistols by their sides not expecting any problems.

The two assassins were inches away from opening Alexander's bedroom door. Roberta readied the laser-sighted scope attached to the top of the MP5, not yet ready to actuate the telltale red beam of the laser.

The master bedroom door opened. She heard the unmistakable thuds of muffled pistol shots and saw the faint muzzle flashes of the two assailants firing into the opulent king-size bed. Pillows had been placed under the covers of the bed to make the appearance of Alexander and a lover sleeping together. After a few shots, they confidently approached the bed and pulled back the covers to find bullet-ridden stuffed pillows.

"Ah, shit!" Realizing they had been set up, the duo immediately ran out of the bedroom and confronted who they thought was Alexander pointing a rifle at them. She instantly fired a few bursts into the two assailants then left their twitching, bloody bodies where they fell. She jumped over them and raced down the stairway toward the third assassin—the one she had to take alive.

Hearing and suspecting his two team members were shot, the living assassin immediately drew his pistol and activated his night googles. To his surprise, a figure was racing down the stairs toward him. He fired wildly up the staircase, uncertain if his shots hit the mark. Confused and nervous, he frantically searched the stairs for the ghost of a woman but found nothing. One moment she was visible, and the next, there was no sign of her. Scared and breathing heavily, the assailant panicked and raced toward the back entrance where they had entered. He had to escape.

When the firing had commenced, Roberta had jumped over the railing and made a safe landing on a nearby sofa. She had purposely positioned the sofa earlier expecting such a reception by the lone assassin. The assailant's 9mm bullets had hit her bulletproof vest, but she quickly determined her injuries were minor.

Racing off the sofa, she found him breathing heavy and running for the back door. Lunging like a wild animal after its prey, Roberta jumped on the man, throwing them both to the oak floor. A life-or-death struggle ensued. The lone assassin came to his senses, clinched Roberta's knife-wielding hand, and slammed it to the floor. She released her grip and the knife slid away. Caught off guard, Roberta tried in vain to escape his grip by rolling them both over while he placed her in a wrestler's head scissors hold. She gasped for air while still trying to free herself and attempting to knock him in the groin area with no luck. The assailant knew it would not be long before she would be dead. He intensified his hold.

"You stupid bitch," the assassin said through heaving breaths. "You are going to pay for what you did to my team and, more importantly, to the Sola Mesa Cartel." He was enjoying seeing the last breaths of Doctor Elizabeth Alexander. The cartel would pay him handsomely.

"Die, you fucking bitch. Die!" he excitedly yelled.

With his legs around Roberta's neck gripping tighter every second, he used a free hand to force his fingers into her eyes. He relished causing her additional pain and agony.

Frantically struggling to free herself from the assassin's stranglehold, she used her last ounce of energy to grab her switchblade knife from the belt beneath her nightgown, now bunched around her hips. Without hesitation, she pressed the button to free the blade. Lightning quick, she forced the blade into the upper part of his knee. Her death grip on the handle pushed the blade deep beneath the kneecap, inflicting a tremendous amount of pain.

"Ahhhhhhhhh, mother of God!" screamed the assassin as he instinctively released his hold on her neck. The agonizing pain radiated out of his knee, causing him to forget about Roberta. He attempted to rise from the floor with the switchblade stuck in his kneecap.

Roberta sucked in deep breaths and ignored the pain in her throat caused by his death grip. Looking up in a daze, she saw the knife sticking out of his kneecap. Instinctively, she pushed the blade deeper and twisted.

"Sweet mother of God, please help me," he cried out, still attempting to stand on his good leg and escape out the door. Bleeding profusely from his wound, he gave up on standing and struggled to crawl away. Unfortunately for him, Roberta found her pin injector and stuck it into his lower leg. The strong dose of anesthesia could put a horse to sleep in seconds. The assassin screamed his last before passing out from the effects of the drug.

Leaning against the hallway wall, she took a moment to regain her senses and get air back into her lungs. Trembling, she surveyed the bloody scene and her close encounter with death. She said a short prayer—thankful for her salvation and deliverance. She always suspected God was on her side, but this truly was the ultimate test of faith.

"Thy will be done," she murmured as she crawled over to the body of the sleeping assassin and placed the plastic zip-tie handcuffs around his wrists. With bruised and strained muscles, she worked to get the blood-soaked nightgown off of her aching body. She found her personal gym bag a few feet away and retrieved her working jeans and blue denim shirt. Now able to stand, she found her way to the downstairs bathroom where she washed and changed clothes. For a moment, she looked at herself in the mirror and saw the many bruises and cuts on her face. Leaving the bathroom, she returned to the sleeping prey.

"When you come to, asshole," Roberta spoke to the sleeping assassin, "you'll believe it was Doctor Elizabeth Alexander knocking the crap out of you—exactly as we planned." She quickly tied a tourniquet above his left knee to limit the bleeding. The downstairs bathroom had several bath towels she used to wrap around his wound. She retrieved her knife, cleaned it, and placed it back in its guard. Thank God it had been there when she needed it.

Roberta was also responsible for searching the bodies for anything that would link them to who contracted them to have Alexander killed. The living assassin only had a cell phone worth any value. Next, she retrieved her prepositioned forensic medical utility bag and small digital camera. She drew the living assassin's blood, took his fingerprints, and snapped his picture.

After limping upstairs, Roberta methodically catalogued the other two assassins. Wading through the pools of blood, she took off the black ski masks of the dead assassins. She was surprised to discover an attractive woman with long brown hair. Taking a minute, she just stared at the pleasant face, attempting to understand the logic of sending a woman on their contract to kill Doctor Alexander. Bending over the bullet-riddled body, she gently patted her face and brown hair, reflecting on what directed her to such an ugly calling. The vision of this woman would linger in Roberta's mind for the days to come. But then again, Roberta pondered what drove her to this "ugly calling?" "Greed and money," she murmured to herself calmly, just like her.

Her smartphone buzzed, bringing her back to her senses. Dejka requested a status report.

"Work accomplished...will have package by the trash pickup...will require attention," Roberta texted. She relayed that the job was complete, the lone survivor would be in a breathable body bag outside near the home's trash collection area, and the survivor required immediate medical care. Roberta knew she would be penalized for providing "damaged goods."

"Back to work," she mumbled to herself. She dragged the larger body from the upper staircase area to the side of Alexander's extravagant, antique king bed. Using every bit of her strength, she hoisted the man's body onto the bed and laid him on his back. Covered with the man's blood and remains of body organs, she retrieved the woman assassin and dragged her into the bedroom also. Hauling the lighter woman onto the bed, she placed her next to the man—side by side. Searching the bodies one last time, she discovered a tattoo of a military parachute badge with one star on the top of the badge on the female assassin's right shoulder. The tattoo signified she had made a combat parachute jump. Startled at this discovery, Roberta was intrigued about who this woman was. She reexamined the body looking for more clues to her background but with no luck.

The forensic team would find her true identity and that of the others. Roberta went back to work arranging the dead bodies on the bed. The man was left on his back, but she had struggled to move the dead woman's body on top of his. She wanted to give the appearance that they were making love. Stepping back, Roberta surveyed the bedroom scene and was satisfied all was in order.

"One last fuck for you, Airborne. Enjoy it," Roberta said as she left the bedroom.

Quickly traveling down the blood-soaked stairway, she went back to the living room where her captive was still unconscious. Roberta reexamined the live assassin and removed the blood-soaked towels and momentarily loosened the tourniquet to allow some blood to flow in the lower leg. Applying more military body packages, she configured a tighter compression to his wound. Figuring he would be at an agency medical facility within a couple of hours, she readied the transferable body bag at the feet of the assailant and slowly started the strenuous task of placing him in the bag for transport. Satisfied he was securely settled, she tied up the bag with support belts and pulled him across the blood-splattered kitchen floor to the back utility door. The outside garbage collection area was adjacent to the four-car garage. Still dark, the sun was just coming up. Roberta quickly pulled the body bag out the door and laid it next to the garbage containers. The body bag and assailant would be picked up soon.

Rushing upstairs, she went into Alexander's huge closet. It resembled a floor at a high-end exclusive department store. Hurriedly undressing and throwing her bloody clothes in a plastic bag, Roberta went to the bathroom and took a quick shower. After drying herself off, fixing her hair, and applying cosmetics, Potter searched for an appropriate outfit to wear to make her escape. She'd once again disguise herself as Alexander.

"OK, these black slacks and this red blouse will do nicely." She put them on and smiled. "My gosh, Elizabeth, how lucky we are to be the same size."

Now dressed, she checked herself in the bathroom mirror and made a few final adjustments to her wig. Satisfied she could pass herself off as Alexander, Roberta made her way to the kitchen where she found several sets of car keys hanging from a key rack near a small table.

She chose the keys to a Mercedes and went out through the door to the garage. Four pristine foreign cars greeted her when she flipped on the light. Too bad Alexander wouldn't be around to enjoy them, but Roberta would enjoy the black Mercedes coupe.

Returning inside to grab her utility bags, garbage containers, and camera, Roberta had one last task to complete before she could depart the house—set the natural gas igniter near the hot water heater in the basement. The specialized and custom-made igniter was a product of the CIA's ingenious clandestine Special Support Division. Properly used by an experienced operator, the igniter could be connected to the main gas line where it hooked to the water heater. After attaching the igniter, the operator would simply set the small digital timer. The igniter would activate when the timer went off, resulting in a catastrophic gas fire. In the history of the igniter, it had never been detected as the cause of the fire. Shoddy installation or an act of God usually took the blame.

In the basement, she set the igniter timer for fifteen minutes then climbed the stairs, picked up her canvas utility bag, and made a beeline for the garage. Punching the Mercedes remote lock/unlock switch, the car lights illuminated and the trunk popped open. Placing a few plastic bags of clothes and her canvas bag in the trunk, she closed it, opened the driver's door, and slid onto the luxurious leather seat. For a short moment, she admired the styling and extravagant interior, thinking about how nice it would be to leave Savannah in this car.

After double-checking her disguise, she opened the garage door and slowly backed the Mercedes out. The sun was just about to come up. Potter could sense a few neighbors watching her leave, mimicking Alexander's daily routine. Once on the street, she headed out of the gated community and saw a Southern Disposal Company truck going the opposite direction. It pulled into the Alexander's driveway. Stopping momentarily to watch in her rearview mirror, she saw two men jump out of the truck in their work coveralls. They headed for the back of the house to the trash area. Roberta was relieved to see the men return carrying what appeared to be the body bag with the live assassin. Little did the neighbors know that morning specially hired agency contractors handsomely paid a security guard at the Southern Disposal motor pool for the use of the truck for approximately a couple of hours.

Satisfied her captive had been picked up, she put the Mercedes in drive and headed toward the interstate. She was going to be well compensated.

"Hello, 911. There was a huge explosion and fire at 2356 Country Club Drive," a neighbor over the phone reported to the Savannah emergency dispatcher.

"Fire and explosion at 2356 Country Club Drive, is that correct?" the dispatcher repeated.

"My God, please hurry before it spreads to the rest of the neighborhood." Hysteria entered the neighbor's voice as the inferno grew a few yards away.

Scrambling to punch the correct radio frequencies on her computerized control panel, the dispatcher directed emergency services to the fire department. She kept the neighbor on the phone to ensure updates and communications continuity. Both the fire and police department had received notification of the fire from the ADT security surveillance call center and were en route.

"Sir, do you see any casualties or people requiring medical care," asked the dispatcher.

"No, I don't see anyone outside the home." The neighbor's voice shook slightly. "It would be impossible for anyone to survive inside the house…impossible!"

"Thank you, sir. Emergency services are on their way. Please stay on the line until they arrive," requested the dispatcher.

Days following the fire, the Savannah Fire Department's Fire Investigation Team began their investigation into the fire at the home of Doctor Elizabeth Alexander. They did not detect the clandestine fire igniter Roberta Potter had installed. According to the official report, the fire was caused by a crack in the internal water heater automated gas control system—an act of God.

Investigators continued to rummage through the black, smoldering house debris searching for any human remains. Scanning with his flashlight through the haze-filled rooms on the second floor, Investigator Wilson Lee turned his light into the master bedroom. Two charred remains appeared to be in some sort of sex act on the burned out remains of a brass king-size bed.

"Hey Phil." Lee got the attention of his partner and pointed to the rather bizarre sight on the bed. "Does that look like what I think it is?"

Getting closer to the two bodies, one on top of the other, they now began a closer look at what appeared to be a couple making love during the fire. However, it was not the couple having sex during the fire that got their attention, but what they were wearing.

"Chief, this is Lee on the second floor in the master bedroom," Lee said into his radio.

"Yeah, go ahead, Lee. What have you got?" the on-scene battalion chief asked.

"Sir, we are going to need the forensic people up here. We have two human remains," Lee announced over the radio.

"OK, Lee," the chief replied. "I'm on my way up."

While waiting for the chief, both investigators were surprised that with the security and fire system sounding out a warning alarm throughout the house that the couple continued their lovemaking.

"Hey Lee, check this out." His partner Phil pointed with his flashlight to the two charred bodies. "It appears both were wearing bulletproof vests."

Lee drew closer and confirmed what his partner had observed—both bodies were definitely wearing bulletproof vests. "Holy shit, Phil. What kind of strange kinky sex do you think they were doing to need bulletproof vests?"

The county coroner arrived on the scene and ordered the bodies to be placed in body bags for their trip to the county morgue. The forensic team would identify the remains there.

On the other side of town, Roberta Potter was listening to a country western radio station in Doctor Alexander's Mercedes heading west on Interstate 16 near Chatham Parkway. She reflected back on her night's work, feeling lucky to be alive.

She smiled and thought about the Savannah Fire Department's surprise when they found of the two bodies in the bedroom making love with bulletproof vests on. She knew eventually the forensic team would identify the two professional assassins and begin a detailed investigation into what they were doing there and question where Doctor Elizabeth Alexander was.

"I'm right here!" a smiling Potter announced, still laughing at her morbid and sick placement of the bodies.

CHAPTER

5

The two SUVs headed out on Veterans Parkway toward Interstate 95 and State Highway 80 to their final stop—Jesup, Georgia. Not a word was spoken by the agents. The only sounds were Doctor Alexander's continuous crying and occasional outbursts.

After an hour of driving in the early morning, the two government SUVs entered the small Georgia town of Jesup.

"Robin, we'll be there in a few minutes—is everything ready?" Dejka asked over his cell phone. "Time is of the essence as you know."

"Joe, understand completely—we'll be ready," FBI Special Agent Robin Stevens replied.

The SUVs drove past the Walmart Supercenter and made a right on US Highway 341 heading west. In a few miles, they turned right onto Bay Access Road. A grand lakeside house sat on top of the hill surrounded by an expansive chain-linked fence. They drove up to the electronic access gate and punched in their code. Luscious gardens and various trees surrounded the house with a spectacular view of the lake.

The owner, Kenneth Raney, was a well-established lawyer who grew up in Jesup and now practiced law in Savannah. He was a boyhood friend of the warden at the nearby Federal Correctional Institution. For years, an army of caretakers from the local community cared for the huge house. On numerous occasions, various organizations leased the facility for parties, conferences, and receptions. During a conference, a few top federal law enforcement officials thought the location made an ideal safe house for the FBI—being close to the federal prison and Army base, but far enough away from Savannah.

Raney relished the idea of federal agents using his property. As a prominent lawyer with large aspirations, supporting the Feds in this venture would certainly pay big dividends in the future. He became the perfect host, and the Feds never forgot his generosity.

All of the local federal law enforcement agents were familiar with the resort and made every effort to attend conferences and meetings there—the catered BBQ meals were considered first class.

Agent Robin Stevens waited to greet Dejka and his team on the bricked front porch, watching the small caravan of SUVs enter the front security gate. Dejka waived at her. There was an unusually high number of vehicles parked in the huge parking lot with license plates from all over, including some government plates.

When Dejka parked the SUV, Stevens ran up and informed him that everything was all set in the basement for the interrogation. Alexander was helped out of the SUV, still crying and shaking from her ordeal. Once out of the SUV, she threw up and begged for a cigarette from one of the agents. None of the agents smoked so one went back into Jesup and picked up a pack at a nearby convenience store.

"Robin, please allow me a minute with Doctor Alexander," Dejka asked. "We both know it is going to be a long, tough day for her."

"OK, Joe. We'll get her cleaned up, something to eat, and some cigarettes as soon as you are through with your talk." Stevens walked to the entrance with the rest of the newly arrived agents.

Dejka held Alexander up as they stood alone in the middle of the parking lot. "Listen to me, Doctor Alexander. It is critical we have an understanding here and now about the seriousness of the situation we are in—time is of the essence."

"What are you going to do to me?" Alexander shook violently, causing her voice to wobble. "Where are we and what am I doing here?"

"In a few minutes, I'll escort you into the basement of this house where you will provide, in detail, yours and Georgia Fried Chicken's associations with the Sola Mesa Drug Cartel, various Bolivian banks, and your involvement with a management trainee named Patricia Turner." He tightened his hold on her arm. "Do you understand me, Doctor Alexander?"

Not waiting for a response, Dejka led Alexander to the front door. They walked into a room with fine furniture and a Steinway grand piano. Several paintings hung on the walls. To the right of the front door, a large stairway led downstairs to the basement where voices of men and women talking and the sounds of equipment and furniture being moved could be heard.

"Alright, Joe. We are just about ready," Stevens called from the bottom of the stairs.

"Coming down." Dejka escorted Alexander down the long stairway.

In the basement, a long conference table had fifteen chairs near one end positioned to face a solitary one at the other end. Various microphones, high-intensity lights, and digital cameras focused on the lone chair.

Dejka sternly guided Alexander to the solo chair and ordered her to sit.

"I demand my attorney right now," a somewhat delusional Alexander demanded, "and I want a cigarette."

"You might find the story on page six interesting." Dejka threw down a copy of the Savannah Morning Newspaper in front of her.

Clumsily, she opened the paper to the correct page. The headline read: "Georgia Fried Chicken Security Officer Roy Baker murdered by unknown assassins at the Savannah Mall."

"Oh my God, oh my God," Alexander kept repeating. She shook her head in disbelief. She could've been next.

"We are sorry we could not get to him before they did." Dejka set a pack of cigarettes next to her. "Like you, he was involved up to his neck, and he paid for it."

"Alright, Agent Dejka. What do you want to know?" Resigned to her fate, Alexander prepared herself for the coming interrogation by fumbling with the package.

"Robin, please notify our guests upstairs that we are ready to begin our talk with Doctor Alexander."

In a few minutes, several men and women made their way down the stairs and took their assigned seats at the large conference table. Each carried a legal pad, some with notes already on them. The attendees included officers and agents from the FBI, CIA, DEA, ATF, and State Department experts on the Bolivian government and drug cartels working in Bolivia. Also, there was a cadre of military personnel dressed in civilian suits that did little to hide their rugged and intimidating appearance.

"Ladies and gentlemen, we will begin the interrogation in a few moments. Please take your seats at this time," declared FBI Special Agent Jim Thompson, the lead interrogator.

Alexander shook uncontrollably despite chain smoking cigarettes. The minutes ticked by slowly as each person took their seats and gazed at her. Their expressions ranged from contempt to pity to disinterest.

"Ladies and gentleman, let's get started." Agent Thompson stood to the left of the criminal to address the gathered group. "I believe I know most you, so I'll be quick with the overall summary of why we are here. Keep in mind, we are very short on time due to the urgency of the situation."

All eyes were focused on the interrogator.

"Earlier this year, the DEA recruited, trained, and assigned one of their top special agents to be an undercover operative in Bolivia. Her mission was to gather intelligence about the expanding operations of the Sola Mesa Drug Cartel."

"Excuse me, sir," one of the ATF agents interrupted. "Our understanding was that the Bolivian government prohibited DEA personnel in their country."

"Thank you, Agent Price, for the question," Thompson acknowledged though somewhat annoyed at the interruption. "It was a calculated risk the DEA was prepared to take—intelligence on the Sola Mesa Drug Cartel, with its expanding footprint in the US, was considered a national law enforcement priority to the point of affecting our national security."

"Please, no more questions till after my briefing," Thompson asked, pausing a moment before continuing his presentation. "Special Agent Bonnie McCord volunteered for the assignment. She would work for Georgia Fried Chicken as an assistant branch manager at the Santa Cruz Mall under the name Patricia Turner."

At the mention of Patricia Turner, Alexander broke down sobbing and yelling about her innocence and how the Sola Mesa Cartel had tricked her.

"No more outbursts, Doctor Alexander!" Thompson sternly warned her then turned back to the attendees. "Henceforth, we will refer to our undercover agent as McCord. Special Agent Dejka, would you please begin your interrogation of Doctor Alexander."

Everyone at the table prepared their notepads and folders, while Dejka took a position to the right of Alexander. He pulled up a seat. An agent ensured the recording devices and video cameras were functioning properly. The electronic media technician at the controls gave Dejka a thumbs-up. All eyes were on Dejka and Alexander.

"Doctor Alexander, time is critical in our attempt to save McCord and we do not know how much more time we have," Dejka emphasized as Alexander broke down again, sobbing and holding her hands to her head not wanting to hear anything further. "We need to understand the full picture of how McCord ended up in Bolivia. The smallest detail could mean life or death. It is in your best interest to tell us everything now without hesitation. Do you understand?"

"Agent Dejka, what do you want to know? Where do you want me to start?" She lit another cigarette, a concession for her cooperation.

"For your information Doctor Alexander, we have retrieved all of your files and computers in your house, including the documents and devices in your wall safe hidden behind your vanity mirror," Dejka informed her. Her mouth fell slack and her eyes widened for she knew full well the many scandalous secrets held in the safe.

"How did you know about the wall safe?" Alexander unconsciously asked Dejka who ignored the question.

"Besides your home wall safe, we have in our possession all of the documents, files and cryptic electronic devices from your office vault at the GFC headquarters," added Dejka. "Bottom line, we have obtained all applicable confidential reports, records, and documents relating to GFC finances and your involvement with Bolivian banks and drug cartels. So now, Doctor Alexander, let's start from the beginning and you can fill in the gaps of what we need to know. You may begin."

Alexander resigned herself to the fact that if she could assist in getting McCord back, it might save her from a worse fate. With the studio lights, camera, and officials at the conference room table now focused on her, she lit cigarette after cigarette as she told them the history of her association with the Sola Mesa Cartel and Patricia Turner.

According to Doctor Alexander, Georgia Fried Chicken had become very ambitious under her watch and expanded too quickly worldwide. They could not financially support their rapid growth. Their credit liabilities soared while GFC sales fell to disastrous levels, due to increased competition and loss of brand identity. Stock prices continued their steady decline after they went public. As a personal favor to an influential and powerful Bolivian bank CEO, GFC established a franchise near the bank's headquarters in Santa Cruz, Bolivia. The bank CEO enjoyed dining at the GFC on his various trips to the US and proposed a deal to Alexander. He was already financing a Steel Rock Café in the popular Santa Cruz Mall and agreed to make the arrangements for a GFC to be located next to the café. She agreed to the terms of the contract but also warned him of GFC's financial instability.

As the interrogation continued, she gradually became more focused on presenting an accurate report on her relationship with Turner, the banks, and the cartel. The interrogators gradually appreciated her direct and factual recollection of events. Her CEO business and survival instincts returned as she continued with the interrogation.

The Bolivian bank CEO already knew about GFC's financial problems and was more than happy to help. According to her, a Pablo Quezada had close relationships with numerous banking officials who would be willing to loan funds to GFC to help bridge the gap until sales improved. Alexander was aware of money-laundering issues in South American banks but was desperate for funds regardless of where they came from—she had to take the risk. GFC accepted a loan agreement with the Bolivian banks. As long as drugs were processed in Bolivia, the banks would be filled with drug money that needed a legitimate home—GFC was one of those homes.

However, Alexander had difficulty finding the appropriate management and staff to run the GFC at the Santa Cruz Mall. The manager of the branch in South America was normally selected by the banking institutions loaning the majority of the funds for the branch—Quezada was just that person. He was well known for his association with the Sola Mesa Cartel's drug processing operation in Bolivia and was anxious to show off his legitimate management skills to the cartel's kingpins as a crafty entrepreneur. Quezada understood his position would literally be a non-working figurehead with GFC's corporate trained assistant manager conducting all of the work—newly hired and trained Patricia Turner.

Alexander explained how GFC Human Resources advertised for the assistant manager position. They interviewed only a few qualified candidates. Patricia Turner was GFC's first choice. She possessed all of the qualifications required for the position, and her mediocre resume showed that she was desperate for work. More importantly, she was fluent in Spanish. It was mentioned, by many of her instructors and staff at GFC's Management Trainee

Institute, maybe Turner was too perfect for the assignment. The Bolivian banks and designated Bolivian manager literally rubber stamped all that Alexander recommended—they were backing her judgment.

Alexander also was briefed on the GFC staff's assessment of Turner and requested a personal interview with the new manager. She knew her relationship with the Bolivian banks and other sources of funds depended on hiring and training a candidate who was "hungry" and dependable—Patricia Turner, on face and paper, was that candidate.

"Doctor Alexander," Dejka broke in, "it has come to our attention through reliable sources that you attempted to have some sort to personal, intimate relationship with McCord at this interview. Is this true, Dr. Alexander?"

"Damn you, Alexander. Tell us the truth now!" Agent Young slammed his fist on the conference table, sending papers and files to the floor. Young apologized to the group for his outburst.

"Yes, yes!" answered Alexander, looking disgusted and ashamed. "I found Turner, sorry, I mean McCord, rather appealing and wanted get to know her better."

"She rebuked your advances did she not?" Young asked.

"Yes, my pride was hurt that a lowly management trainee would turn down my offer of an intimate relationship with me. Who would turn down the CEO of a major corporation?" Humbling herself, she knew she had nothing to lose—there were no more secrets. All pride was lost with her answers and recollections and becoming more accurate and clearer. "I was going to show that pretty management trainee that no one turns me down."

"Tell us, what were your actions after McCord turned you down?" Agent Dejka asked.

"I was angry. No one turns me down." Alexander took a long drag and slowly breathed the smoke out. "Something troubled me about McCord, like a sixth sense or something. So, I ordered a more in-depth background check on her. My security director, Roy Baker hired an expensive, very reputable security investigation service. Baker even checked with his paid informants in the government to validate Pat Turner's true identity."

Alexander acknowledged that McCord indeed arrived in Bolivia and professionally setup and organized the GFC branch in Santa Cruz. No one would confirm Patricia Turner was Agent Bonnie McCord, but they weren't denying it either, which evoked more suspicion.

Emotionally distraught and covering her face with her hands, Alexander explained that during a routine board meeting, Baker called and said he needed to talk with her immediately. Despite her ire at the interruption, Alexander met him outside at a secluded lunch bench in a park near corporate headquarters. Baker told her that Turner was really a DEA agent named Bonnie McCord. She immediately returned inside, opened her office safe, and retrieved a special, secure cell phone to contact her partners in Bolivia. She told them about her suspicions about the true identity of the current GFC assistant manager—Patricia Turner.

"Doctor Alexander, did you ever consider the fatal consequences of reporting the identity of a possible undercover federal agent—especially to a drug cartel?" Thompson shook with anger and his eyes bulged. "Did you consider what they would do to McCord if they discovered she was indeed a DEA agent?"

"I honestly felt they would simply fire her from GFC and send her home and that would be the end of it," she reasoned. "You know, just send her back to the States."

The audience was dumbfounded. She was either naïve, stupid or possibly a syphilitic moron. Possibly all three.

Most of the members of the conference carried a firearm. Each would not give a second thought to putting a bullet in her brain. Her safety depended on her ability to help them rescue McCord.

"What can I do? What can I do?" a distraught and scared Alexander repeated while clumsily finding one of the last remaining cigarettes in her pack. Dejka struck a match to light it. Everyone sat silently listening to Doctor Alexander's sorrowful statements and empty offers of help.

An unidentified FBI agent entered the conference room carrying a medium-sized carrying case and handed it off to Dejka who in turn returned to his seat next to Alexander.

"Doctor Alexander, all of the contents in your security vault at the GFC corporate headquarters are in this case, including various secure cell phones." Dejka rested his hands on the worn leather case and slowly opened it, ensuring Alexander a view of its contents. "We obtained them last night and our team of analysts have reviewed them thoroughly.

"Doctor Alexander, we are going to lay out before you all of the contents in the case and allow you to review them," Agent Dejka said.

"What am I reviewing them for if you have already done so yourselves?" asked Alexander.

"We are going to give you an opportunity to personally review the contents of your office safe to ensure we are not overlooking or missing something of importance," Dejka explained. "Something that may seem insignificant to us, may hold great value and importance to you or your associates. Do you understand?"

"Yes, I'll do whatever you want." Alexander nodded her head in approval and took a deep breath to try and regain her composure. There might be a chance of getting McCord back with her review of the safe documents. "Mr. Thompson, may I ask a question, sir?"

Thompson nodded his head in approval.

"Sir, do you truly believe that another review of my documents will make a difference?" Alexander asked, searching for some action to pin her hopes on.

With his experience and background in cartel operations, Thompson knew the chances were slim to none that she would discover that unforeseen bit of information the FBI analyst had not already found, but she had to try. "Who knows, we might get lucky," Thompson thought to himself.

With a Winston cigarette dangling from her lips and ashes dropping everywhere, she diligently reviewed the documents and took notes on a plain yellow notepad. The officers began making their formal reports of the interrogation for their respective head-quarters. Once complete, the reports were electronically forward-ed to their respective bosses. The attendees then headed back to their hotels or plane connections in Savannah. Only Agents Dejka and Thompson were left to monitor Alexander's progress.

"Agents Dejka and Thompson, here is what I have outlined so far." A tired Alexander handed Dejka a few pages from her legal notepad. Both agents began scouring the pages and comparing them to the summary from the analysts. They were frustrated that her statements mirrored the contents of the safe and her recent interrogation.

"Not sure if it means anything, but..." Alexander trailed off while lighting another cigarette. The smoke only added to the foggy atmosphere in the basement.

"But, what?" Thompson snapped, but she held his undivided attention. Maybe this was the piece they were missing.

"Do you have federal agents at the US Embassy in La Paz?" She was trying to recollect some of her earlier conversations with her Bolivian bank point of contact, Pablo Quezada.

Both agents looked at each other with inquisitive stares, attempting to comprehend what Alexander just asked.

"No, the United States Government does not have federal law enforcement agents in the Bolivian Embassy," Dejka replied, knowing agents did reside in the embassy in the guise of special assistants to the ambassador. He moved his chair closer to Alexander. "Why do you ask?"

"Well, when I called Pablo about the identity of Agent McCord, I could swear I heard someone in the background comment that they had known about McCord's true identity from one of their people in the embassy."

Dejka made sure the recording equipment was switched on. Then the two sat with notepads and prompted Alexander to continue her thought process. Both agents stressed the critical importance of anything else she could recall.

"From what I understood of the background conversation, some embassy worker knew McCord and saw her at the Santa

Cruz Mall's GFC franchise and deducted she was working undercover," Alexander nonchalantly relayed.

"Dr. Alexander, can you recall, or do you know, the name of the person at the embassy that identified McCord?" Dejka asked.

"The Bolivian GFC designated manager, Pablo Quezada, is the only person I know of," Alexander recalled.

Immediately, the agents made secure encrypted phone calls despite the lateness of the evening. Besides finding and rescuing McCord, they now had a prospective federal employee in Bolivia working with the cartel.

CHAPTER

6

"Besides a missing a DEA undercover agent in Bolivia, you're telling me we have a possible double agent assigned to our embassy in La Paz?" FBI Deputy Director Alex Stuart roared and threw his hands in the air. A handful of government officials were gathered in his secure conference room in the FBI Headquarters in downtown Washington D.C. "What the hell is a DEA agent doing in Bolivia? Didn't they kick you all out a few years ago?"

"Stuart, we prepared this undercover operation for months and decided the risks were worth sending in an agent," DEA Deputy Director Glen Flint countered. "We were fully aware of the possible dangers involved, but we had to take that chance."

"What is so important in Bolivia that you had to break Bolivian law and send in an undercover agent?" Stuart stood and paced around the small conference room table. "Besides being arrested by the Bolivian authorities for entering their country, the drug cartels would love to capture this agent and possibly work a trade for some of their people in our prisons." Calming down, he sat in his chair. "Who is the agent?"

"The agent's name is Bonnie McCord," Flint answered.

"You stupid fuckin' assholes! What were you thinking sending a female agent?" Stuart pointed a beefy finger in Flint's face. He was close to throwing a punch into the DEA deputy's gut. "Do you realize what is probably happening to her as we speak? Fuckin' morons!"

"Gentlemen, let's all calm down. We need to figure out how we are going to deal with Bonnie McCord's possible abduction in Santa Cruz and a compromised federal employee working in our embassy in Bolivia." FBI Director Al Schmid held his hands up, trying to bring back a semblance of order into the meeting. "We don't have much time. When was the last time we heard from Agent McCord?"

"McCord was punctual in keeping contact with her handlers at DEA headquarters via her secure cell phone. Also, McCord's routine sales reports sent to GFC headquarters were also monitored at DEA headquarters as a backup check on her operations. Two days ago, we began receiving questionable situational reports that were confirmed to be bogus—fakes," Flint reported.

"When you say bogus situational reports, what does that mean?" Schmid asked.

"Sir, these reports were either drafted under duress or were written by someone else," Flint explained. "For example, McCord misspelled certain keywords in her reports. These are missing in the reports from the last two days. We are confident that McCord was tortured into providing the report protocols to show that operations were normal. No agent would divulge these protocols unless under extreme stress.

"However, every message has the sender's own style and various personal quirks. It's obvious someone else was sending the messages for McCord," Flint continued.

The top leaders of all the federal law enforcement agencies in the room just shook their heads in disgust at the DEA's risk taking in Bolivia.

"I would now like to introduce Special Agent Bill Warren, Assistant Deputy for Operations for the DEA." Flint pointed to a quiet man at the end of the table. "Special Agent Warren will brief you on the events leading to where we are today."

"After losing a positive contact with McCord, DEA followed unaccounted for or missing agent protocol with no success," Warren advised. "We made the usual contacts with our clandestine agents and paid informers in Bolivia, requesting any information about McCord, but with no success.

"However, while monitoring the communications of the known members of the Sola Mesa Cartel, we realized they had her in their possession. We have reason to believe they are holding her at a hacienda owned by the cartel kingpin, Juan Castillo." Warren momentarily paused his briefing.

The large overhead projection screen showed a satellite picture of the hacienda a few miles from Santa Cruz. An elaborate system of barbwire fences and several men guarded the compound. High-intensity floodlights illuminated the grounds.

"Are you telling me Special Agent McCord is in that compound?" asked FBI Director Schmid.

"Analyzing the secured and unsecured communications from the cartel leaders, we are highly confident Special Agent Bonnie McCord is in that hacienda," Warren confirmed.

"Deputy Director Flint, in your experience, what can we expect to find if she is in the hacienda?" FBI Director Schmid asked somberly.

Not a sound could be heard while Schmid waited for an answer from Warren—which seemed to take forever.

"Sir, I can answer that question." DEA Foreign Operations Director Manuel Toro stood, preparing to answer Schmid. Everyone in the quiet secure conference room stared at Toro, anxiously awaiting his brief.

"Who might you be?" Schmid turned and pointed his shaking finger at Toro. "Get your ass up to the podium now and begin your analysis of what is happening to McCord."

Flint glanced at Toro and nodded his head in approval, relieved not to be conducting the briefing.

"Toro got her in there, now he can get her out," Flint thought to himself.

While Toro got up from his seat and made his way to the podium, an official photo of a man of Hispanic descent appeared on the screen. The caption read: DEA Special Agent Enrique Camarena Salazar. Everyone in the room knew or had heard stories about Enrique. He was considered a hero in all law enforcement circles. His death continued to haunt many federal agents working undercover in foreign countries.

"Good morning ladies and gentlemen, I am Manuel Toro, the Director of Foreign Operations for the DEA," Toro said with a great deal of anguish. "Yes, I am the officer responsible for McCord's undercover assignment to Bolivia."

"Fire the son of a bitch."

"Hang the bastard."

Ignoring the harsh commentary, Toro coolly adjusted his microphone and addressed FBI Director Schmid.

"Director Schmid, you asked the question, 'What could be expected of the treatment of McCord if she is indeed held by the Sola Mesa Drug Cartel.' A similar situation occurred in Mexico a few years ago when our DEA undercover agent Enrique Camarena Salazar was abducted in broad daylight by corrupt Mexican officials. These officials were also working for the major drug cartels." A large, guarded hacienda ranch displayed on the screen behind Toro. "Just outside of Guadalajara, the well-guarded hacienda you are viewing is owned by a past director of the Mexican Federal Judicial Police. It is where Camarena Salazar was held and tortured to death."

"Damn it, Toro. We all know about happened to Camarena Salazar," a now frustrated Schmid asked. "For God's sake, we need to know what McCord is in for if she is indeed in the cartel's hands?"

Not a sound was heard in the room as Toro wiped the sweat from his brow. His hand twitched slightly, betraying his nervousness. Everyone in the conference room expected the worse, but they hoped Toro's intelligence briefing would offer something positive.

Toro nervously clicked the slide remote control. Another satellite imagery of a hacienda appeared with the caption: Santa Cruz, Bolivia.

"There are two possible scenarios we are confident to predict," Toro said. "First, the cartel may possibly treat her as a prisoner and a valuable bargaining chip in some sort of agreement with the Feds. The cartel may ask the US government to trade McCord for a few of their men in US custody. It has happened in the past."

"Do we currently have any key Sola Mesa members in custody?" CIA agent Beryl Williams asked.

"In the research we conducted, we found fourteen Sola Mesa Cartel members we may consider for a trade," Toro responded with a little more confidence in his voice.

"What is the protocol for offering a trade?" Williams asked. "How would we contact this cartel boss, Juan Castillo, about the trade?"

"Yes, I understand your question; however, please realize that what I am going to tell you is highly classified and could jeopardize the lives of our paid informers—some working for the cartel and others working for the government or police," Toro said. "Rest assured, I have an informer that will carry our deal to Castillo and bring back an answer. When we conclude this meeting, I'll make the contact with our man who will get the offer to Castillo as soon as possible."

One could feel and hear the sighs of relief that a trade could possibly be made for McCord. However, the deal would be counter to US policy and would require presidential approval. The conference members were at little more at ease until Director Schmid brought the room back to attention.

"Director Toro, you initially stated there were two scenarios you foresaw with the McCord abduction. What is the second scenario based on your experience?" Schmid asked.

"Worst case, Special Agent McCord is being held in that hacienda as a DEA whore and is being screwed by every Sola Mesa Cartel member who the Castillo deems deserving." Toro cringed at hearing the words spoken aloud.

Several profanities followed at varying volumes.

"Alright, let's settle down. We are going to need everyone to work together to save her from this tragedy." Schmid's voice was calm, hiding his desire to bust Toro in the mouth and then hold him accountable for this tragedy of tragedies. "Director Flint, what about the DEA Rapid Response Teams? Isn't their mission to rescue agents in trouble overseas? Have they been activated?"

"Yes, sir. You are correct. Our Rapid Response Teams are responsible for deploying worldwide to assist special agents requiring assistance in high-risk and dangerous operations," Flint briefed. "Our teams are headed by a former Navy SEAL and are comprised of retired or separated special forces members."

"Well that's fuckin' wonderful Flint." Schmid stood and angrily pointed his finger at Flint screaming, "is the team heading for Bolivia as we speak?"

"No, sir. They are not," Flint nervously replied.

"Listen you fuckin' son of a bitch, you get that team mobilized now. Do you hear me? Now!" Schmid ordered.

"Sir," Flint addressed a red-faced Schmid, "when the DEA Operations Center was confident that we had lost an agent, the Rapid Response Team was mobilized and began preliminary planning for their deployment to Bolivia. However, the team was ordered to stand down."

"Stand down!!! What the fuck for? That is the reason for the team, is it not? To get agents out of danger like this?"

The various law enforcement and military officers in the room were beside themselves not understanding the DEA's refusal to send in a rescue team to save one of their agents.

"I need to know right now, Flint, who gave the order for the team to stand down?" Schmid and the members in the room all anxiously awaited Flint's reply.

"The Director of the DEA and the head of the DOJ were personally told by the President of the United States and the Secretary of State to stand down. There would be no rescue attempt in Bolivia," Flint briefed.

Grumblings and angry discontent followed this information. Why couldn't the DEA rescue their operative?

"You got her in there. Now you get her out," a shaking angry Schmid ordered, poking his finger in Flint's chest.

Toro stood at the podium, not saying a word. He knew full well that a rescue mission was not possible—militarily or politically.

A deal with the devil was the only way to get McCord back alive. Or could the cartel be fooled in thinking a prisoner swap was possible while a clandestine rescue mission was being planned?

"Is our man in Bolivia...oh what is his name?" Schmid demanded. "Is he aware of the situation with McCord?"

"Sir, I believe you are referring to Doctor Jose Mercedes," Deputy CIA Director Reynolds replied, "and no, sir, we have not asked for his involvement in this situation. However, I am sure he is aware of this incident based on his numerous contacts and associations."

"Let's get him involved immediately and ask him to start spreading the word that we are working a deal for a swap," Schmid urgently requested of the Reynolds.

CHAPTER

7

Departing the beautiful and impressive main entrance of the US Embassy in La Paz, Bolivia, Jose Mercedes entered the white-walled courtyard. He stopped and admired the quiet beauty and serenity of the chirping birds who had built their nests in the trees.

"Bellíssimo y tranquillo," Mercedes mumbled as he left the courtyard and headed for the embassy's main security entrance on Avenue Arce. The Marines on duty came to attention when he passed the gates—he was a fellow Marine from years past and the detachment had not forgotten his service—Semper Fi. Mercedes saluted with a huge grin and reflected for a moment on his days in the Corps.

Avenue Arce was a busy and noisy main thoroughfare in the central part of La Paz. Jose had made this walk at least a thousand times as the ambassador's special assistant for economic partnerships with US companies.

Mercedes was a dark and handsome man of medium stature with obvious characteristics of a native Bolivian. Growing up and educated in Bolivia's elite private schools, he excelled in soccer and other various sports and was passionate about learning the English language. On his way home from soccer practice passing the embassy, he enjoyed practicing his English with the Marines guarding the entrance. The Marines were more than happy to exchange a few words with this enthusiastic school student to a point where both student and Marines look forward to their informal afternoon meetings. He often expressed his wishes to live and study in the United States.

"Mercedes, have you ever considered joining the Marines," a Marine sergeant of the guards asked. "We'll have an information package tomorrow regarding enlistment."

"Thank you, sergeant. I'll be here tomorrow and review it." Mercedes knew his parents would forbid and prevent any thoughts of him joining the US Marines.

While he had enjoyed growing up in Bolivia, his father's job transferred them to the US while Jose was in high school, giving him access to a completely different life. He had always admired the Marines and jumped at the chance to join them. After obtaining his US citizenship, he became an officer and won several awards for service to his country. After retiring as a colonel, his doctorate in international business opened up an opportunity in his native Bolivia.

"How would you like to return to Bolivia and work at the US Embassy as a special assistant to the Ambassador?" was the offer made to Mercedes. He jumped on it.

Several defense intelligence agencies were struggling to gain accurate third-party intelligence on the phenomenal growth of coca and the production of cocaine since the unexpected expulsion of the Drug Enforcement Administration by the Bolivian President Evo Morales. The unexpected departure of the DEA ushered in a new era in Bolivia's relationship with the coca leaf and established drug cartels.

With the typical walk and swagger of a retired Marine, Mercedes enjoyed the morning walk down Avenue Arce where many Bolivians knew and recognized him with much respect. He was affectionately known around the embassy and local populace.

"Buenos días, Doctor Mercedes. Como estas?" came from many people passing Mercedes on the streets and boulevards.

"Bien, Bien, muchas gracias mis amigos," replied Mercedes with a huge smile on his face.

Upon reaching Calle Cordero, he turned right at the busy

intersection and headed for a local coffee shop he frequently visited called the Caffettino. The small, relaxed shop was usually frequented by local small business owners and Bolivian government and municipal workers whose offices were nearby. The café had its regulars who frequented the café, not because of the relaxing ambiance or coffee, but for the widely known informal meeting area. Mercedes was there for one purpose this beautiful La Paz morning—to do business.

"Hola mi amigo. Como se encuentra usted?" Señor Manuel Vargas greeted Mercedes. Vargas had owned and operated his shop for over thirty years and prided himself on all the influential and famous people that frequently visited his establishment.

"Here you are, Doctor, your usual." Vargas handed Mercedes a large cup of his favorite espresso.

"Manuel, you are way too good to me. I don't deserve friends like you." Mercedes carefully handled the hot espresso in one hand and the morning's paper in the other. It was no accident that Vargas had a strong bond and appreciation for Mercedes. A couple years back, local gang members attempted to strong arm and threaten Vargas into paying "protection fees" to the gang. Vargas refused and his family was threatened, his home broken into, and his beloved Caffettino was ransacked. It took months to rebuild the shop. Though a fairly new customer at the time, Mercedes offered to look into the incident, seeing the connection as beneficial for his work. It didn't take long for the gang leader's death to make headlines, fortifying the new friendship between Vargas and Mercedes.

There was no doubt in Vargas's mind that the abrupt end of the gang's intimidation and threats against him and his family were a direct result of Señor Mercedes' intervention. He was eternally grateful.

This morning, Mercedes took the paper and espresso outside to a small, simple wooden table under the shade of an oak tree. The leaves swayed in the wind while the birds chirped a relaxing melody. Situated on the main boulevard, the café was a great place to watch the lively community.

"Señor Mercedes, is there anything else we can do for you this morning?" a young waiter asked Mercedes.

"I do have a request this morning," Mercedes politely asked, looking up from his morning paper. "When available, I would like to have a quick word with Señor Vargas, please."

The waiter politely excused himself to find Señor Vargas who was busy working behind the counter taking orders.

Vargas ordered someone take over the counter, shed his white logo apron, and made his way outside to meet with Mercedes. This request was nothing new. Mercedes would not have asked him to meet privately if it was not important.

"You requested to see me, old friend." Vargas found his friend reading the paper with his legs crossed in apparent relaxation. Mercedes didn't fool him one bit.

"Ah yes, mi compa." Mercedes stood, moved to his friend's side, and put his hand around the shorter man's shoulder as a sign friendship to those passing by the Caffettino. "I have an informal business meeting this morning and I would like to meet with him here for a short discussion—is that OK with you?" Mercedes whispered.

"Certainly, old friend. I'll ensure you are not bothered by my staff and other customers."

Exactly what Mercedes had expected.

While finishing his first cup of espresso, he noticed an elegantly dressed man in a well-tailored blue summer suit approaching the Caffettino from the tree-lined street. He looked out of place walking the streets with the rest of the La Paz masses. Approaching the Caffettino, he immediately spotted Mercedes, grinned, and made a beeline to his small table.

"Francisco Perez, so wonderful to see you. Thanks for taking the time to see me," Mercedes warmly said while shaking the other man's hand and giving him a short, friendly embrace.

Childhood friends, Francisco had remained in La Paz, becoming a very successful and well-known attorney for an international bank—the Banco Mundo of Bolivia.

A few years back, Francisco was arrested for his involvement in a money-laundering operation linked to a local drug cartel. He had created shell companies to hide the money and investments in overseas financial institutions; however, he was caught and tried and spent four years in a Bolivian prison. It was widely known he took the hit for the Sola Mesa Cartel. After his release, some quasi-legitimate bank officials, with suspected links to the Sola Mesa, found a position for him as a lawyer at the Banco Mundo of Bolivia.

Mercedes had vouched for Francisco and assisted in his release, despite the potential damage to his reputation. Francisco would never forget his old friend's efforts in his early release, but was not ignorant to the fact this generous assistance would not be forgotten. Francisco had a sixth sense he was about to payback that assistance.

"Ah, my old and dear friend, what a pleasure to see you." Francisco smiled and embraced Mercedes.

"How good it is to see you," Mercedes said with affection. "I see you must have recovered from your old soccer injuries by the way you are walking."

"Yes, I had a hip replacement," Francisco laughed. "Too many run-ins with you on the soccer field during our early days."

The waiter refilled Mercedes' cup and brought one for Francisco. Francisco took out two premium Havana cigars and handed one to Mercedes. The flavor of the cigars paired well with their coffee.

Francisco slowly pulled a twenty-four-karat gold cigarette lighter from his coat pocket and lit the cigars. Mercedes took a long draw and exhaled the aromatic blue smoke.

"Many thanks, amigo," a smiling Mercedes said. "You certainly know how to start the day off right."

For a few minutes, both men sat back, drinking espresso, smoking cigars, and catching up. However, both men knew the underlying purpose for the meeting. Mercedes was aware of what Francisco wanted from him—everything else was just a nice façade, a game leading up to the real purpose of the meeting.

"Ah Francisco, as we all know, you are a man of many talents and you have done well with your hard work and skills as a mediator and lawyer. We have always been grateful for your assistance in the past and are again asking for your help, which only someone of your expertise can accomplish," Mercedes trumpeted, building up his friend's ego.

"Enough of this bullshit," Francisco thought to himself playing this charade out of respect for his old friend and again grudgingly remembered, "paybacks are bitches."

Mercedes knew anything he said would be transmitted to Juan Castillo. Wearing electronic listening devices, commonly known as wires, their conversations would be guarded and benign. Each man knew the most modest, simple words or statements would be understood without further clarification. Both knew the protocols well.

"Francisco, we need your assistance in locating a US citizen who was working as an assistant manager at the Georgia Fried Chicken in the Santa Cruz Mall—the one next to the Steel Rock Café." Mercedes came to the purpose of their meeting. "I assume you are familiar with the chicken franchise."

"Por supuesto, I have been there on a few occasions," Francisco said.

"The embassy has tasked me with finding the assistant manager of this chicken restaurant. Apparently, the family and the Georgia Fried Chicken corporate headquarters have lost contact with the manager." Mercedes did not mention her other job as a DEA undercover agent.

"Have you contacted the police for assistance in finding this woman?" Francisco clenched his teeth at his mention of "this woman." Mercedes had never said if it was a male or female. Francisco let him know that he knew the whole situation.

"Thank you for the advice, but we've had no luck in finding the missing assistant manager—Patricia Turner." Mercedes drank his last few drops of espresso and waived to the waiter for more. Friendly chatter of people passing by and the relaxing sound of the tree leaves blowing with the wind above their small, secluded table only hid the underlying tension between the two men—discussing life and death.

"How can I help you, old friend?" Francisco was anxious to

get to the point of this "friendly meeting."

"Francisco, we have reason to believe that US citizen Patricia Turner was abducted from her work at the Santa Cruz Mall by members of a cartel operating in that area." Mercedes laid down his first card as if in a high stake's poker game. "I am personally seeking your assistance in finding and releasing her. I would look at it as a personal favor, my old friend. With your various contacts, I hope, with your persuasion, they would be willing to set her free, for a substantial reward of course."

"If I was able to make contact with individuals who knew about the abduction, I trust they would want to know what the reward would be?" asked Francisco, steering the conversation to what was in it for him and the cartel.

"Please relay to those having information on her disappearance that we are willing to release five members of their organization, who are currently being held in a federal US prison." Mercedes flicked the ashes of his cigar in the ashtray. "That is the deal."

Francisco had expected this deal as did his contacts in the Sola Mesa Cartel. They were simply waiting to officially hear it from the United States Government.

"As a longtime friend, you and I both know the winds of change are coming to Bolivia. Numerous popular uprisings of oppressed and impoverished people are making things difficult for those in power." Mercedes' intelligence forecasted major political changes in Bolivia, and he had one final offer for Francisco. "You may need friends at the embassy, and we would be grateful for your assistance."

"I'll make contacts and relay your offer to some friends who have dealings with the cartel." Francisco wanted to end the meeting on a positive note. He might need his friend's help one day.

The waiter returned, refilled both cups of espresso, and asked if they wished to see a lunch menu. Both politely refused, stating they had to get back to their offices soon.

"I'll get back to you as soon as possible with the reply. If a deal is accepted, we can meet back here to settle the arrangements."

Francisco felt uncomfortable about being the mediator between the United States Government and the Sola Mesa Cartel. He didn't have a choice. He owed Mercedes this accommodation.

Finishing their espresso, they returned to reminiscing about the promising days of their youth.

"Thank you for meeting with me, my friend." Mercedes rose from his seat and laid three one-hundred-dollar bills on the table to be shared among the staff for their first-class service and respect.

Embracing Mercedes in a friendly hug, Francisco discreetly slipped a small, white envelope into the side pocket of Mercedes' suit without him noticing.

"This will be my priority this afternoon," assured Francisco as he shook Mercedes' hand one final time and headed back down the now-crowded street.

Mercedes left the table and walked to the owner's office in the café to thank him for the superb service and accommodations. Manuel Vargas was in the rear kitchen overseeing the lunch preparations and preparing some chicken for baking. As always, he wore his signature white shirt and black tie covered by a white waiter's apron. Seeing Mercedes approaching, he hurriedly took off his apron, fixed his tie, and wiped the small amount of sweat on his forehead with a cloth. Vargas' actions were standard protocol when in contact with Mercedes.

"My dear friend, thank you again for your most trusted friendship." Mercedes gave Vargas a quick embrace, smiled, and left to return to the US Embassy.

Sitting back in an old wooden swivel chair, he began reviewing the arriving lunch orders when a thought struck him. He got up from his chair and discreetly called the waiter who had served Mercedes. The loyal waiter made a quick beeline to his boss' side.

"Señor Vargas, what can I do for you?" Renaldo asked politely.

"Renaldo, do you know who that gentleman with Mr. Mercedes was?"

"Si, señor. I know him only by reputation," Renaldo said. "Francisco was known as a well-connected broker for one of the drug cartels while serving as a Bolivian national bank vice president. I believe it was the Sola Mesa. Word on the street is he was arrested and served time at the federal prison for embezzling and laundering drug money, among other things."

Vargas listened intently to his well-informed and loyal waiter.

"Entonces, I am curious about the connection between Francisco and Mercedes."

Calls for a waiter rose louder with each passing moment. Now was not the time to have this conversation.

"Renaldo, please make it point to see me when your shift is over. OK?"

"Si, mi jefe," Renaldo politely replied then returned to the service area with two hot containers of coffee.

Señor Vargas had a sixth sense that his friend and protector, Señor Mercedes, maybe heading into a trap.

CHAPTER
8

Casually walking back to the embassy, Mercedes recalled the thousands of furious protesters who filled the streets only a few weeks earlier. They demanded the resignation of President Evo Morales. Mercedes had met the president on several occasions as a representative of the United States Embassy regarding various issues, including the expulsion of the DEA. The country was the second-largest grower of coca in the world, supplying approximately 15% of the US cocaine market. Analysts believed that exports of coca paste and cocaine generated well over one billion dollars annually, surpassing Bolivia's legal exports. Nearly everyone understood that Morales was a corrupt tyrant who discreetly allowed the cartels freedom to do as they pleased—as long as he got his cut.

Seeking a fourth presidential term, Morales rigged the election. His "votes" surpassed the threshold to win in the first round, avoiding a risky runoff. The sixty-year-old socialist claimed victory while his opposition claimed fraud.

The heads of the armed forces and national police also called for him to resign. Morales, soon after, boarded a plane with his millions in drug money to Mexico. There he lived in exile.

Mercedes wanted nothing more than a peaceful transition of power to stabilize his homeland and to challenge the cartel's drug operations. It was likely wishful thinking. He shook his head and refocused on his mission to help rescue the captured DEA agent.

Returning to the embassy main entrance, he produced his Government Common Access Card (CAC) and punched in his personal code into the access reader. The turn stalls unlocked and allowed him entry where a Marine sentry double-checked his credentials.

"Thank you, sergeant," a smiling Mercedes said to the Marine guard opening the door. He made his way to the main lobby and took the elevator to the seventh floor to his suite of offices. Opening the door, staff members inundated him with requests to discuss their assignments.

"Please, set your appointments with me through Helena," Mercedes politely but sternly directed his staff. He was anxious to get in his office to review his meeting with Francisco and hear news from the cartel.

"Señor Mercedes, before you go into your office," his private secretary Helena Vaca said, "the ambassador would like to see you this afternoon at five in the basement for a conference call. It sounded urgent."

"Thank you, Helena. I'll plan on being there," he politely replied while entering his office. He securely shut the door behind him.

Going to the basement was code for a session in the embassy's Sensitive Compartmental Information Facility, known as the SCIF. The SCIF was a highly secured complex where the most sensitive and top secret information could be discussed. Access to the SCIF required the highest-security clearances available in the United States. Few personnel at the embassy had the security clearances or the need to ever visit the SCIF.

Mercedes reasoned it could be anything, but his best guess was the recent circumstances behind President Morales' resignation and exile to Mexico. Who would be the next President of Bolivia and how could the US influence the new president's relationship with the United States?

"Helena, please ensure that I am not disturbed for the next hour," Mercedes announced over the intercom system. He removed his jacket and placed it on a hanger on the office's coat rack.

"Yes, Doctor Mercedes." Helena suspected he needed some time to catch up on his mountain of paperwork. As Mercedes' executive support person, she knew about the various responsibilities and non-disclosed duties Mercedes had at the embassy—in particular, his role with the CIA.

Adjusting his tailor-made blue wool coat on the metal hanger, an old military habit, he noticed a folded piece of nondescript white paper in the coat's side pocket. The coat was picked up from the cleaners the previous night. He assumed the paper would not have survived the cleaners. Instinctively, he grabbed a pair of disposable gloves from the utility shelf and put them on before removing and investigating the curious white paper. He gently pulled the paper from the coat pocket and unfolded it to find a short message:

You have an informant for the cartel in the embassy.

Moving to his cluttered desk, he sat down and read the contents of the paper again and again. He refrained from showing any emotion in case a hidden device had been placed in his office. Quietly, he pulled a large brown mailing envelope out of his desk, placed the white paper inside, and wrote the day's date on the front.

Sitting at his desk as if nothing unusual had occurred, he nonchalantly placed the envelope in the side drawer of the antique, wooden desk and locked it. He would move the envelope to his secure personal safe when the opportunity presented itself to avoid raising the suspicions of anyone watching.

Reviewing the stacks of reports on his desk concerning the recent protests in Bolivia, he tried to find answers to why the protests continued and what or who was inciting them. President Morales had already been ousted and granted political asylum in Mexico.

Taking a pause, Mercedes sat back in his chair and rubbed his forehead. Morales had won a landslide election in 2005, promising democratic reform for the small nation. Implementing social programs that aligned with the demands of the many social movements, he nationalized the gas and oil industries to fund social services and infrastructure projects. The efforts attempted to close the gap between the rich and the poor while bringing forth incredible economic growth. New schools provided access to education and opened more markets to farmers, resulting in a significant increase in income and food security. Women won a significant victory with the changes to the electoral law that required that 50% of each political party's list be women. The current Bolivian legislature had a female majority.

"What more could the country ask for?" Mercedes turned to look out his window. "Now we are back to facing the same protests in the streets by various political groups while the drug cartels grow stronger and stronger during this new government transition."

"Dios mío," Mercedes thought to himself, turning back to the stacks of papers requiring his attention. "What happened?" Bolivia's democracy had one of the most socially inclusive constitutions in the Western Hemisphere that truly empowered minorities.

Mercedes knew the age-old passage too well. "President of the people" simply meant: more money, more prestige, more praise. Helena buzzed his intercom to remind him of his upcoming meeting with the ambassador, interrupting Mercedes' reflections.

"Helena, have we an agenda for this afternoon's meeting?" Mercedes asked.

"Sir, I understood the meeting was to review the various scenarios surrounding the new government," Helena briefed. "Also, the ambassador's aide, Barbara Martinez, mentioned something about a missing US citizen in the Santa Cruz area. She implied you knew something about this."

"Many thanks. I'll be in the basement at five."

In Mercedes' estimate, the newly appointed ambassador, the Honorable James Burton, was a political hack. He had been a large fundraiser for the current president's campaign, but did not speak Spanish and knew absolutely nothing about Bolivia and its current issues relating to the interests of the United States. He looked at himself as solely a figurehead who only needed to attend embassy cocktail parties and schmooze with government and commercial officials. The ambassador's naivety and ignorance about Bolivia meant Mercedes drafted the position papers, correspondence, and speeches for all the critical decisions and actions of the embassy. This suited Mercedes just fine as everyone at the embassy knew he was the de facto ambassador who literally called the shots.

Always praising and supporting Burton in public, Mercedes led the ambassador to exactly where he needed to go. On a few occasions, Burton disagreed with Mercedes' recommendations and guidance, which resulted in great embarrassment and damage for him and the US Embassy. Naturally, Burton put the blame on Mercedes and his staff for supplying him with wrong information and not aggressively supporting his positions. Mercedes took it all in stride knowing the ambassador would think twice before wandering off in his own direction. The ambassador was conditioned to listen and follow Mercedes' recommendations, or guidance— diplomatically speaking.

In preparation for the upcoming meeting with the ambassador and his staff, his briefings and point papers were complete for presentation. However, he wasn't sure how much the ambassador had been briefed on the missing DEA agent. As usual, Mercedes would lead the ambassador's decision by providing possible rescue scenarios using the top secret intelligence they had recently received from the DEA and CIA.

"Helena, I am heading down to the basement." Mercedes rushed past her, putting his suit coat on. He ensured his briefing documents were in his leather briefcase.

"Are Hugo and Juan ready to go?" Mercedes expected his top aides to attend the briefings.

"Sir, I was informed the conference this afternoon would be with Ambassador Burton, Deputy Ambassador Betty Woolman, Deputy Chief of Station Judy Casey, Military Attaché Colonel Warren Weaver, and yourself—no one else was on the invite list," answered Helena.

Mercedes could only remember a few times when other critical staff members were not invited to attend conferences. The ambassador wanted to limit the number of witnesses to his lack of independence at the embassy. More importantly, he didn't want to show his ignorance regarding sensitive diplomatic matters in front of the entire embassy staff and potentially get into a heated discussion with Mercedes. As the CIA Director of South American Operations, he was well aware of Ambassador Burton's shortcomings but had free rein in his actions.

In Mercedes' mind, Deputy Ambassador Betty Woolman was a hard-working, career State Department officer who was well-respected in State Department circles and took her job as deputy seriously. However, she was new to Bolivia and frequently sought the advice from Mercedes. He was glad to have her in his corner, but knew she in lockstep with Ambassador Burton.

The Embassy Defense Attaché, Colonel Warren Weaver, was an ambitious Army officer who still had dreams of future promotions. Weaver and Mercedes had crossed paths many times while serving in Iraq and Afghanistan. After work, they often could be found together at one of their favorite watering holes near the embassy. If there were differences, it came down to which branch was better and tougher—the Army or Marines. When the chips were down, which they had been several times with the current uprisings in Bolivia, Mercedes could always count on Weaver's support.

"Hey Enrique, do you mind holding the elevator for me?" Mercedes rushed to the elevator, tossing a couple of mints in his mouth. Inside, he punched the button for the basement level and clumsily pulled out his CAC card that authorized his access to the basement for the ambassador's secure conference room. While going down, he mentally went over his notes.

A Marine sergeant greeted him when the doors opened. "Doctor Mercedes, may I see your CAC card and your government identification?" Double-checking the documentation, he asked for Mercedes to open his leather briefcase and checked for unauthorized cameras or electronic listening devices. Mercedes never minded these checks, knowing they worked to keep the facility secure.

"Doctor Mercedes, sir, you are cleared to enter the conference room." The Marine pressed the button that allowed Mercedes to go through the turn stall into the conference room. Pushing the turn stall's bar doors, he heard a buzzer as he entered the conference room.

Mercedes made his way to the computer controlling the audio/visual viewing screen. His slides had already been loaded into the computer, but he checked to ensure all was in place. Taking his assigned seat at the large conference table, he again reviewed his notes while waiting for the ambassador and other staff members to arrive. He was always early, out of habit.

Hearing the loud and boisterous voice of Ambassador Burton entering the security checkpoint followed by Colonel Weaver and Betty Woolman, Mercedes checked his watch. Burton was on time for once; however, he was sure to subject them to his usual round of bragging about how well he was doing. "Oh, a god sent to Bolivia," Mercedes whispered, amusing himself.

Rising from his seat, Mercedes greeted the trio as they entered. They took their seats. Everyone but the ambassador placed folders and reports on the table. Mercedes would be the first to report and was anxious to get started, before something else catastrophic happened in the country.

"Good morning, everyone," Burton began. "Before Mercedes begins his situational awareness report, I would like to inform you all that the vice president called me today. He said he had heard through the State Department that we were doing a superb job keeping the diplomatic channels open with the new government here in Bolivia. The vice president, I, and several of the president's staff go back a long way. Our good work is likely to lead to a handsome promotion. So let's keep up the good work."

Everyone politely nodded in agreement having heard his narcissistic bullshit a hundred times before. They kept the embassy running despite his incompetence.

"Understood!" Burton emphasized while looking directly at Mercedes knowing full well Mercedes had his own agenda during the crisis in Bolivia. Technically on paper, Mercedes worked directly for the ambassador, but his duties and operations came from the CIA, which annoyed and upset Burton.

"Yes, sir," Mercedes obediently replied while Casey and Weaver acknowledged Burton's statement by nodding in agreement.

"Alright then. Mercedes would you provide us with your update." Burton glanced at his watch. "I have an important reception tonight at the Canadian Embassy, so let's just get to the point." Woolman and Weaver gave a quick glance to each other and sarcastically nodded their heads, holding back their laughter.

"Yes, sir." Mercedes used the remote control to start the slide show and began the briefing.

Mercedes discussed the rapidly changing political tragedy currently evolving in Bolivia while the former President Evo Morales sought asylum in Mexico. His popularity began declining when commodity prices dropped and the economy slowed—the government literally ran out of money. With this, Morales submitted a referendum to run for a fourth term as president, but the Bolivians rejected his candidacy. However, he pressed forward and declared himself a winner. The Organization of American States' audit found the election to be a fraud with forged signatures, hundreds of polling stations reporting 100% of votes for Morales, and absentee ballots outnumbering the number of eligible voters.

As a result of the self-declared win by Morales, fires, looting and chaos in La Paz and other parts of the country had been reported by international newspapers. Confrontations between Morales' supporters and those who contested the election were still taking place. When the Bolivian military and police sided with the demonstrators and recommended Morales resign for the good of the country, he announced his resignation and sought asylum in Mexico where they embraced him as a hero.

A usually disinterested Ambassador Burton stopped eyeing his watch and mobile phone and began taking notes during the briefing. No doubt, he understood he might be held accountable for possible embassy involvement. He also realized if he did not take appropriate diplomatic action, Mercedes would.

The Bolivian constitution mandated that when a president resigned, an election had to take place within ninety days. Morales' opponents wanted to take power. Recently, Jeanine Anez, the interim president, had declared herself president without the required parliamentary session to appoint her.

"May I interrupt for a moment." Burton asked Mercedes. The ambassador was unusually engaged and interested in the past few days' events in Bolivia. He was taking more notes and asking pertinent questions. For weeks, Mercedes had attempted to update Burton on significant political events to no avail. Mercedes figured someone at the State Department had been asking him questions and he couldn't provide answers.

"You all are aware that the President of the United States has welcomed the resignation and departure of President Morales." Burton's warning to Mercedes not to take any actions contrary to the president's directive was subtle as he addressed everyone at the table. "You may continue, Mercedes."

Mercedes thought it might be best for Bolivia and the US if the ambassador departed for his reception. He could impress the Canadians with his chaotic diplomatic skills.

Moving on, Mercedes got to the point about the current situation in the capital, La Paz. Bolivia's largest city, Santa Cruz, remained chaotic and was possibly escalating into a civil war with a military takeover. The ousting of Morales had opened a power vacuum that people and organizations hostile to democracy were trying to fill. Bolivians had lost faith in the electoral process. Any election would now be challenged for its legitimacy.

Mercedes summed up his report with the obvious. "The most critical need for Bolivia now is to end the violence and reestablish the legitimacy of democratic institutions before they are destroyed forever."

"Thank you, Mercedes, for the update and summary. Betty, Warren, do you have any questions or concerns?" Burton asked.

The discussion went on for another hour. Mercedes fielded most of the questions while Ambassador Burton sporadically interjected that the President of the United States did not like Morales.

After repeatedly glancing at his watch during the additional discussions with Woolman and Weaver, the ambassador hurriedly wrapped up the conference. Grabbing his briefing papers and carelessly throwing them into his classified briefcase, he found his coat jacket and clumsily put it on while staring at his smartphone.

Mercedes, Warren, Casey, and Woolman, out of respect for the ambassador, stood while he readied to depart the room.

"Before I head off to the Canadian Embassy for an evening of fine wine and food, is there anything else of extreme importance that needs to be addressed?" Burton knew no one would want to complicate his exit.

"Yes, sir, there is, and this may take some time," Mercedes softly directed his statement to the departing ambassador who abruptly stopped and turned around to face the director as he had many times in the past two years.

"Alright," Burton said impatiently while taking off his coat and briefcase on an empty chair. "I suspect you want to discuss something not on our agenda for today's meeting. Let's get it over with."

With a possible informant in the embassy, as evidenced by the questionable note found just recently in his suit pocket, Mercedes was not taking any chances. He requested the conference room security systems to be checked and confirmed they were safe prior to continuing the meeting. An annoyed Burton uncharacteristically slammed his briefcase on the table, disappointed that he was not making it to his reception on time.

"Ambassador Burton, sir, with your permission, I would like another security check of the room," Mercedes requested.

"Fine!" Throwing his hands in the air in frustration, Burton authorized the check.

The Marine guards took a few minutes and accomplished the check.

"Mr. Mercedes, everything checked out," said the conference room security specialist.

"Thank you, sergeant. Would you please ensure no one has access to this room during the remainder of this meeting," asked Mercedes.

"Sir, as a reminder," the specialist said, "please turn off any smart phones or electronic devices immediately."

"Yes, sergeant," Mercedes said.

The conference room was announced sealed and secured with a bright rotating red light reminding the attendees that secure classified conversations were authorized.

"OK, Mercedes, what needs my attention?" asked the disgruntled ambassador as he threw his reading glasses on the table and shook his head.

"Sir, we need to discuss missing DEA Special Agent Bonnie McCord and where we stand in our rescue attempts," Mercedes stressed as he made his way to the podium, preparing to take an onslaught of questions. "Time is short, and we need to act now."

Ambassador Burton trimmed his fingernails, obviously annoyed and bothered by Mercedes and this particular issue.

"As the CIA regional director for this region, I made contact this morning with Señor Francisco Perez, our informal friend and go-between with the Sola Mesa Cartel," continued Mercedes. "I provided him with a proposal that has been approved by the DEA and the Justice Department to trade five Sola Mesa Cartel kingpins, currently in custody in US federal prisons, for the safe return of Bonnie McCord."

Burton sat motionless not prepared to comment on Mercedes' update.

"Ambassador, at this time, the approved proposal is, I presume, being reviewed by the Sola Mesa leadership." Mercedes glanced at his watch. "Knowing Francisco's track record, we should hear something soon concerning the deal."

CHAPTER

9

"No more screwing the DEA bitch until further notice," Juan Castillo yelled down the hallway to the cartel members waiting their turn in the small conference room near his office. The anxious men voiced their displeasure loudly and begged him to reconsider the order.

"No, it stops now. Do you hear me? Now!!!" yelled Castillo as he and his bodyguards chased the men waiting in line out of the hacienda. The cartel members left grumbling that they did not have the opportunity to "fuck the bitch" and voiced their anger to Castillo.

"That's too fuckin' bad. Now, get out of here while I sort some things out." Castillo returned to his office and pushed the intercom button. "Maria, would you please come to my office."

"Si, Señor Castillo. I will be right there, sir."

While waiting for Maria to arrive, he picked up the secure phone and called Doctor Francis Valdez. He had been treating Special Agent McCord since her arrival at the hacienda.

"Buenas tardes, Francis. Your assistance is required here at the hacienda," Castillo asked politely but anxiously. "An unexpected situation has developed, and your skills are needed."

"No hay problema," Valdez replied. "Is your concern over a certain visitor staying at your ranch?"

"Si, a major development," an excited Castillo replied.

"I'll be there around six this evening." The doctor was somewhat surprised at the sudden need for his services. Recently, he and Castillo had scheduled his visits to the hacienda, but this was a deviation. Something must have happened.

"Fine." Castillo put down the phone and took a draw of the cigar he just lit.

Castillo looked out the window in his office to watch the cattle grazing on the pastures next to the hacienda fence line. A few of his security guards patrolled the area, ignoring the cows on the other side of the barbed wire. Smiling, he looked out at the panoramic view and took a moment to admire the fleet of aircraft parked in hangars near the hacienda's well-maintained runway.

Besides being the head of one of the largest drug cartels and money-laundering groups in South America, Castillo was considered one of the top "Narco Cattlemen" in Bolivia. Various drug cartel bosses had established bona fide cattle ranches to disguise their true business. After evading justice for several years, he developed and operated a ranch and was now known as a respectable cattle rancher in the fertile Santa Cruz farming and ranch region.

"Dios mío, I cannot believe our fuckin' luck!" Juan Castillo yelled out unable to contain his excitement. "Unfuckin' believable!"

"This calls for a shot of tequila." He reached for the bottle on his desk, poured himself a glass, and sat back. Francisco Perez had come through again. If Mercedes brokered the deal, Castillo knew it was real. While he didn't like the traitor, the man excelled at informal negotiations and was a straight shooter.

What luck! Five of their most experienced and loyal lieutenants had been rotting in some American prison for the past few years. They could have the gringo bitch. An easy exchange would force their competition to step aside. Sola Mesa would win the cartel war.

A knock on the door interrupted his thoughts.

"Señor Castillo, you wished to see me?" Maria asked.

"Yes, please come in," a now cordial and appreciative Castillo replied. "I have a special job for you. It needs to be done now."

"Si, señor. What do you wish me to do?"

"Maria, I want you to put all of your energy into taking care of our DEA woman. We need her healthy and presentable," directed Castillo.

Maria was surprised and couldn't believe what she was hearing from Castillo. Knowing what this poor woman had gone through in the past few days, with the none-stop sexual orgies, how was Maria going to help bring her back to health?

"Get her cleaned up, take care of her needs, and ensure her room is cleaned. I can only imagine the state it is in now." Castillo took a sip of tequila. "The doctor will be here this evening to take care of her medical needs. The DEA woman will have no more visitors. Do you understand, Maria?"

"Si, mi jefe. I will begin immediately." Maria turned and headed to the storage room to organize the supplies she would need. She paused and thought about how strange it was that it was DEA bitch or DEA whore for the past few days, but now, he referred to the gringo as DEA woman.

Castillo again told his people that all scheduled and future cartel sessions with the DEA woman were canceled. Her need for rest for future pleasure was the only reason given.

That afternoon, Castillo convened a short meeting with a few of his key lieutenants and staff at the hacienda conference room. The basement room had mahogany paneling and fine leather chairs. He offered each one an imported Havana cigar to smoke. He briefed them on the deal offered by the embassy for the safe return of DEA Agent McCord. Several men voiced their disappointment that their "play thing" was leaving, but they reasoned that getting their fellow friends and associates back was well worth the sacrifice. They'd get another gringo bitch eventually.

"Right now, Maria is cleaning McCord up to determine what kind of shape she is in and her health needs." Castillo lit the cigar, took a long drag, and exhaled. "The key to this trade is her being alive and well when we deliver her."

"Last time I saw her, she looked rough…too much of a good time." One lieutenant elbowed another while wagging his eyebrows.

It was obvious to everyone, especially those who had taken advantage of McCord, that she was in terrible physical shape.

"Doctor Valdez will be here soon to determine if it is possible to make her presentable," Castillo said. "If not, you all are aware of the consequences."

"When we do get her health back, how will the trade take place?" Roberto Gomez hoped to take advantage of the situation and secure himself a higher position in the ranks.

"We'll work out the details of the transfer later, but for now, we have to get the gringo's health back or everyone loses—the gringos, our people in US prisons, and most of all, the woman."

"What if the deal falls through and the gringos change their minds on the swap?" another cartel leader asked.

"I am afraid that if the gringo bastards change their minds on the deal." Castillo's mouth lifted up at the corners in a sinister smile. "McCord will go back to work for us."

The cartel members nodded their heads in approval.

With the conference over, the visiting cartel leaders finished their lunch and headed out to the hacienda parking lot. Many gathered in small informal groups to discuss the news about the trade. All agreed that they were looking forward to getting their old friends back. They returned to their vehicles and went back to work.

Castillo found a comfortable chair on the front porch and continued to savor his cigar. Doctor Valdez would be there soon. Hopefully, he'd be able to work a miracle on the woman. The sun began to set behind the Parque Nacional Ambora, a few miles west of the hacienda. A lone black Range Rover approached the security entry point at the main entrance.

The doctor had finally arrived. After parking his vehicle, Valdez exited and opened the rear hatch. He took out his basic medical bag and two other large bags filled with various health items and equipment. He knew the gringo had been in bad shape the day before, so he brought with him everything he thought she might need. Knowing her health was precarious, he hoped he could work a miracle.

"Ah, Doctor Valdez, como está?" Castillo stood to greet his friend as the doctor made his way to the front porch.

A little tired from carrying the heavy bags from the parking lot, he gratefully took the offered seat next to Castillo. A house waiter arrived, and Valdez ordered an iced tea and anything that was ready to eat. It had been a long day at his clinic in Santa Cruz. Soon, the waiter arrived with a large pitcher of tea and a couple of beef tamales, which Valdez devoured quickly.

Sitting back enjoying the company of his good friend, Castillo watched Valdez finish the tamales off in short order. He waited for the doctor to be ready for what he was going to spring on him. Valdez wiped his face of the remaining pieces of food and refilled his glass with tea.

"Francis, you are not going to believe our luck," Castillo said. "The gringos at the embassy offered us a trade: five of our members, currently held in US federal prisons, for the fucked-up DEA bitch."

Valdez was surprised, almost relieved, to hear the offer and looked at Castillo now understanding the reason for the short notice.

"Are you considering making the trade?" a curious Valdez asked.

"Depends. If we don't have anything to trade, amigo, the negotiations are worthless." Castillo shrugged his shoulders. "We'll just say we have no information about a missing DEA undercover agent in Bolivia. But if we did have something of value to trade, we'd proceed."

"So, I suspect you want me to use my medical skills and rehabilitate the gringo back to a presentable state." Valdez hoped he had brought enough supplies, knowing what the DEA agent had been through the past few days.

"Yes, mi amigo. Use all of your powers. Having our loyal and experienced members back will be invaluable to us." Castillo puffed on his cigar and blew out a blue ring of smoke. "With the other cartels moving in and taking our business, we are going to need them more than ever."

"OK." Valdez collected his thoughts for a moment while outlining a potential plan of care in his head. "No one touches her except me and possibly Maria. My plan for her recuperation must be followed to the letter. I don't want all of my work to be for nothing. Keep your thugs from knocking at the door."

Surprised at his friend's directness, Castillo nodded his head in approval while examining the blue smoke rising tranquilly from the cigar,

"Also, with your permission, I would like to provide Maria the food and liquid requirements that McCord will need for the next few days—will you approve that?" Valdez asked.

"Por supuesto, whatever you need," Castillo agreed. "When can you start?"

"We have to start immediately," Valdez urged. "God only knows what kind of sexually transmitted diseases your people gave her and dangerous bruises to her groin area."

"Are you concerned about the drugs you gave her to keep her going for us?" Castillo reminded the doctor of his contribution in keeping the agent a sex slave to the cartel.

"We will start immediately with a detox regiment—if it is not too late…" Valdez directed, knowing full well his complicity.

"We'll move her into one of the guest suites. Maria is ready to assist."

"My friend, it is imperative that this deal is made," Castillo reminded Valdez. "I expect you to use all of your skills to make McCord presentable. Our future depends on it."

Valdez nodded, knowing her health could have implications for him and his family. Castillo's sinister stare confirmed the threat.

"Juan, if you will excuse me, I have work to do." Valdez took a final swallow of his tea and, with the help of the waiter, moved additional medical bags and supplies into the guest suite.

Maria was already in the guest suite arranging for McCord's move when Doctor Valdez entered and began expertly arranging his supplies and equipment. After an hour of carefully getting the suite ready, Valdez sat down with Maria at a small writing desk and began drafting instructions for McCord's care. Besides food and drink, he prescribed some medicines necessary for her recuperation that Maria would administer. She had always been a competent helper for the doctor.

"Maria, do you have any questions?" Valdez asked. "If not, let's move the agent to her new room."

Maria rolled her small service cart alongside Valdez. The cart contained various supplies she thought they may need, including bed sheets, women's t-shirts, simple cotton gowns, and blankets.

With no questions asked, they moved to the room where McCord was staying. The stench of bodily fluids, blood, and stale cigarettes brought tears to their eyes. What was left of the woman lay on stained sheets with her hair matted and dirty. A small 60-watt lamp on the nightstand gave an eerie glow to the empty beer cans and liquor bottles strewn around piles of filthy rags.

Without the drugs that had kept her going, the woman appeared lifeless. Her chest barely rose and fell. Valdez grabbed his doctor's bag and pulled out a couple of pairs of surgical gloves. He handed a pair to Maria and they both put them on.

Beneath the disgusting sheets, the once beautiful woman was covered in bruises. Her ribs were visible beneath the remains of a tattered cotton nightgown. Gently picking her up from the worn mattress, Valdez and Maria wrapped a cotton comforter around her and carried her out of the purgatory she had been in for the last few days.

"No, no. Please, no more," McCord mumbled as she awoke from a drug-induced sleep. Disoriented and confused, she began crying hysterically and, using every ounce of remaining strength, attempted to free herself from the clutches of the doctor who had been giving her the drugs from the start.

"Mi amiga, todo esta bien ahora," Maria murmured while holding the other woman's hand.

Attempting to care for McCord the best she could since her arrival, Maria had held back the anguish and tears she had felt, but no more. Teardrops fell unbidden down her cheeks as she used a wet towel to clean McCord's dirty face.

Valdez and Maria carried McCord to the designated guest suite that would be her new room for the time being.

Opening the suite's door, Valdez and Maria laid McCord's fragile body on a large queen size bed with clean sheets and blankets. The doctor immediately opened his medical bag, administered an IV, and began his examination. He was relieved to use his medical skills to save her, but he'd have to live with the guilt for what he was responsible for inflicting on this woman. He was following orders from the cartel. It was her life or his. But now, he had a chance to redeem himself, if he could save her. He prayed this deal could be made for this poor woman's sake and freedom for five cartel members. McCord was both a prisoner-of-war and a despised spy. He shuddered to think about what would happen if the deal fell through. What would happen to McCord? And to that end, to him and his family.

Valdez and Maria were totally in tune as they cared for McCord. The doctor applied drugs and took vitals while Maria traveled between the well-stocked bathroom and the bedroom, attempting to clean the days' worth of filth caked on McCord.

"Como esta?" Castillo ventured into the suite, eyeing what resembled a rural hospital room. Medical equipment and monitors were strewn on either side of the bed.

"Juan, we've done all we can do for now. Her recovery looks promising, but time will tell." Valdez placed his stethoscope back in his bag. "We'll continue working with her on a daily basis, but a lot will depend on Maria."

"Maria!" Castillo called while looking around the room for her.

"Estoy aquí, mi jefe," Maria replied from the bathroom where she was rinsing out towels.

"Si Maria, I would like you to stay here and care for the woman on a full-time basis for the next few days." Castillo knew he was asking a lot from his longtime, loyal housekeeper. She did have a large family to care for at home.

"No hay problema, mi jefe." Even without orders, Maria would have stayed and cared for McCord.

"Bien. Do whatever you have to do and keep me updated on her progress." Castillo left the suite and headed back to his office where several issues awaited his attention regarding the deal with the embassy. His plant in the embassy had failed to tell him about the deal before Perez. Had his plant been compromised or had the offer come through other channels? Regardless, Special Agent Bonnie McCord would be alive and well for the trade.

Once inside his office, he immediately went to the huge antique oak desk overlooking a window. The panoramic view of his estate didn't hold his attention today. His mind was occupied with the upcoming deal. There had been countless deals and exchanges in the past, but this one was big and had catastrophic consequences if not followed correctly. Weighing his options in his mind, they could either use McCord for their pleasures until she died pleasing the cartel leadership or trade a living McCord for five Sola Mesa kingpins held in US prisons. He was bothered by the prospect that all of this talk of releasing the five cartel members was just a ploy by the DEA. Did they even know he had the agent?

If it was a ploy, contacting the embassy through Francisco Perez would confirm the Feds' suspicion that Castillo had knowledge about her disappearance and possibly knew where she was. To avoid such a fate, he needed another source to confirm the offer. He wanted that confirmation from his informant in the embassy. Without that confirmation, they might as well take the recovering agent outside and blow her brains out—all this getting her back to her health would be a waste of time.

Castillo made a few secure phone calls to a few of his close associates and paid informers at Washington D.C. to confirm the legitimacy of the deal.

CHAPTER
10

"It is cold out tonight." Raul Lopez glanced furtively side to side as he walked among the gravestones in the Cementerio Jardin. In a low nervous voice, he said over his secure cell phone, "Señor Castillo, this is Raul Lopez. I understand you urgently needed to talk with me."

Lopez made his calls on a regular basis from the Cementerio Jardin, near his apartment south of the US Embassy in La Paz.

"Yes, Raul, I need you to find out about a tentative deal regarding a missing DEA agent named Bonnie McCord."

Raul was the "rover" for the embassy, handling mail distribution. Thanks to his mother's position as the Director of the Cultural Affairs Office, he received the position after returning from the US. His job duties included providing administrative and secretarial support for the different sections throughout the embassy and he possessed a top secret security clearance. He was one of few in the embassy that had access to most of the classified messages coming in and out.

Despite his mother's best efforts after his father passed, Raul was constantly in trouble with the authorities. He had moved back to Bolivia after a dishonorable discharge from the Army was reversed to a general discharge. The entry-level position started off boring until he realized the sensitive information he transported for the embassy.

The new start in Bolivia seemed short-lived as Raul got in-volved with drugs and partying shortly after arriving. His mother kicked him out of her condo after finding the place a mess following one of his parties. Raul moved into the Rendezvous Hostel. Located close to his work, it was in the middle of the La Paz district—known for its fun, partying, girls, and drugs.

Life was going well for Raul. Many of his new friends had the telltale signs of cartel members with their swagger, stylish clothes, extravagant jewelry and watches, expensive cars, and beautiful women.

Rumors began to circulate about Raul's new lifestyle, which did not reflect the image of an embassy staff member. However, people liked Raul and did not want to cause any controversies for his mother, so kept their observations secret.

Unfortunately, Raul was prone to brag about his position to his new friends, eventually garnering the attention of the Sola Mesa Cartel boss, Juan Castillo. After looking into the rover, Castillo decided that mentoring Raul would prove valuable for the cartel.

Raul had naively suspected that the cartel valued his views on US policies toward Bolivia and agreed to meet the cartel boss. Arriving at the La Paz Alto International Airport in his favorite Cessna Turbo 206 aircraft on a sunny afternoon, Castillo was promptly whisked away by two cartel members to the Café del Mundo on the outskirts of the city of El Alto.

The nondescript black Mercedes sedan arrived at the restaurant. Castillo emerged with his signature Cuban. The host escorted him and his associates to a small separate dining room in the back. Raul rose and shook hands with Castillo. They engaged in small talk about Raul's background and work at the embassy while enjoying a meal of top choice Bolivian steaks.

"Raul, my people here in La Paz are truly impressed with your position and connections at the embassy. We need a reliable inside person like you to advise us on various political matters." Castillo was building on Raul's low self-esteem. "We would like to offer you a position with us as a part-time contractor to advise us on certain political and domestic matters. You would be well compensated."

Castillo paused and watched the greed light up the rover's eyes. He had him right where he wanted him. "Well, what do you think, amigo? Are you ready to reciprocate our friendship and enjoy the fruits of our new association and build yourself your own career in Bolivia?"

"Yes, Señor Castillo," an excited Raul replied. Both men stood and shook hands then Castillo immediately left the restaurant and went to the airport. Dreams of money, women, and luxury cars filled Raul's mind as he walked to his old, rusted-out Toyota sedan and headed home.

Within a few weeks of their association, his information steered the cartel away from several drug and money-laundering investigations planned by the government. The most valuable intelligence Raul gave to the cartel and the most tragic for the US was the disclosure of names and identities of US Federal Law Enforcement agents working undercover in Bolivia, including DEA Special Agent Bonnie McCord. After learning of McCord's undercover identity, a small force of Sola Mesa Cartel hitmen abducted her in the middle of the night from her high-rise apartment near the mall. McCord put up a good fight against the intruders and wounded one of her abductors with her Barretta service pistol. She was immediately subdued, wrapped in a blanket, and quickly driven to the Sola Mesa Cartel boss at his hacienda for interrogation. Castillo had no illusions she would not survive this ordeal.

Raul Lopez had no clue of the gravity of the situation he was responsible for, nor the pain and agony he had caused. Raul's mother, the US Embassy, and US Law Enforcement would pay a heavy price for his thoughtless actions.

Back at the embassy, Raul found an abandoned storage room to screen classified messages. Raul knew well enough not to be too overt in seeking information. He had to rely on embassy message traffic and informal conversations by embassy personnel. Having unlimited access to all areas in the embassy, he knew more about the inflow and outflow of information and communications that anyone else, including the ambassador and his senior staff.

"Let's see, the DEA agent's name is Bonnie McCord," he said to himself as he looked for both her name and the DEA.

"Ah, here we go," Raul commented as he reviewed that morning's classified messages. A classified message from the State Department asked for more information on the prisoner trade for McCord. After writing a short summary, he would relay the contents of the message to Castillo the next evening.

CHAPTER
11

"As directed by the CIA director for this region, I made contact this morning with Señor Francisco Perez, our informal friend and go-between with the Sola Mesa Cartel," Mercedes briefed.

"I authorized him to disclose the approved deal made by the DEA and the Justice Department to trade five Sola Mesa Cartel kingpins, currently in custody in US federal prisons, for the safe return of Special Agent Bonnie McCord."

There would be no deal with the cartel for McCord's release. The top secret decision was known only by a few key intelligence and State Department officers. The bogus deal served two purposes: to attempt to find the informer in the embassy and to buy the DEA time to form and execute a covert rescue mission. It was determined that the DEA had nothing to lose by fabricating a prisoner swap deal for McCord—the odds of her surviving were zero.

Mercedes was the only person in the embassy that knew the true nature of the proposed swap with the Sola Mesa Cartel.

Back at the embassy conference room, Burton sat motionless unprepared to comment on Mercedes' update.

"Ambassador, at this time, sir, the approved proposal is, I presume, being reviewed now by the Sola Mesa leadership." Looking at his watch, Mercedes commented, "Knowing Francisco's track record, we should hear something soon concerning the deal."

CHAPTER
12

"Good afternoon, this is Mercedes," he answered his secure cell phone. It was late. The day's situation conference had run longer than expected.

"Buenas noches, Doctor Mercedes. Como estas?"

Mercedes hurriedly flipped the recording function for future playback. "Bien, Francisco, y tu?"

"I spoke with some people who are very interested in the proposal you offered this morning," Francisco said. "Will this be a straight trade of five to one with details to be worked out later for a possible exchange?"

"Yes," replied Mercedes while he took a seat in his desk chair. "I estimate it will take us a week to make all of the arrangements for our guests to travel. Can your friends be ready by then?"

"My friends would like to confirm again the names of people that may be traveling." Francisco wasn't prepared to provide an estimate of when the cartel would be ready for the exchange. He had only heard informal reports on McCord's condition.

Mercedes relayed to Francisco the names of the cartel leaders slated to be traded. Most of them were detained at the maximum-security prison in Florence, Colorado.

"Thank you, Mercedes. I will forward the names to our mutual friends and see if they have any questions or comments," Francisco said. "However, I do not foresee any problems. Do you happen to have any idea of the target date for the exchange?"

"I'll check to see when the five prisoners are scheduled to leave the prison in Colorado for a prison in Texas and their flight to Mexico," Mercedes said.

Mercedes reasoned with Francisco, "It would be much easier for the Department of Justice to discreetly and quietly transfer the five to the Mexican authorities for safe keeping until released to Bolivia."

"I suspect McCord would be transported to the US Embassy in Bolivia in the middle of the night—yes?" Francisco asked.

"Agreed," Mercedes replied.

"Have you had the opportunity to review the names of those prisoners being released?" Mercedes knew they were all Sola Mesa Cartel leaders.

"Ah yes, my friend," Francisco replied. "I suspect the prisoners selected will be acceptable."

Upon completing his conversation with Francisco, Mercedes thought, "No doubt, we are giving them their top leadership back, but only in their dreams."

Grinning, Mercedes pulled out a bottle of bourbon and poured himself a glass. He leaned back in his leather office chair and slowly savored the amber liquid. It had been a busy week from populace riots and uprisings in the streets of La Paz to the rescue operation for an undercover DEA agent. His mind went back to the note he discovered that morning in his coat pocket, placed their most likely by Francisco.

How did the Sola Mesa Cartel know details of the trade that Mercedes hadn't disclosed? The note pointed to a traitor at the embassy, but who had access to top secret information they could relay to the cartel? Whoever it was had to have access and the ability to move about without suspicion.

Mercedes pulled out an embassy roster tucked into a desk drawer. He took another drink as he perused the list. Most were career State Department officials and vetted contractors with high-level security clearances. However, there was one name that drew his attention—the embassy rover, Raul Lopez. The carefree partier was known to live beyond his means as a low-level employee. Mercedes went to his computer and accessed the secured personnel records and reviewed the file on Lopez. Mercedes was concerned with what he reviewed combined with the rumors of Raul's wild and partying lifestyle. He would have an immediate session with the embassy security manager in the morning to discuss a security breach and Raul Lopez.

"Yes, Mercedes, we can track all of Raul Lopez's movements around the embassy with our security cameras," the security manager said. "Is there anything in particular you are looking for?"

"Any unusual contacts or stops in the embassy that you suspect are questionable or not part of a rover's duties," Mercedes instructed.

"Can you tell me what this is all about?" asked the security manager.

"I'll talk further with you about this today, but I suspect various messages are leaking out of the embassy." Mercedes said no more but agreed to meet with the manager later to discuss details.

"OK, Mercedes, I'll get back to you later with what we discover."

Mercedes returned to his office where a mountain of reports and documents required his attention. He turned on the coffee maker, prepared for a long night.

CHAPTER
13

The abrupt ringing of a phone woke Mercedes. He reached for the phone, which had fallen to the floor next to the sofa and answered. "This is Doctor Mercedes." He looked at his watch. The sofa beneath him was not as comfortable after a short night's sleep.

"Sir, this is Gloria," the ambassador's executive officer said. "The ambassador requests your presence at an emergency executive session this morning at nine in the basement conference room. Can you attend?"

"Just a moment please, Gloria." Mercedes ran his fingers through his hair and rubbed his eyes. He glanced at his watch to see if he had enough time for a shower. "I can be there. Is there an agenda for the meeting?"

"Not that I'm aware of. However, the ambassador says it is imperative for you to attend."

"Alright, I'll be there." Mercedes hung up and checked his watch again. He had half an hour before he needed to make his way to the conference room. He walked to his private bathroom where he showered and shaved. The hot water cleared the sleep from his mind.

With so much happening in Bolivia, he focused his attention on what the ambassador might want that morning. After preparing all of his classified situational awareness reports and placing them in his brown, leather briefcase, Mercedes viewed himself in the mirror. Satisfied, he made the walk down to the basement. He grabbed a couple of breakfast burritos from the embassy café and wolfed them down on his way to the elevator and the short ride down to the basement.

"Doctor Mercedes, sir, you are cleared to enter the conference room." The Marine security guard opened the heavy, secure door.

Thanking the sergeant, Mercedes found the other executive members sitting in their assigned seats, reviewing their reports and updates for their areas of responsibility—unsure about the nature of the meeting. Knowing Ambassador's Burton's past track record of emergency meetings, most likely, it was something trite and insignificant like a street vendor making a derogatory comment about his wife.

"Ladies and gentlemen, the ambassador," the Marine guard announced before closing and securing the conference room door after Burton. The ambassador took his place at the front of the table and quickly began reviewing several urgent, classified documents from his folder.

"Good morning." The ambassador rose and went to the podium.

Mercedes figured his use of the podium was some sort of demonstration of his importance over the rest of the executive council. Mercedes was in no mood for the narcissistic clown's antics and simply rolled his eyes.

"Doctor Mercedes, we just received a classified notification this morning from the State Department," the ambassador confidently announced. Mercedes looked up with a snide smile upon hearing his name. "In regards to the exchange of five Sola Mesa Cartel members currently imprisoned in the US for who we believe to be undercover DEA Agent Bonnie McCord, the President of the United States has canceled authorization for the exchange."

Mercedes, acting shocked, rose after hearing the announcement while the others in the room were confused and speechless at this tragic change. He was particularly concerned that the ambassador might have leaked that the exchange was a ruse.

"Mr. Ambassador, are you absolutely sure?" Mercedes asked convincingly. "The deal had been approved by the Justice Department, DEA, and the Secretary of State. Could you convey to the State Department that the offer is already on the table and it appears the cartel is preparing to make the swap, as are we. We cannot turn back.

"Mr. Ambassador, McCord's survival depends on this trade," Mercedes emphatically pleaded with much theatrics. "Why is the president negating the trade?"

The ambassador was stunned by the insubordination and immediately censored his behavior in front of the others. He asked the other officers present to leave the conference room to have a private meeting with Mercedes.

Mercedes could not have played it better. He had been looking forward to the ambassador announcing the president's decision about McCord. Knowing it wouldn't happen, he had continued to press forward for the trade. However, for the sake of the intelligence leak in the embassy, the trade had to look like it was going through all the official channels.

"Please reconsider having the others leave the room," Mercedes requested while the others were unsure whether to leave or stay. "We are discussing a situation here that possibly impacts the life of one of our own agents following her orders.

"No one is left behind!" Mercedes angrily pointed at the ambassador. "We never leave our people behind in any conflict, and we are not going to start now if there is any possibility of getting Special Agent McCord back." Those with military service knew exactly what Mercedes was referring to—the informal protocol that no US service member man or woman would be left behind on a battlefield—dead or alive.

"All embassy staff, leave the conference now!" an angry red-faced Ambassador Burton ordered. "Except for you, Mercedes." The conference room emptied except for Mercedes and Ambassador Burton. Both men settled down as soon as the conference room door was closed and secured.

"Doctor Mercedes, you will never again question my authority or my directives in front of the embassy staff again," Burton said, pointing his finger at Mercedes' chest. "Do you understand me?"

Mercedes slowly took his hand and grasped the ambassador's index finger on his chest and moved his hand away, making his point.

"Mercedes!" Burton ordered. "I'm calling your boss right now to have you recalled and sent home."

"Mr. Ambassador," Mercedes said with deadly calm. "Sir, why don't you and I have a seat and we can discuss some options you laid on the table this morning?"

Surprised and relieved that Mercedes was now calm and respectful, the ambassador nodded his head and took a seat across from him.

Both Mercedes and the ambassador understood the discussion up to this point was just for the effect of the other staff members in the room. Each man knew they needed each other. Burton depended on Mercedes because he literally kept the embassy operating well. Mercedes needed Burton just to stay out of his way.

"Ambassador Burton, please hear me out on a few issues." Mercedes kept his voice calm and respectful. As a seasoned and experienced Marine officer and a cunning CIA agent, he planned to lead Burton to exactly where he needed him to go.

"First," Mercedes began slowly. "I recommend that you respond back to the Secretary of State that in your view the trade for McCord should proceed as originally authorized and planned."

"Now Mercedes, I explained to you that this came from the president. No deal would be made with the cartel," Burton said, "and I am not going to question my orders from State."

"Sir, you do have the authority, under State Department directives, to question and even deviate from orders if you view the change would jeopardize the safety of a US citizen." Mercedes knew the ambassador had limited knowledge of State directives.

"Mercedes, this decision comes directly from the president and I will not use my authority to change the directive—that is final," replied a now flustered Burton.

"Alright, Mr. Ambassador," Mercedes quietly said while pulling out a couple of large envelopes from his leather briefcase. He handed the stack to Burton. "These are for you. Please open them up."

Burton eyed the envelopes with suspicion. He took out his pocketknife, opened the blade, and slowly opened the first envelope. He pulled out several eight-by-ten color photos of his wife in compromising sexual positions with the Spanish Ambassador. Breathing heavily, he tore his gaze away and opened the second envelope. More photos fell on the table, these showing his own homosexual love affair with a Bolivian contractor.

The conference room was silent. Burton took several deep breaths as he attempted to regain his composure. Mercedes waited patiently for the ambassador to speak. It was good that no one else witness the discussion between Mercedes and Burton.

"Alright, Mercedes. What do you want?" Burton's shoulders slumped in resignation. His life, career, reputation, and family were in Mercedes' hands.

"Here is what you are going to do." Mercedes spelled out exactly how the ambassador would handle the situation with DEA Agent Bonnie McCord. He hoped he was not too late to save her.

The ambassador would reach out to the Secretary of State to request a reversal of the president's decision. Burton would lean on the precarious change in the Bolivian government as motivation for continuing to move forward. The life of an American citizen was at stake.

"Make sure the communications are clear. We want whoever is listening to the conversation to know the deal will go through as planned. Do you understand?" Mercedes asked.

"I can't and will not put out a message of that nature," Burton staunchly protested.

"If you don't, I will," Mercedes said to the sobbing ambassador.

"OK, OK, write what you deem necessary. My assistant will make sure it goes out." Burton put his head in his hands. "Anything else?"

"We are going to need a continuous stream of message traffic from the embassy to the State Department with regards to the status of the trade," Mercedes directed. "The messages can be true, bogus, falsehoods, unsubstantiated—whatever, but it has got to show the appearance that the trade is still happening or being worked."

"State will go nuts if I begin sending the useless messages you described," the ambassador protested, knowing it was useless to argue.

"As long as we send them to some low-level office staff member, it should be fine," Mercedes said. "The messages should denote that all is on course with the trade and any issues are being worked by you and the embassy.

"For your own safety and security, you do not need to know anything further. You are responsible for making sure these messages go out on a regular basis." Mercedes gave the ambassador a tissue and offered him a cup of coffee.

"Please tell me, why are you so concerned by one DEA agent's disappearance when she shouldn't have been in Bolivia in the first place." The ambassador's hand shook as he brought the steaming cup of espresso to his lips.

Mercedes just stared at the ambassador in disbelief, wanting to slam his fist into the cowardly man's face; however, that would wait. He would need the ambassador to do more of his bidding in the very near future for the possible release of McCord.

CHAPTER
14

"That's him," local CIA contractor Alberto Montana whispered to a napping Mercedes in the front of seat of a black Chevrolet Suburban with blackened windows.

He woke from a much-needed nap while Montana produced a thermos of coffee and poured Mercedes a cup. Nodding his head in thanks, he slugged down the coffee in short order and devoured the two cold chicken wraps offered to him.

"Hey boss, what do you want with this wild partying punk?" Montana asked. "Isn't he some sort of mail room clerk at the embassy?"

"I have good information and a sixth sense that he is providing sensitive information to a cartel, and we are going to find out for sure this evening." Mercedes put down the last of the wrap and the empty cup. The other CIA contractor, Pablo Cortez, was snoring in the rear seat. Both Mercedes and Pablo viewed the sleeping Cortez and laughed before waking him.

"Same procedures in picking this guy up before taking him to the safe house?" asked Montana.

"Yes, absolutamente," replied Mercedes, "and let's ensure it is quick, smooth, and without incident."

Parked just down the street from Raul Lopez' favorite night club, Club Nocturno, the men in the SUV watched for a couple of hours from the nearby Falcon Gym parking lot. According to their observations, he usually left the bars just prior to midnight where he headed back to his apartment and managed to sober up and change clothes prior to returning to his job at the embassy.

"Go get him." Mercedes ordered as Lopez left the bar and walked awkwardly toward his parked vehicle.

The two men slid out of the SUV dressed as a couple of wild local partyers and made their way up the sidewalk to Club Nocturno. Discreetly following behind Lopez down Calle Linares, Lopez was taken in a split second and carried to a nearby discreet alleyway. The rover kicked and screamed as they carried him. Pablo subdued him with a nonlethal chokehold, immediately stopping his outbursts. A black cloth sack covered Lopez' head, his hands were cuffed, and he was thrown in the cargo area of the waiting SUV. The SUV was parked in an empty, unlit parking area where no one could hear Raul's cries for help.

"What do you want with me, where are you taking me?" a very frightened and confused Lopez muttered from his head sack.

"Mr. Lopez, please behave and no harm will come to you if simply follow our instructions. Do you understand?" Pablo nonchalantly said. "We are on our way to a place where we can visit in private. Now sit back and enjoy the short ride."

Pablo grinned while Alberto simply shook his head. Mercedes glanced at the pathetic Lopez then worked on his report and checked his smartphone for messages. All three men had gone through this same procedure a few times before and knew their various roles for the reception of Raul Lopez.

The SUV entered an industrial area just north of the La Paz International Airport. The steady sounds of aircraft landing and taking off would drown out their planned activity in the quiet warehouse. The SUV stopped in front of the large, galvanized steel doors of the Electrico Internacional warehouse. Two nondescript Toyota sedans were parked in the lot beneath the neon sign.

Alberto clicked a remote and the doors opened. They parked the SUV inside then waited for the doors to close. Mercedes got out and flipped on the fluorescent lights.

Alberto and Pablo escorted Lopez out of the vehicle and into what appeared to be a typical office complex of rows of cubicles surrounded by various offices on the side. They directed him to the small, makeshift interrogation room. With the dark canvas bag still tied around his head, Lopez sobbed and pleaded for a cigarette. Everyone knew, from their years of experience in this clandestine business, the interview with Lopez would be quick and easy to the point of being pathetic.

A woman peered out of one of the office windows, catching the men off guard. She didn't bother to turn to greet them. Instead, she stood like a cat waiting to catch its prey. Roberta Potter's reputation preceded her. CIA contractor Roberta Potter was specifically requested by Mercedes to assist him with the McCord rescue attempt. Besides speaking fluent Spanish, she had very unique skills required for this particular mission and she worked well alone in the most dangerous of situations. She would be required to do just that.

The interrogation room was equipped with various listening devices and digital video cameras and a small, simple wooden table surrounded by folding chairs in the center of the room. Alberto and Pablo pushed the crying Lopez into a wooden chair. He kept muttering that he didn't do or know anything. If Mercedes was convinced that he was not the leak at the embassy, he would be set free with the condition that nothing unusual happened this night—he just partied too late into the evening.

Mercedes' absence from the interrogation was on purpose. Since he worked in the embassy, he did not want Lopez to have any type of interaction with him. Or to know what his real role at the embassy was. If Raul was questioned by the cartel, knowledge of Mercedes' true role in releasing McCord would be disastrous.

Pablo turned on the recording devices and nodded to Potter. She approached Lopez, took the bag off his head, and threw it on the floor. Surprised, Raul squinted in the bright lights. Snot ran down his chin, a pathetic sight.

"I did not do anything." The grown man wailed like a small child. "What do you want?"

Pablo tossed a box of tissues to Lopez who blotted his tears. He blew his nose loudly.

"Now, Mr. Lopez, let us get started," Potter asked politely.

"What do you want to know?" a confused Lopez asked, trying to regain his composure.

"Start with what you do for the embassy." Potter began the interrogation with something easy for him to answer. After a half hour of listening to his relationship and work at the embassy, Potter questioned him on his outside associations. He mentioned his advisory work with a front company for the cartel.

"For your benefit, Raul, we are aware of your passing classified messages and documents to the Sola Mesa Cartel and your association with Juan Castillo," Potter said right in his face. She showed pictures of him with Castillo at the restaurant and him making copies of documents at a secluded embassy office with a copying machine.

Potter instructed Lopez that she had some critical questions that he needed to answer immediately—especially in regard to his knowledge of the abduction of DEA Special Agent Bonnie McCord.

"Yes ma'am. I was aware through the State Department's classified message traffic bulletins. The bulletin advised an undercover DEA Agent working as a manager at a fried chicken franchise in Santa Cruz," Lopez regaining his senses answered, wishing to placate Potter as she held his life in her hands. "It was my understanding that some executive at the chicken franchise headquarters had blown the whistle on McCord, and I was just confirming what they already knew."

Lopez continued to tell Potter, to the best of his recollection, all of the information he had passed on to the Sola Mesa Cartel. From all the details about disclosing the true identities of American agents to planned Bolivian law enforcement drug raids, Lopez began to open up. At the end of his confession, he had realized the gravity of his situation and the extent of the damage done—especially to McCord. There was complete silence in the interrogation room. Potter just stared at Lopez.

"Ms. Potter, where do we go from here?" a sobbing and tearful Lopez said with his head down in his lap. "What can I do to attempt to make things right?"

Having interrogated countless individuals like Lopez that unwittingly were drawn into the cartels, Potter now turned her attention to the immediate task ahead for Lopez. "Listen to me very carefully because, frankly, your life depends on it."

Lopez sat in his chair shaking with fear but attentive.

"At a predetermined time in the near future, you will discreetly be released from your duties at the embassy and be reassigned to the United States where you will face the full weight of the Justice Department for your actions here in Bolivia," Potter sternly said as Lopez began uncontrollably crying.

Potter knew that the odds were good that Lopez could keep up the façade of the trade deal being worked, but she was concerned he could abruptly turn and flee the country or attempt to hide out somewhere in Bolivia. She would need to balance the repercussions and penalties of his actions with an incentive to remain on their side.

"However," Potter started with the carrot or stick approach. "If you follow our instructions to the letter, we'll ensure that your cooperation is documented and forwarded to the presiding judicial officials."

"What can I do?" Lopez looked up, eager to hear more while Potter grabbed a yellow legal pad from the table to take notes.

"You will continue to work at the embassy in your current position," she directed, "and you will continue your association with your friends from the Sola Mesa Cartel."

"Ma'am, I don't understand," a perplexed Lopez asked. "With all that has happened, you want me to continue at the embassy and stay connected with the cartel?"

"Starting now, we will provide you with all the message traffic and intelligence reports that you are to pass on." Potter gave him a deadly stare. "Of course, it will all be bogus and fake, but it will appear credible to your friends at the cartel. Do you understand?"

Potter wanted nothing more than to perform a "contractor interrogation" on Lopez, but her employer needed him intact and without bruises—for now.

"But if they find out that I am passing off false information, they'll know I have been compromised," a fearful Lopez said. "They'll kill me."

"Yes, Mr. Lopez. Our sources tell us they plan on killing you just as soon as you are no more use to them." She paused to take a drink of water. "Now, let us stop bullshitting around and get to work. Life will go a lot easier for you if you cooperate. You are going to help us get Agent McCord back alive—are you not?"

Lopez began twitching, rubbing his face and hair with shaky hands. He was in a no-win situation, working with the cartel had caused him enough anxiety. But going behind their back was the stuff of nightmares.

"Besides revealing the true identity of Agent McCord, what else have you given to your cartel friends regarding clandestine DEA operations in Bolivia?"

Lopez remembered many insignificant and routine reports involving the DEA. The messages to the ambassador regarding the prospect of an exchange of five imprisoned Sola Mesa members for McCord intrigued him. He recalled from experience that the US never exchanged cartel leaders for the lives of American citizens. He admitted passing on the exchange proposal to the cartel and surmised it was bogus—i.e., fabricated by the CIA.

"For your benefit, Lopez, and you listen to me carefully, eventually there will be a swap for McCord, but it is taking time to convince the president to reverse his decision," explained Potter, not revealing a hint of the time being bought for a rescue mission.

"What if time passes and there is no deal?" Lopez timidly asked while staring at the floor.

"Then she dies, we would have done everything possible to save her, and you would be held responsible," Potter answered factually while Lopez began to whimper.

"Listen up Lopez," Potter emphasized, "if you are convincing enough to keep her alive for the next week or so, we'll have a good chance of getting her back alive. Meaning your chances of survival have increased significantly...do you understand?"

"Yes ma'am, I understand and will follow your instructions."

"Good." Potter nodded her head with approval. "Now listen up."

"We have pretty good intelligence that McCord is literally being used as a DEA trophy whore—most likely doped-up and fucked by various cartel members—as a result of your help." She knew she was getting worked up and more hostile toward Lopez and wanted to smash his face in. With a few deep breaths, she calmed herself. She was getting paid well to see this mission through.

A warning in her small earphone from Mercedes told her to move on quickly. They didn't have that much time left before they had to get Lopez back to the embassy for his daily routine.

"Everything needs to appear normal for Mr. Raul Lopez," Mercedes warned Potter who acknowledged him by nodding her head.

"I didn't know, I didn't know..." Barely able to control himself, Lopez lowered his head onto his folded arms and began crying. His eyes were bloodshot, and tears trickled out of the corners. "What is going to happen to me?"

Potter moved to a small table in the corner of the room where she picked up a brown folder filled with various embassy messages, documents, and internal memorandums. She laid the folder in front of Lopez and directed him to quickly review it.

"You will relay the information in this folder to your contacts, friends, whatever with the cartel," she ordered. "The cartel members prisoner exchange for McCord must take priority in your communications. They need to be convinced it will take place in the very near future—and hopefully it will."

"Why am I providing them information on a trade that isn't taking place?" Lopez wiped his eyes and picked up the folder. Several tabs with dates on them organized the information within.

"It is best you don't know all the details, but you must be very convincing that a deal will occur soon. Just ensure they believe you," Potter stressed.

"One other item we'll require from you before we drop you off near your apartment." She paused to let the reality of his situation sink in before continuing, "Listen to your cartel associates very carefully. Report back to me any information you can about McCord, but don't be too obvious." She handed him a nondescript secure cell phone.

"Ma'am, what do you mean by the word 'trivial,'" he asked.

"Anything you hear about her, forward it to us, and we'll decide if it is useful or not," she replied. "The more you help us, the more we can justify helping you when you return to the States."

Lopez took the phone and placed it into the pocket of his pants.

"Also, if you should unfortunately decide to turn on us." Potter pulled out her Beretta 92FS service pistol and pointed it at Lopez. "I will personally find and kill you and your mother. Do you understand?"

Lopez paled.

"Alright, you know what is expected of you. The gentlemen who brought you here will drop you off at a discreet location near your apartment. Now put this on." Potter tossed him the black cloth bag he'd worn on his ride there. "When you get to your apartment, get something to eat, drink some coffee, and get ready to go to the embassy—no deviations." Potter grabbed his arm and squeezed it tightly out of pure disgust for the pawn. She moved in close, her lips nearly brushing the cloth near his ear. "Listen you little prick, you try to fuck us again, and they'll find your mutilated body in a cesspool near the dump."

"Yes, ma'am," a quivering and hysterical Lopez responded.

Alberto and Pablo entered the integration room and looked at Potter before proceeding. With a nod of her head, the men took hold of Lopez and escorted him out and into the waiting SUV. The early morning sounds of the commercial jet airliners could be heard thundering into the brilliant dawn sky. Nothing was said in the SUV except for the high volume of Alberto's favorite morning radio playing "Thriller" by Michael Jackson.

Arriving at a high-rise parking area near the Rendezvous Hostel, Alberto entered the garage and drove to the third level. He parked in a corner spot. Pablo exited the vehicle to check for any type of camera or monitoring device. He found one and quickly disabled it. A quick scan of the floor revealed that they were alone. He opened the back door, grabbed Lopez by the arm, and hauled him out of the vehicle. They walked three parking spaces down before Pablo released his grip.

"Lay down and count to two hundred before taking the bag off your head. Do you follow?"

Lopez nodded, laid down, and began a slow count in his mind. The cool concrete reminded him he was still alive.

Pablo hopped back into the SUV. Alberto put it into reverse. In short order, the SUV disappeared in the smog-filled streets of La Paz.

Slowly taking the bag off, Lopez looked around and recognized the parking garage just around the corner from his apartment. Tired and disoriented, he slowly made his way out of the garage to the Rendezvous Hostel lobby. It was a familiar site in the Hostel to see the early arrival of Raul Lopez wandering to his apartment after a full night of partying and then a half hour later, seeing him showered, dressed, and heading for his job at the embassy.

"Ah, there goes Raul," the concierge shook his head. "Another rough night of partying, pobrecita."

"America's finest preparing for his hard work at the embassy." The desk clerk laughed.

The concierge chuckled then excused himself to go outside. He walked to a small employee lunch table near the back-alley entrance. He lit a cigarette and briefly looked around for any other employees. Seeing none, he reached for his cell phone, punched a preset number, and waited for an answer.

At the click of someone answering, he said, "Rover went by as usual. Too much to drink but headed home."

"Muchas gracias, mi amigo," replied the voice before the line went dead.

The concierge had reported on Lopez since before the cartel began working with him. Juan Castillo liked keeping tabs on his informants. The shifty-eyed informer could turn on him at any moment, but all was well. Castillo needed Raul to confirm the validity of the embassy's arrangement for McCord. He wasn't taking any chances.

"Good morning, Raul. Another rough night?" The guard at the embassy's main entrance couldn't keep the condemnation out of his voice. No matter how many times the guards reported suspicious activity surrounding Lopez, nothing seemed to happen. Being the son of a top embassy officer had its perks.

A hungover Raul Lopez made his usual rounds and discovered a top secret dispatch that required the ambassador's immediate attention. He snuck into one of the men's bathroom stalls to review the dispatch.

TOP SECRET. No Foreign Dissemination
For the Ambassador's eyes only
To: Ambassador Burton
From: Under Secretary of State, Dr. Cory Epler

The President of the United States has denied the request by your station to proceed with negotiations for the exchange of five Sola Mesa Cartel members, detained in US federal prisons, for undercover DEA Special Agent Bonnie McCord. The reasons for this denial are as follows:

1. No tangible information on the status of McCord or where she may be detained.
2. The standing US policy is no drug cartel prisoners exchanged for hostages.
3. Injecting five highly valued cartel leaders back into Bolivia would result in increased violence and coca production.
4. With the current change in governments in Bolivia, covert prisoner exchanges with the US have been denied.

5. The DEA is prohibited from entering Bolivia under any circumstances. It was made clear to the Director of the DEA that no agents were to be assigned to Bolivia prior to McCord's arrival.

6. The President of the United States, under the circumstances and national security interests, sees McCord as expendable.

No further action will be taken by you or your embassy in securing the release of DEA Special Agent Bonnie McCord.
For the Secretary of State
Dr. Cory Epler
Under Secretary of State

After reading the dispatch, Lopez clumsily placed the classified dispatch in its top secret pouch and remained in the stall thinking about what he had just read. He was torn between two deadly realities—lie to Juan Castillo about the prisoner exchange for McCord or tell him the truth, which meant immediate repercussions from the CIA and DEA, plus a long prison term.

Lopez continued his normal job routine while attempting to hide his growing panic. Preparing himself mentally for the call he would make that night to Juan Castillo, he thought of the various contingencies that awaited his decision, trying to determine the lesser of the impacts to his life.

"Señor Juan Castillo please," Lopez asked the cartel member answering Castillo's private phone.

"Is this Raul?" the answering member asked. "Juan asked me to take any information you have. I assure you he will receive your update tonight, ok?"

Lopez relayed the false dispatches provided to him. Conveying the lie that the exchange was still being negotiated and was proceeding as planned. However, Lopez emphasized that the Feds wanted proof that McCord was alive and in good health for the exchange to move forward. He was relieved the call had been made.

CHAPTER
15

"Como te sientes, señora?" Maria moved to McCord's bedside with a warm washcloth. She had been monitoring McCord's progress for the past few days, enjoying the help she could give the young woman. Though saddened by what the woman had gone through, she looked forward to the homecoming of the cartel members—they were all old family friends.

McCord opened her eyes and glanced around furtively. Fear filled the green depths.

"Would you like something to eat?" Maria had prepared a plate of fruit and yogurt and placed it on the small dresser next to the bed.

"Who are you?" The sedatives had left McCord dazed.

"Si, señora. My boss asked me to take care of your needs."

"Why now?" McCord tried to sit up, but her arms were weak.

"Aquí, let me help you," Maria offered as she helped the thin woman to a seat. She winced when Maria hit a bruise, but there were too many to avoid.

"Why are caring for me now?" asked McCord. The movement to a seat had exhausted her. Her breathing was labored from the small effort.

"Creo que, I believe it best if Señor Castillo explained the circumstances to you." Maria peeled a banana and attempted to feed the younger woman.

Just mentioning his name caused McCord to noticeably tremble.

A man knocked at the bedroom door. "May I enter?"

"Si, mi jefe." Maria rose to greet Castillo who walked into the bedroom.

"How is she doing? Has Doctor Valdez been in to see her today?" He stared at his valuable bargaining chip unable to hide a smile.

"Bien, mi jefe. Bien," Maria answered. "The doctor has given me a list of things I need to do for the señora."

"Keep me updated on her progress." Castillo moved closer to the pathetic woman's bedside and took a seat in a chair next to the bed.

As Castillo stared at McCord's bruised and cut face, he was somewhat relieved that a prisoner exchange had been offered by the gringos. He figured her current condition would be a stark warning to the DEA not to send any more undercover agents to Bolivia. Even with more time to rehabilitate her, she'd show the effects of her time at the Ranch. Her release would prove beneficial for the cartel beyond the release of his lieutenants from US custody.

Fear threatened to overwhelm McCord as she stared at the devil himself. She remembered the sadistic torture he had put her through. Her body shook uncontrollably. Was he just there to torture her some more? Heal her only to break her some more?

"McCord, do you understand you are very lucky to be alive?" Castillo leaned back and crossed his legs, getting comfortable.

"No," a faint whisper could barely be heard from her swollen and cracked lips. "Why stop now?"

"That is a very good question. I would like to share the answer with you."

McCord, expressionless, just stared at Castillo.

"Frankly, McCord, I don't care if you live or die here. In fact, we were having so much fun having you as our guest, we truly did not want to give you up." Castillo paused a moment to relish her discomfort. "Entonces, I received a credible offer from the embassy that they would release five of my men for your return."

McCord sucked in a breath not believing a word he said. She was not supposed to be here. The DEA wouldn't trade cartel bosses for her. It had to be a lie, something else he was using to torture her.

"Naturally, as a prominent businessman and respected rancher in Santa Cruz, I agreed to have my people look for you." Castillo's cruel laugh echoed in the room. "We just so happened to find you before another cartel could cause more harm to you—gracias a Dios! Naturally, we needed to get you cleaned up to make the trade possible. So you see, everyone benefits."

Hope flared in McCord for a moment. Maybe there was a chance she'd escape with her life.

"Take advantage of our hospitality and get healed, you—" Castillo stopped short from calling her various repulsive names. He simply rose from the chair and motioned for Maria to follow him to the door. Pulling out a Cuban cigar, he savored the distinct aroma of the cigar before lighting it while Maria waited.

"It appears McCord is recovering." Castillo kept his voice low. "Continue the good work and take whatever time you feel is necessary to continue the progress."

"Si, mi jefe. No hay problema." Her customary reply satisfied Castillo who left, closing the door behind him.

Maria returned to McCord's bedside. Despite their differences, the housekeeper enjoyed the company of another female companion. Most of her time was spent caring for the gringo. Thankfully, the woman was fluent in Spanish. Maria's English was limited to a few basic phrases. Conversations usually centered around past loves, Hollywood, movie stars, and their families. Some days, the two women would talk for hours to the point that Castillo would abruptly warn Maria to stop the unnecessary chatter—if she had nothing else to accomplish with McCord, she could return to her normal duties at the hacienda. Regardless, a friendly informal relationship was building where they looked forward to their duties and visits.

On a routine visit, Doctor Valdez determined it was beneficial for McCord to get some simple exercises and fresh air. They decided the spacious patio adjacent to the large kitchen and outdoor dining facilities was a safe place for her to go.

Castillo reluctantly agreed, commenting, "I'm not running a health club for gringo sluts. The bitch needs to hurry up and heal." His bad mood increased with each passing day.

"Juan, a few short trips to the patio will increase her healing," the doctor said, trying to appease the cartel boss.

"Alright, I'll have Maria escort her to the patio a couple times a day." A frustrated Castillo huffed. "I liked it better when she was fucked all night by my soldiers."

"Yo entiendo, my old friend," Valdez replied and asked the question many cartel members had recently, "How is the deal going for the five?"

"Why don't we take a short break out on the patio and enjoy a smoke?" Castillo pulled two cigars from the special custom-built humidor in his office. Both walked a short way to the private chairs and table reserved for Castillo and his guests. They took a moment to savor the cigars. "We can talk more comfortably here."

"How certain are you that this is a true, authorized exchange and not just some scheme the Yankee gringos dreamed up to buy time?" Valdez enjoyed playing the devil's advocate. He generally learned more without raising Castillo's ire.

"I have wondered the same thing, but regardless it is a win-win for the cartel," Castillo explained. "Either the exchange goes through for the five or McCord goes back to work for us as our trophy—all cleaned up and ready to go back to her undercover work."

Both men laughed.

"Francis, I have a rat in the embassy. His job is to distribute classified documents, messages, and reports to the various offices in the embassy. He contacts me every day with any pertinent information he believes is of interest to the cartel." He took a draw on the cigar and exhaled. "Our rat confirms that the exchange is a done deal. He has even provided me official documents confirming the authorization for the exchange."

"That's good news."

"Not to mention, the CIA dick stationed at the embassy, some guy named Mercedes, has been in contact with our go-between at the bank and he also confirmed the United States' commitment to make the trade."

"It all seems legitimate then?"

"Sin duda. What would be the purpose of the gringos to make up such a scheme?" Castillo sought his friend's opinion to be sure he hadn't missed something.

"The Americans know your situation with the other cartels. They must realize how desperate you'd be to have your five lieutenants back." Valdez pondered a moment before adding, "Trading for McCord seems a reasonable request, if they thought she was still alive."

"They are not sure whether she is alive or dead, but they threw down the dice, betting that she is alive when they contacted us with the offer. I suspect they have their paid sources pointing to the Sola Mesa Cartel," reasoned Castillo laughing. "Everyone has their paid sources."

"Juan, please humor me for a minute. Is it possible that this exchange deal is just a setup to keep McCord alive until a possible rescue mission can be organized to free her here at the hacienda?" Valdez hoped he hadn't pushed Castillo too far. "The gringos are not in the habit of making deals with the cartels as you know."

"Yes, we are aware of the DEA's Special Response Team. We have had conflicts with them in the past when the DEA were allowed in Bolivia," Castillo recalled. "But since our dear President Evo Morales kicked the DEA out of Bolivia a few years back, an illegal undercover DEA agent found in Bolivia is an embarrassment to their government. I understand from our people in Washington that no rescue team is in the works. The current President of the United States wants a new start with our new president and government.

"Anyway, we have half of the off-duty Santa Cruz police force and Argentinian mercenaries guarding the Ranch. I doubt they will try anything stupid like attack the hacienda." Castillo leaned back content with his assessment of the situation. "If they attempt a rescue, we'll just shoot McCord and place the blame on the rescue team."

"Sounds like you've thought of everything." Valdez was surprised by his friend's thorough assessment of the situation. Normally, the doctor had to remind him of the possible dangers.

"We have nothing to lose by keeping McCord alive for a possible exchange. We win either way—our captured leaders or our whore back." Castillo grinned sadistically. "Entonces, our new government will file a formal complaint with the President of the United States about a DEA agent's presence in our country. That will be fun to watch."

"Those Americans need a taste of their own medicine." Valdez thought the US interfered too much in their affairs.

"We'll continue to care for McCord as long as we receive positive updates on the exchange." Castillo looked out over the horizon, his lips curling in a devilish smirk. "Otherwise, I'll have the honor of being the first to screw her."

CHAPTER

16

"Thank you, gentleman, for your quick response to our urgent request for your services." Retired DEA Special Agent John Franklin, Foreign-deployed Advisory and Support Team (FAST) Chief, addressed a seasoned team of retired military special forces members in a conference center at the Federal Correctional Institute near Big Springs, Texas, formally Webb Air Force Base. They all had worked with the DEA and CIA on a part-time contract basis as needed.

"Each of you has worked various clandestine missions in South America against the major drug lords." Franklin looked at the team of men ranging from a retired Army DELTA to a former Air Force Combat Controller. "You know the language, the customs, and more importantly, how to blend in with the population. Sorry, I cannot provide you further details on the mission, but, so far, the planning has been very fluid based on the intelligence we have gathered.

"Now gentlemen, I would like to refer you to this large screen behind me," directed Franklin. "I would like to introduce retired United State Marine Corp Colonel, Doctor Jose Mercedes."

"Thank you, Mr. Franklin. Good morning, gentlemen. I am Doctor Jose Mercedes, Special Assistant to the Ambassador of Bolivia and regional director for the CIA," Mercedes began explaining that his classified Zoom conference was coming from a CIA safe house in La Paz.

With Mercedes, monitoring the teleconference, was CIA contractor Roberta Potter who had recently flown into La Paz overnight to participate in the mission planning. If she had questions, she would write them down and have Mercedes ask for her. Both believed it best to keep her participation secret until the actual execution of the rescue mission. She could not afford to let her involvement be compromised due to her planned sensitive, undercover tasks in Santa Cruz and the cartel's hacienda.

"Your video teleconference reception is good here," answered Team Chief Franklin guardedly. "For us old retired, military types, we are using facilities at what once was Webb Air Force."

"Very good, thank you," Mercedes said, doing his best to keep his cool. "I trust you are aware of the circumstances of DEA Special Agent McCord's abduction after her cover was blown. Allow me to summarize to make sure we are all on the same page. Agent McCord was abducted by members of the Sola Mesa Cartel two weeks ago upon departing from her undercover assignment at the Georgia Fried Chicken franchise at the Santa Cruz Mall. We are 80% confident that she is being held at the Ranch, owned by the Sola Mesa boss, Juan Castillo, ten miles outside of Santa Cruz in the middle of the nation's cattle and farming region."

"Thank you for that valuable information," Franklin snapped sarcastically. His tone hinted at long-held antagonism between the two. "Doctor Mercedes, are you familiar with the mission of a DEA FAST Team, sir?"

The tragic death of DEA Special Agent Enrique Camarena Salazar had hung between the CIA and DEA ever since. The FAST chief's cool reception of Mercedes' involvement made it clear that the animosity between the agencies hadn't waned in the years since.

Camarena Salazar was believed to be targeted by the cartel as a result of his superior work in breaking up huge marijuana operating rings in Mexico. Also, he architected hitting the cartels where it hurt the most—money. Camarena Salazar devised the successful operations of chasing and auditing the cartel's money sources vs. chasing the drugs, which proved so successful that the cartel, in retaliation, ordered his capture and murder. By coincidence, McCord's undercover work in Bolivia was from the same playbook.

Recently, the US Department of Justice began reexamining the case after a federal court tossed the convictions of two men implicated in Camarena Salazar's death, leading federal authorities to re-interview several of the witnesses. While interviewed, three former Mexican police officers, who worked security for the drug cartel bosses, told investigators that the CIA was present at the meetings when the kidnapping plot was planned.

The CIA was implicated in both the DEA agent's death and the growing strength of the Mexican cartels. The CIA aided the easy distribution of drugs in the US in exchange for a share of the profits. The money went to aid various "freedom fighters" around the globe.

Continuing to seek justice and revenge for the murder of one of their own, the DEA took justice in their own hands. A FAST team kidnapped the cartel doctor who helped keep Camarena Salazar alive during his torture. Unfortunately, the doctor was released when a federal judge dropped charges against him. The DEA, dumbfounded at his release, saw CIA involvement in protecting the drug cartels once again.

McCord's undercover work mirrored the success and now disaster of Camarena Salazar. It was no wonder the tension in the room was high.

"Thank you, John. I am familiar with the mission of the FAST team." Mercedes tried to hide his annoyance. He could understand the tension in Franklin's voice, but they needed to work together. A speedy resolution was necessary for the safe return of McCord.

"Before I move forward with my updates, let it be known my only involvement and resolve in this mission is to assist in the release of Agent McCord. I have no other agendas," Mercedes emphatically briefed his audience, but it was obvious to all he had something up his sleeve in addition to freeing McCord, who was just a means to an end. Franklin, expressionless, just stared at Mercedes on the large conference screen—it was obvious, they did not get along.

"Doctor Mercedes, would you liked to be introduced to our team," asked Franklin.

Mercedes, viewing his conference monitor in Bolivia, could make out the familiar faces of the team. No introductions were necessary, he had known or worked with the team in classified operations in the past, but he was intrigued with the Air Force Combat Controller—Rob Madden. Mercedes understood the reputation in the special force's community of the Combat Controllers and was curious who recruited him and why he had volunteered for this mission.

"What is the mission?" an impatient DELTA member asked. Like him, most of the team members assumed it would be another reconnaissance and intelligence mission aimed at the drug cartels, like many they had been on in the past few years.

"My God, she is fucked," came a knee-jerk response from an Army DELTA Force team member. "What in the hell was she doing there in the first place?"

Rob Madden thought that he could provide the full briefing to the FAST members, but he found it prudent to sit back and keep quiet to see if there were any further developments. He figured that if this rescue team did not start out quick, he would fly himself to Bolivia and attempt a rescue.

Air Force retired sergeant and combat controller, Rob Madden, introduced himself and discussed his long association with Special Agent McCord. He briefed that McCord had saved his life on a mission in New Mexico and wanted to repay the favor.

Navy SEAL Chief Petty Officer Nathen Black rose and said, "I am aware of the qualifications of a combat controller and am relieved to see him on the team."

Madden just smiled and nodded his head. He did not dare mention his true intentions for volunteering to save McCord—his reasons were from the heart. He was romantically linked to her. The other team members just assumed he was a retired and skilled adventurer seeking another mission in life—and money.

Mercedes was particularly relieved that one of the Army DELTA members was a seasoned physician's assistant, whose services would be critical if they got as far as rescuing McCord. Ben Gray was a commercial cargo pilot who had flown agency missions around the world in various types of short-take-off-landing aircraft—similar to the types of aircraft used by the cartels to smuggle drugs out of Bolivia.

Mercedes had to hand it to Franklin. He was a competent team leader.

The team discussed a clandestine rescue mission. Mercedes offered to assist the cover up. The team would be linked to a rival cartel or disgruntled Bolivian military junta. Several cartel members owed him a favor.

The rescue team members spent the next few hours reviewing the intelligence reports and satellite photos of the hacienda and the surrounding roads and airfields used by the drug cartels. In particular, the team was most interested in knowing more about the security of the hacienda and the well-maintained small airport. They were intensely studying and reviewing all the documents while attempting to build a consensus on the best course of action to free McCord—if they were lucky to get that far. All the team could do now was study the documents and brainstorm a rescue plan.

"Doctor Mercedes, do you believe this is the most opportune time to introduce our special guest?" Franklin asked while the team members looked at him curiously. Looking at the conference room's security checkpoint and entrance, Franklin nodded to the security officer. A prisoner in an orange jumpsuit and handcuffs entered, escorted by four prison security guards.

"My God, it's Mario Fernandez," a DELTA team member inadvertently said.

The middle-aged Bolivian aristocrat smiled like a movie star approaching his admiring public. He waved a shackled hand as he shuffled to his designated seat at the end of the conference room table. He momentarily stopped to view the pictures and documents scattered all around the table, recognizing the information.

"Ah, la hacienda mis amigos," Fernandez mumbled and smiled, realizing his use to the DEA.

The DEA team members recognized the prisoner as the former Bolivian government anti-drug czar.

Mercedes was visibly uncomfortable seeing Fernandez and his participation in the rescue planning. While working for the CIA, Mercedes had many classified meetings with Fernandez when he was the anti-drug czar for Bolivia. Many of which could be very embarrassing for the United States and the CIA.

"Fernandez will have to be dealt with after this rescue mission," Mercedes thought to himself.

"If I can have your attention, please." Franklin paused a moment as he waited for the team's undivided attention. "I trust the DEA team members recognize and know the story behind Mario Fernandez; however, for the rest of the team, I'll take a minute to enlighten you. Fernandez was intercepted and arrested by US federal authorities in Panama for smuggling over five hundred pounds of cocaine from a Chilean port to Miami, Florida. He pled guilty on all charges, was sentenced to twenty years, and incarcerated at the nation's highest-security prison near Florence, Colorado, nicknamed the Alcatraz of the Rockies."

Mercedes glanced at Fernandez. His long gray ponytail and orange jumpsuit did little to detract from the caged lion within. Fernandez captured the CIA director's gaze and grinned.

"More important for us at this moment are his ties with the Sola Mesa Cartel, particularly Juan Castillo. Fernandez made frequent visits to the hacienda, called the Ranch." After the statement from Franklin, everyone in the room realized Fernandez' knowledge and familiarity of the hacienda and its operation would make the rescue mission possible. All the team members were anxious to pepper him with questions.

Mercedes stared uncomfortably at Fernandez, remembering the confrontations they had had in the past years. As the corrupt anti-drug czar, he bilked the CIA out of hundreds of thousands of dollars in the name of combating the drug cartels. They found out later from a paid CIA informer that Fernandez used the funds for his own luxurious lifestyle and compromised a couple of anti-drug officials. As payback, Mercedes was the one who alerted the Miami authorities of his smuggling cocaine into the US using Bolivian government aircraft.

Fernandez was also uncomfortable with seeing the CIA operative again. Sitting as comfortable as possible and relishing the attention being given to him, Fernandez had made a lucrative deal with the Feds for his information. Mercedes was completely unaware of any deal made with Fernandez and wanted him taken care of as his usefulness to the rescue mission was complete. However, Fernandez had made his deal with the US Justice Department—not the CIA.

"With the assistance of the FBI's research department, we found a Bolivian cartel member in one of our prisons who could be swayed to provide us with information on the workings of the Sola Mesa Cartel," Franklin relayed to the team. "To make a long story short, Fernandez was transferred yesterday from his prison in Colorado.

"Fernandez and his lawyer agreed to a lucrative deal in exchange for answering all of our questions regarding the hacienda and providing us with his thoughts and recommendations on rescuing McCord," Franklin said. "Fernandez does not speak English, so all of the conversations, questions, and briefings will be in Spanish." Since all the team members were fluent in Spanish, Franklin knew this wouldn't be a problem. In fact, this was the best situation since there left no error for interpretation.

"Sir, I do have a quick question," a Navy SEAL member asked. "What is the incentive for Señor Fernandez to assist us in this rescue mission?"

"Thank you for your question, but much of the arrangement with Fernandez is classified. However, I can say this, with the deal we made, he has everything to gain if McCord is found alive and rescued." Franklin checked his watch. "If there are no more questions for me, we can get started."

The team wasted no more time getting down to business. They brought satellite maps and placed them in front of Fernandez. The questions went on until late in the afternoon. Fernandez provided invaluable information to the FAST team. From pointing out the backup generators to underground passages into the hacienda, his information appeared to be surprisingly accurate and relevant. The designated team planner and scribe, Army DELTA member Matt Ruster, sorted, recorded, and organized all of the information Fernandez provided and quickly drafted a report for the team to study on their flight to Bolivia.

"It just might work," an excited Mercedes said while closely following the planning.

After the team exhausted their questions, the security officials escorted Fernandez back to his holding cell. While leaving, he stopped and looked at the team and wished them well.

"Good luck in rescuing your DEA agent McCord," Fernandez said, knowing this comment would get the attention of the team members.

Struck by this parting statement, Franklin glanced at Mercedes on the conference room screen then calmly asked Fernandez, "What do you know about McCord?"

"Ah amigo, we probably receive more information in prison than you could imagine. A captured DEA agent is a big deal, but a trade for the release of five cartel members in prison—that news travels fast." Fernandez shrugged. "Many of us hoped we'd be one of the five chosen, but then I got the chance to make this deal."

"If you thought you'd be one of the ones traded, why did you accept our deal?" Franklin asked.

"No sé. The DEA's never made a trade like that before. It seemed too good to be true. You're rescuing that woman, no?"

"What do you know about her?" Franklin ignored the convict's question, more concerned with any additional information they could learn about McCord.

"I heard the cartel was fucking the shit out of McCord, keeping her alive just for their pleasure." Fernandez paused to relish the disturbed looks on the other men's faces.

Rob Madden had a white-knuckle grip on the conference table. It was the only thing keeping him from launching over the table to wipe the smirk off Fernandez' face. He had to keep his emotions in check if he was going to save her.

"Not sure how accurate what I am going to tell you is, but I heard that with the pending exchange, Juan Castillo has had his people stop screwing and beating McCord," Fernandez said with everyone intently listening. "In fact, it is believed the cartel is attempting to rehabilitate and clean up McCord for this possible prisoner exchange.

"If Castillo gets wind that he has been double-crossed, and he eventually will, your friend will die a slow, painful death," Fernandez surmised nonchalantly.

Madden winced and shook his head, envisioning what his Bonnie was going through. His pent-up rage would have to be controlled until he got to Bolivia.

"Can I have more of that BBQ we had for lunch?" Fernandez eyed the serving lunch table with the platters of leftover BBQ brisket. Franklin nodded his approval to the prison warden, and Fernandez filled a couple plates to take back to his holding cell.

While walking in step with the prison guards, he stopped for a moment and looked back at the team. "There is one item you also may be interested in. If I can come back to the table, I'll show you something."

"Proceed." Franklin nodded to the security guards who walked him slowly back to the conference table.

"Can I see the aerial map?" Fernandez held the two to-go boxes of BBQ while the map was laid out on top. A team member saw the awkward position Fernandez was holding the containers and offered to hold them until he finished.

"What do you see, Señor Fernandez?" Navy SEAL Black asked.

"Do you see this large barn, hangar, whatever, and a road leading from the barn to the runway?" Fernandez pointed to a large building near the airfield. "Inside is a very nice Beechcraft Super King aircraft that is always fueled and ready for takeoff. It is Castillo's personal aircraft, available for use day or night."

"Have you ever ridden in it?" a team member asked.

"Si." Fernandez laughed. "As the anti-drug czar for Bolivia, I have had to make many trips in that airplane—to fight the drug cartels of course." He winked at Franklin.

"Gray, do you have any questions about the aircraft?" Franklin looked at the team pilot.

"Can you tell me what model the aircraft is?" Ben Gray pulled up the manufacturer's website while waiting for a response.

"No sé. I'm an anti-drug czar, not an aeronautical engineer," Fernandez joked, causing a few chuckles. "It was only a few years old last I saw it. Castillo had just put in some long-distance fuel tanks. Does that help?"

"Very much so, thank you," replied Gray.

"Ben, worst case, how many people could we load in the King Air if necessary?" asked Franklin.

"Sixteen, but it would be cramped," Gray estimated.

"And the range?"

"Count on around 1,200 miles, but with modified fuel tanks, could be longer," Gray concluded.

A Beech Super King Air aircraft, a couple hundred yards from the hacienda, opened up the possibilities for a quick rescue operation.

Franklin and the rescue team members appreciated his sense of humor and wished him well as he picked up his closely guarded BBQ and departed with his guards.

"See you at Disneyland," Fernandez said, implying he was heading to the witness protection program if the rescue mission succeeded. It was obvious Fernandez would be a marked man for cartel execution if word got out, and it would, that he assisted in the rescue of McCord and the downfall of the Sola Mesa Cartel.

Regardless, the critical information Fernandez had given them filled the team with hope.

CHAPTER
17

"Please take your seats." Franklin wiped the remnants of BBQ sauce from his mouth with a paper napkin. With his belly full, he could concentrate on creating the rescue plan. "Dr. Mercedes has some ideas for blending in with the natives."

"Juan Castillo is not only the leader of the Sola Mesa Cartel, but he is also a respected cattle rancher. It is not uncommon for cartel bosses to pose as cattle ranchers. They buy land in remote areas close to Santa Cruz where they can have privacy and access to their own airport aircraft hangar. Dressing like a cowboy will help you blend in with the workers in the area and attract less notice of those on patrol at the Ranch," Mercedes said.

"So we're supposed to be a bunch of cowboys?" one of the guys scoffed.

"Yes, complete with boots, blue jeans, belts, and straw hats." Mercedes couldn't help grinning, imagining these hardened combat officers as local cowboys.

A couple of men groaned.

"Interestingly enough, they earnestly portray themselves as legitimate ranchers. They even join breeding associations and formally register their cattle," Mercedes continued.

"What kind of cattle does Castillo breed?" a SEAL team member asked.

"He breeds Zebu. It is a cow with a large shoulder hump, originally developed on the Indian subcontinent, but they are well-adapted for hot environments like Bolivia. The breed is becoming a top meat producer in the country."

"Why do we need to blend in with workers on the Ranch?" a Navy SEAL asked.

"Because you are going to be faculty members from Texas A&M University on a government sponsored field trip to Bolivia for the purpose of briefing the results of experiments in successful cloning of Zebu cows," Mercedes briefed.

Nothing but inquisitive looks came from the team members.

"With incredible luck, we have a small-time cartel member on our books who also breeds Zebu cattle on his ranch near the town of Salina, just a few miles from Castillo's hacienda. The State Department commonly sponsors cattle and ranch experts to discuss new techniques and research on cattle breeding. Since we know you don't know shit about breeding cattle, we had some Texas A&M professors draw up some papers that explain the details in layman's terms." Mercedes looked at the disbelieving faces staring back at him and shrugged. "Gentlemen, it's the best we could come up with."

"Sir, so we are just supposed to illegally enter Bolivia disguised as university cattle researchers, take over a drug kingpin's hacienda, rescue an abducted DEA undercover agent, and fly back to the United States without being noticed? You sure there's nothing else?" one of the DELTA Members asked Franklin.

"Sergeant, don't forget about the Aggie jackets you'll also be wearing. The maroon color should match your eyes." Franklin just smiled. "In all seriousness, we have arranged for an agency member who graduated from A&M and understands cattle breeding to accompany you on the first leg of your mission. He'll explain the quirks of being an Aggie to help you pass off as legitimate graduates."

"They are not paying me enough for this shit," voiced a Navy SEAL while the rest of the team shook their heads and laughed. "We'll be the stupidest looking gringos in the Bolivian prisons."

"At ease, gentlemen. We'll leave in an hour for Dyess Air Force Base. From there, a Texas Air National Guard C-130 cargo aircraft will be waiting for you. You'll refuel in Panama before continuing on to Bolivia."

"This particular C-130 aircraft is used often by the Governor of Texas. The VIP suite includes conference tables, sleeping facilities, a well-stocked galley, and a steward to prepare meals."

All the team members smiled and nodded their approval after hearing the plush amenities on their aircraft.

"Once we get wheels up from Dyess, we'll finalize our plans, inventory our deployment bags, and get some sleep," briefed Franklin, understanding that all of his members knew the reference to deployment bag was a nice and unnoticeable way of saying tactical weapons and equipment duffel bag. This bag contained a wide array of weapons, communication equipment, and everything an operator would require in preparing for an ad hoc, make-it-up-as-we-go mission.

"If you find the equipment and supplies are missing or damaged in your bags, contact me immediately," Franklin ordered. "We'll make a call to our contacts in Panama to ensure you receive the correct equipment and supplies. In addition to the deployment duffel bags, you'll pick up a carefully-prepared carton of C-4 explosives in Panama." This statement got everyone's attention.

"Why are we taking a ton of C-4 with us?" a DELTA member asked.

"Thank you, sergeant. Madden, care to take this one?" Franklin asked.

"Gentlemen," Madden stood and faced the team. "I have been tasked with destroying the hacienda when we depart the area. The C-4 will make that possible with little chance for mistakes."

"Thank you, Madden," Franklin commented. "Besides the C-4, we will ensure a destructive gas leak is ignited at the same time Madden sets off the explosives."

"Regardless of whether we find Agent McCord alive or dead, the entire hacienda is coming down—with everyone in it," Franklin said. "If any other cartel has ides of abducting and torturing a federal agent, they can expect the same to happen to them."

A stone-faced Madden just nodded his head with the rest of the team members.

"OK, pack your personal gear and be ready to depart in an hour," Franklin ordered. "Meet me at the bus in the front of this conference center."

The team packed up their papers and documents from the table.

"Remember, all phone calls are prohibited unless authorized by me—no deviations," Franklin directed as the team began filing out of the room.

DELTA member Steve Wilson caught up with Navy SEAL Hector Espada as they walked out of the conference room. They stopped near a cluttered storage room.

"Steve, I don't understand," Espada quietly asked. "Why in the hell are we risking our lives for some DEA woman agent who is most likely already fucked to death by the cartel who captured her?"

"If there is the slightest chance that we get her out alive, so much the better. Regardless of the risks, this is what we are good at—lighting fireworks and knocking off bad guys." Determination glinted in Wilson's eyes. "Think about this, Hector, if that person being held was one of our own, would we even hesitate?"

"Good point! We leave no one behind." Hector grabbed his gear from the closet. "Alive or dead, let's get her out of there."

CHAPTER

18

"Lookie here, sarge," the security police guard at the Dyess Air Force Base main gate commented to his supervisor. "Another group of college professors heading out on another government-paid boondoggle. Where are they from?"

"According the base access list, they are from A&M."

The private luxury bus stopped at the Dyess AFB entry control point where Franklin exited with the team's authorization documents. While he was inside reviewing the documents with the supervisor, one of the gate guards entered the bus for a routine inspection. The guard was bewildered by what he saw. The passengers were not the typical university professors passing through Dyess for research work in South America but appeared to be some sort of special operations types dressed in typical Texas rancher wear. The team stared at the guard until he made a quick exit from the bus, wondering who they really were.

"OK, Mr. Franklin, you and your team can proceed to the passenger terminal near base operations." The gate supervisor handed back the authorization documents. "Are you familiar with where it is?"

Franklin nodded and climbed aboard the bus. He sat and handed the driver a map with the destination highlighted. They weren't headed to the passenger terminal, but a secret, nondescript aircraft hangar specifically used for staging special forces missions in Central and South America.

In front of the hangar stood a Texas Air Guard C-130 cargo aircraft being readied by the ground crew for an immediate takeoff.

The team remained on the bus, waiting for the word to depart. A lone figure wearing a standard green Air Force flight suit left the hangar and headed for the bus. Franklin opened the doors and hopped off.

"Are you, Franklin?" the young major asked as he approached the bus.

"Yes. Are we ready to go?"

"Yes, sir. Please have the driver move the bus into the hangar where you will offload and gather your equipment," the major instructed. "We are aware that we need to get you off the ground as soon as possible."

"Very good, major. Let's go!" Franklin was relieved the ground crew had a sense of urgency.

The bus moved into the hangar and each team member grabbed their bags. All baggage was checked and inventoried, then double-checked their information on the passenger manifest. The manifest justified the mission. It also contained alias passenger names as a normal protocol to protect the mission and team members during special operations missions.

"Thank you for your patience, gentlemen. The aircraft is ready for loading." With that, the team picked up their personal items and headed to the waiting aircraft. Four large turbo propeller engines blew hot exhaust and dirt on the loading passengers. The team found their seats and prepared for the long flight.

"Sir, the takeoff checklist is complete," announced the pilot Major Dave Schnor of the Texas Air Guard and contract pilot with the CIA. "We are cleared for takeoff."

Schnor taxied to the active runway for an immediate takeoff. The old but still powerful engines gradually gained speed as it rolled down the runway and climbed above the West Texas prairie. A half an hour later, Major Schnor announced they were at cruising altitude and cleared to move around the aircraft.

The aircraft crew chief got up from his seat in the cockpit and returned to the cargo area to configure the necessary tables and seats for Franklin's team. The task had become routine since the state began leasing the Guard's aircraft to the CIA. Once finished, he gave a thumb's up to Franklin and returned to the cockpit.

"Gentlemen, may I have your attention," Franklin yelled across the cargo area where most of his team and support members were taking advantage of some rest while they could. The team members gathered their briefcases and took their places around the stowed conference table in the middle of the cargo bay. The modified drop-down lights illuminated the planning area well.

"Ruster," Franklin called out, "would you please inform us when you will have the draft rescue plan ready for briefing?"

"Yes, sir!" Ruster was a well-seasoned warrant officer in the Army's DELTA force. The thirty-year veteran had become one of the best planners for ad hoc contingency missions—especially on short notice with only the available resources at hand. "I need about an hour for your concept briefing. You can expect it a couple hours prior to landing at Panama."

"All right, Ruster. Work your magic and we'll convene again in an hour," authorized Franklin, confident Ruster would draft the best plan under the time constraints they were facing. He had worked with Ruster on various occasions in Afghanistan and Iraq and was sure his team would have the best plan possible under the circumstances. While Ruster was intensely engaged in his mission planning, including checking various documents and contacting Mercedes several times, the rest of the FAST team laid back for a couple hours of sleep.

While the Texas Air Guard C-130 cargo aircraft made its way across Texas and the Gulf of Mexico, Mercedes worked feverishly with his friendly contacts in the Nueva Confederación Cartel, a rival of Sola Mesa. Mercedes was relying on the inherent animosity between the two to get the FAST team access to the hacienda and the abducted agent. The rival cartels had so far only engaged in petty turf battles, not the full-scale attack the FAST team planned on the Ranch.

Unfortunately, Mercedes thought, the CIA actions against the Sola Mesa Cartel would build up the Nueva Confederación's power in Bolivia. There was no telling if that would be better or worse for the native population. If word got out of the CIA's involvement in the power struggle, heads would roll. For right now, the only friends the team had in Bolivia was the Nueva Confederación. Mercedes smiled and mumbled, "And they don't abduct and rape DEA agents—at least for now."

CHAPTER
19

"Ruster, are you ready?" Franklin approached the planning table where Ruster had spent the past few hours.

"Yes, sir." Ruster took off his reading glasses and rubbed his temples, attempting to relieve a little stress.

Franklin went around the aircraft and woke up the rest of the team. They headed to the conference table in the cargo bay with their notepads. The steward brought a cup of coffee to each one.

"Gentlemen, before we have Ruster provide us the plan, I need to emphasis again," Franklin sternly stressed, "we all are frustrated that this situation happened so unexpectedly and quickly that there was no time for a formal, solid mission plan. We'll go in with what we got with much being ad hoc."

"As long as Castillo believes they are getting a trade, we have a high likelihood of finding McCord alive. We can only hope we move fast enough. Without further ado, Ruster lay out the plan." Franklin sat and took a drink of the black liquid steaming in his cup.

"Thank you, Agent Franklin," Ruster politely acknowledged and grabbed his file of loosely arranged briefing papers.

For the next hour, Ruster provided the team a best guess timeline for team actions, where the team would be hunkered down, the vehicles and assistance required from the supporting rival cartel, and how the team would evade and escape after finding McCord.

"Thank you, Ruster, for your incredible work," Franklin announced. "All this draft planning will be solidified once we reach our staging area where we can share details with our new friends from the Nueva Confederación Cartel."

The team members returned to their seats and reviewed the draft plan with their areas of responsibility. After making a quick study, their attention was directed at Franklin.

"Gentlemen, could I please have your attention please," Franklin said. "We are now on our way to the Panama International Airport that was at one time Howard Air Force Base. We will exit the plane with our equipment to an out-of-the-way terminal specifically operated by the US government for various missions that support the government's interest in this region, including legitimate support for our embassies, consulates, country advisory groups, etc. Your baggage and equipment will be loaded on a truck and driven to the Central Air terminal at the main commercial ramp."

"You will board a chartered modified and updated Central Airlines Curtiss C-46 Commando aircraft." Mercedes could see the team's stunned faces at the prospect of flying more than two thousand miles in an old World War II troop carrying aircraft that was older than their grandparents.

"Don't worry, gentlemen. I understand it has been converted into a very comfortable and reliable aircraft used extensively for making embassy runs." Ruster looked at his notes for a moment. "After a seven-hour flight, we'll deplane in Santa Cruz at an out-of-the-way terminal, specifically used to support government assistance groups arriving in Bolivia."

The team members began talking amongst themselves, confused and concerned about what they had just heard. They all had spent time in South America as special operations operators or agents, working for the US or as private contractors, and knew their fate if apprehended by Bolivian government authorities

"Let me get this straight," a frustrated DELTA member asked, "you and Mercedes expect us to deplane at the Santa Cruz International Airport with false documents, passports, and enough weapons to arm a militia while looking like a bunch of cowboy college professors to boot?"

"Permit me to take that question, Ruster," Mercedes' voice came across the conference call radio on all of the team member's headsets.

"Please, Colonel Mercedes." Ruster turned up the volume on his headset.

"Gentlemen, I own the men managing the government's cargo port at the Santa Cruz airport. The only thing they know is that a bunch of college professors from the States are arriving to do some sort of genetic research on Zebu cattle using their own equipment," Mercedes reassured the team. "Numerous livestock and agricultural experts arrive frequently in Bolivia to provide US government assistance and research. You will just be another assistance team helping the ranchers and farmers have a better life.

"Also, please let me remind you, gentleman, corruption has a firm hold on Bolivia's military, security, and most of the government departments. We will take full advantage of that for this mission," Mercedes noted with sarcasm. The team fully understood this corrupt environment and was relieved that they were taking full advantage of it.

"If there are no more concerns or questions, Ruster will continue to inform you of our plan to free Agent McCord and finish off the Sola Mesa Cartel," Mercedes concluded.

The team members were surprised to hear of a secondary mission of destroying the Sola Mesa Cartel, but just remained quiet. They hadn't expected anything but freeing Agent McCord.

Rob Madden listened to Mercedes' incidental remark about destroying the cartel. He figured Mercedes had his reasons, probably some sort of international CIA scheme, and Madden had his—rescue his love, Agent Bonnie McCord, and then deal with her captors.

Madden figured he would use Mercedes to the maximum extent possible to exert catastrophic pain on Bonnie McCord's tormentors. Madden would ensure, regardless of what Mercedes or Franklin said, each cartel associate in that hacienda would be horribly tortured. He would keep them alive for the purpose of extended torture—as the cartels did with abducted US officials.

CHAPTER
20

"As is routine for agriculture assistance visits, the sponsoring cattle ranch, La Vista Grande, and cattle association, Bolivian Association of Zebu Breeders, will provide transportation to the ranch," Ruster explained. "Dr. Mercedes has assured us that a customs officer will be there to greet us when we depart the plane. He will walk us out of the terminal, ensuring our bags are not checked by the authorities. The La Vista Grande Ranch is located near the town of Montero about twenty miles from the Ranch off a busy highway."

"Please gentlemen, don't be shocked to learn the owner of the La Vista Grande Ranch is a cartel kingpin, Felipe Formosa, of the Nueva Confederación Cartel," said Mercedes. "The man is as dangerous and ruthless as our target Juan Castillo, but he is on our side."

"Felipe Formosa is certainly a bastard, but he is our bastard," Franklin explained.

"Like Castillo, he also masks his narco operations while posing as a legitimate Zebu cattle rancher in a remote area where his organization has set up clandestine airstrips and warehouses—far enough away from the town of Montero," briefed Mercedes. "As a front, like Castillo, Formosa is a bona fide cattle rancher. He frequently opens his ranch up to outside visitors, such as yourselves, for the appearance of furthering the Bolivian cattle production and helping the growing country's economy.

"We have left Formosa alone because he runs a small, insignificant cartel—for now. Also, whenever we needed some sort of assistance such as boarding or hiding some of our covert operations against the drug cartels, he has allowed us to use his facilities, saving him from Bolivian police drug raids and various other government agencies," Mercedes said, resulting in bewildered looks from all the team members.

"Formosa's people will pick us up at the airport and transport us to a rather modern bunkhouse at the La Vista Grande Ranch where you will find additional tactical weapons, Bolivian Federal Police uniforms, and your personal equipment, including medical supplies." Mercedes could understand the astonished faces of men who could not believe what they were hearing. To each team member, it was risky enough entering the hacienda masqueraded as college professors, but as federal police, that was something else entirely.

"Mr. Franklin, I do have a question, sir," stern-looking SEAL member Black asked. "Maybe I missed something, but what is the explanation behind the Federal Police uniforms?"

"Thank you, Chief Petty Officer Black that's a very good question—I apologize for not briefing this earlier," Franklin said, "but, basically, it is the only way we can raid the hacienda. They'll be surprised as hell and, most likely, will put their guard down with the Feds. By the time they figure we are not the Feds, it will be too late for them. We'll already be inside." The rest the team perfectly understood the rationale.

Excited and loaded questions came from all the team members at the conference table. Ruster and Mercedes continued briefing the ambitious and risky rescue plan.

Franklin and the entire team suspected Mercedes was attempting to take full advantage of the McCord crisis. He saw a major opportunity to destroy the major drug cartel in Bolivia, which would cause havoc amongst the other cartels who would try to fill the void after the destruction of the Sola Mesa Cartel.

Sitting at his desk in a highly secure CIA safehouse on the outskirts of the capital La Paz, he monitored the planning session via secure satellite communications. He felt good about the plan Ruster was about to begin briefing.

However, Mercedes realized the success of the operation depended on the fake messages about the prisoner swap being passed on to Juan Castillo and the Sola Mesa Cartel. Knowing full well that if Castillo got wind that the messages were a scheme to keep McCord alive, her fate would be painful and deadly.

To ensure the safety of the unpredictable and useless Raul Lopez, Mercedes had asked Roberta Potter to monitor his movements to ensure he kept to their agreement. If he strayed, his dead body would be found hanging from a tree in an apparent suicide.

Mercedes came back to his senses when he heard over the secure radio that Ruster was beginning to brief the details of the rescue plan to the team members.

"Mr. Ruster, thank you for your patience," Mercedes acknowledged and grabbed the radio headset on his makeshift desk. "Please proceed with the plan." Mercedes was well aware of the details of the plan—he and his associates had been working on it for days without coordinating with Franklin and his team. Mercedes was going to take the team exactly where they needed to go.

Just before landing in Panama, a tired and stressed Ruster had completed briefing the plan to the team, emphasizing again that execution of the plan had to be soon with much of it ad hoc—if necessary.

"Gentlemen, could I have your attention please for one further comment," announced Franklin. "We will be landing soon, and I would like to remind you of a few points prior to exiting the aircraft. You are university professors here to assist the Bolivian ranchers, and if asked questions by customs, while unloading your equipment, refer them to me or their supervisor.

"I hope Mercedes greased the right palms or we are in a world of shit," Franklin halfway joked, but he and the others knew everything depended on Mercedes' contacts.

CHAPTER

21

"Mercedes, this is Roberta Potter." She kept her voice calm, knowing she had catastrophic news to share. "We lost track of Raul Lopez."

"Do you have any details?" asked a bewildered Mercedes.

"It appears his new friends picked him up at one of his watering holes last night and took him to another bar," Potter said. "I understand through contacts at Raul's hostel that four men, no doubt cartel members, broke into his apartment and cleaned it out completely—nothing was left behind."

"Oh sweet Jesus, what have we done?" Mercedes mumbled over the phone. He tried to get his composure back, knowing the actions and consequences of the news he had just heard. The complete and false scheme to trade five Bolivian cartel members for DEA Agent McCord was no doubt known by Juan Castillo and the Sola Mesa Cartel. Mercedes knew it would be a matter of hours before McCord went from recuperating back to the cartel's whore.

Tears came to his eyes as he thought about the torture and pain she probably would be enduring soon. Mercedes tried to reason that he and the others had done the best they could to get her out, but the circumstances were insurmountable to overcome. Trying to rationalize their failure to achieve the mission did little to make him feel better. Mercedes got a hold of himself and remembered that he was a decorated Marine Colonel—a tough and smart guy whose career was based on beating-up and destroying enemies such as Juan Castillo.

"Mercedes, are you there?" Potter's voice broke through his thoughts. "Mercedes, are you there? Damn it, we have tons to do now in light of this new information."

"Damn you, Mercedes, you weak dick, mother-fucker, get your shit together and let's get our girl out of there!" Potter roared into the phone. Mercedes was somewhat brought back to life with her yelling.

"OK, Roberta, thank you for the reality check," Mercedes acknowledged. "Are you prepared to move forward with the little contingency plan we discussed in the event the prisoner swap was discovered to be a hoax?"

There was silence on the line as Potter was deep in thought.

"Potter, you still there?" Mercedes asked.

"Are you offering me the option?" Potter said. "There appears no other way to get McCord out of there halfway alive is there?"

"Your call, Potter," Mercedes hoped and prayed Potter would take the option they had discussed earlier.

"Mercedes, let me get this option or deal straight with you," Potter confirmed. "I make my way into the hacienda, find McCord, and literally protect her until you and your team show up—did I read it back correctly? Also, your agency pays me two hundred thousand dollars for my services, plus any money or valuables I take off the dead cartel members."

"Damn it, Potter. We are not sending you in there so you can collect cash and Rolex watches from the cartel members you kill—do you understand?" Mercedes had had enough of Potter's bullshit and stupid bravado. "Your only job is to protect McCord until we can get there."

"All right, I'll give it a try," Potter calmly replied. "Just ensure your team enters the hacienda as soon as possible after I find McCord."

"Thank you," Mercedes calmly replied. "How do you intend on getting into the hacienda and finding McCord?"

"Like you, I was monitoring the debriefing of the one-time drug czar of Bolivia, Mario Fernandez. He had some very useful information about the various security systems and their operation. I'll be able to handle it," affirmed Potter. "Also, he mentioned a couple of underground, basement-type passages leading out of the hacienda to a small patio complex only accessible from a small staircase via Castillo's office."

"How did you find out all this additional information from Fernandez. You did not ask for any additional information at the conference call you monitored with me," Mercedes curiously asked.

"I helped place many bad prisoners in the prison in Colorado where Fernando is housed. I simply called the warden and stated I needed more information from Fernando. The warden agreed to give me fifteen minutes on the phone with him. I obtained most of the information I needed."

"OK," Mercedes mumbled, shaking his head in amazement at her resourcefulness. "One last question before we organize the team and head out toward the hacienda. How do you plan to get from Santa Cruz to the secluded underground passage inside the hacienda?"

"Easy! I plan on dressing and acting like an expensive drug whore and have a taxi driver take me from the red-light district to the large bunkhouse at Castillo's Ranch. Once at the Ranch, I'll mention I am looking for a strong cowboy to fuck me."

Mercedes just put his head down and shook his head in disbelief but was going to hear her out—this was something new even for him.

"Most likely, they'll want to screw me immediately in a pickup truck or, if they can wait, take me out to one of their barns," she stated nonchalantly. "Regardless, I'll have enough sedative in a drug injector to put him out for a long time. I'll ditch him and the truck and head over to my planned entry point. Anyway, we might need the truck."

"One last item for your benefit, Mercedes, and this will cost you extra," she directed. "When I get to McCord's room, I'll give you a status update over the tactical radio. If she is dead, you can cancel the raid, and I'll find my way back to Santa Cruz." She paused. "However, if she is alive, I'll give her what assistance I can and hold back any cartel members wanting to fuck her. But, you had better be right around the corner. You got that, Mercedes?"

Potter was either the craziest contractor Mercedes had ever dealt with or very cunning and brave. He thought about the many obstacles facing the team. Time was growing short if they were going to rescue the agent before there was no chance of her survival. Then the raid would be all for naught, except for destroying the Sola Mesa Cartel—an act of vengeance for McCord's murder. However, if Potter could somehow gain access to McCord's room, they might have a chance. If anyone could pull this off, it would be Potter. With a now confident smile, he was assured the questionable and missing aspects of the plan were now coming together.

"No problem, Mercedes. I can pull this off; however, are you going to be able to uphold your side of the operation," Potter asked. "I need to know when you plan on being at the hacienda. The operation's success depends on our efforts coordinating perfectly. Where do we plan on meeting up after your team does their work?"

"Initially, we'll plan on meeting up at the large aircraft hangar located between the hacienda and the Ranch complex—if it is available," briefed Mercedes. "If not, we'll head back to the La Vista Grande Ranch and take Felipe Formosa's offer to fly the team to an airport in Argentina that is US friendly."

"Shit, Mercedes." Potter smothered a laugh. "Let's see, a rival drug cartel saving the DEA's butts with their aircraft, flying you all to a safe haven in Argentina."

"There is no other way." Mercedes had resigned himself to the fact he had made a deal with the Devil to save McCord. He did not share with Potter that in his mind, the deal with the Devil was his agenda to destroy the Sola Mesa Cartel and using any excess of force as an excuse to save McCord—the Sola Mesa's destruction would be a warning to other cartels attempting to abduct US federal agents.

"All right, I'll be awaiting your call at the safehouse, dressed to kill," an amused Potter said.

"I'll give you an hour's head's up prior to us reaching the hacienda."

"How does your team plan on entering the building?" a concerned Potter asked.

"We are literally driving up to the hacienda checkpoint in four brightly marked Bolivian Federal Police SUVs. All of the team members will have on custom-made uniforms."

"Good idea! I'll await your call," Potter replied. "We'd better be quick!"

CHAPTER

22

"How stupid of me! How stupid of me!" Juan Castillo yelled into the phone. The cartel member had been following Raul Lopez since before he became their informant in the embassy. Unfortunately, the rover had failed to disclose the latest information, which Castillo found out through one of his plants in the State Department.

Turned out, the US President didn't agree to the trade. With the DEA operating illegally in Bolivia, the DEA agent could expect no help from the US. The president saw no need or obligation to work the diplomatic channels to get her out. The US didn't want to jeopardize the fragile relationship with the new Bolivian government.

McCord was expendable.

The cartel member on the phone had tracked Raul Lopez down at one of his favorite bars. He and another trusted member had received the transfer of classified documents to Castillo regarding the prisoner exchange. The two men told Lopez that Castillo needed to talk with him that night about the quality of his work. Lopez joined the two members in a Porsche sedan, somewhat honored to be invited to the hacienda to speak with the boss.

At the hacienda, the men whisked Lopez into the large conference room where they searched him for weapons and cell phones. They threw the shaking man into a chair at the end of the table and handcuffed him.

Castillo walked in the room with his lieutenants, carrying files of the fake exchange documents doctored by the CIA and Mercedes. All were smoking expensive cigars and chattering amongst themselves. Ignoring the crying and hysterical embassy rover.

"Alright, Raul, we are aware of the fake documents coming out of the embassy regarding the prisoner swap for McCord," Castillo calmly said. "We need to know who recruited you to pass false information to us. Start from the beginning and give us every detail."

Begging for mercy and forgiveness, Lopez explained to those present in the conference room, from start to finish, his association with Mercedes and his CIA associates. Several questions were directed to Lopez throughout the afternoon about the CIA's involvement and classified operations at the embassy.

Suddenly, Castillo jumped up from his chair in a rage and slapped Lopez across the face—nearly knocking him senseless. Threats and insults followed from the other cartel members.

Pleading for forgiveness and his life, Lopez offered and agreed to begin funneling bona fide classified documents to Castillo for his mercy. Castillo, continuing to smoke his cigar in his left hand, threw his glass of bourbon in Lopez' face.

"Of course, I will be more than happy to start over with you. We can begin with you giving us true classified documents— no fakes," Castillo sarcastically said then put his glass down and slapped Lopez again. "In regards to the undercover DEA agent you told us about, McCord is her name, would you like to meet her?

"Ever since you provided us the true identity of the DEA agent working at the Georgia Fried Chicken restaurant and those official-looking documents about a prisoner exchange for McCord, we literally have been treating her like a queen," Castillo added. "We wanted to make a fair trade with a healthy-looking agent."

"But now, what are we to do? We cannot trade her now, so I suspect she will just have to work for us for the time being." Castillo motioned for Lopez to stand and walk with him down the large well-lit hallway. They passed an informal bar and card room now used to entertain cartel members waiting in line for some fun with McCord.

"You see, friend, I have McCord all clean and rested for her second shift," Castillo commented sadistically. "In fact, as of now, I am having her moved from her plush rehabilitation bedroom back to her working bedroom."

"What do you think, Raul? Would you like to meet the DEA agent you informed us about?" Castillo laughed hard. "But then again, you tried to save her with this lie of a prisoner swap. Dios mío, Raul, do you want to save her or kill her?"

An outburst of laughter came from cartel members following Castillo on their way to the bar where they waited their turn to experience the pleasures that McCord provided.

Quivering with fright and attempting to hold back tears, Raul prayed the walk in the hallway would lead to the front patio and parking lot.

"Hey, amigo." Castillo held Raul close to him in a false gesture of friendship. "Would you like to meet DEA Agent McCord? Better yet, would you like to screw her?" Uncontrolled laughter from Castillo and his lieutenants could be heard all over the hacienda.

"Come on, Raul. Why don't you screw the woman who is here because of you?" Castillo physically pulled Raul down the hallway to McCord's working bedroom.

Castillo opened the bedroom door and shoved Raul into the putrid-smelling room. He stumbled slightly and grabbed the bedpost for support. He was startled to see a skeleton of a woman lying in a fetal position on the grossly stained bed. Moans of pain and agony echoed in the small room as the woman tried to pull the sheets over her naked body. Raul just stared in shock unable to find the words to free him of what he had done.

"McCord, welcome back," Castillo taunted McCord.

"Kill me, please, for God's sake, kill me, PLEASE!" McCord struggled to sit up. "Kill me, PLEASE!" Using all of her energy, McCord slumped back down on the mattress.

"Hey bitch, are you familiar with what happened to DEA Agent Enrique Camarena Salazar in Mexico?" Castillo knew that there wasn't a DEA agent who was unfamiliar with the tragedy. He was given drugs for the purpose of keeping him alive for continued torture by the cartel and corrupt Mexican federal law enforcement officers.

McCord went into convulsions hearing this and struggled to free herself of her hopeless situation with no possible alternatives.

"Stephen," Castillo said to his top cartel lieutenant. "You and Francisco get a hold of her and sedate her for a while. She'll need her energy when she begins entertaining the troops tomorrow."

McCord was sedated and loosely tied to the old, military-style bedframe with a surplus cotton mattress. Castillo was now more afraid of McCord attempting to kill herself. According to Castillo, they would kill her when she no longer had value for the cartel.

After giving the appropriate orders to his lieutenants, he ushered a pale-looking Raul out of the bedroom and into the better-smelling hallway. Raul complained to his overseers that he thought he was about to throw-up. Bending over in the hallway, he began to dry heave. The lieutenants immediately straightened him up and pulled him forward.

"Just think, Raul, due to your wonderful connections at the embassy, you provided us with this prize." Castillo enjoyed taunting the rover, who seemed distraught at his complicity in the abduction and torture of the female agent.

While physically escorted down the long heavily used hallway by Castillo's bodyguards, Raul stopped suddenly, falling to the floor and vomiting as a result of what he saw. One of Castillo's guards radioed for Maria to clean up the mess.

"Pendejo," said one of the bodyguards. He pointed to the wet spot on Raul's pant leg, causing a hearty laugh among the men.

"God, I am so, so sorry for what I have done," Raul murmured beneath uncontrollable sobs. The men elbowed each other while making fun of the pathetic man.

"After you help Maria clean up this mess you left, my men will take you back to your apartment in La Paz," Castillo ordered. "We expect all of the classified reports involving drug cartels in South America from two years ago. Do you understand, bastardo?"

Sobbing and shaking profusely, Raul continued to apologize to Castillo for breaking his trust. The cartel boss responded with a swift blow across his face, knocking out two of his teeth. Blood flowed from his mouth.

"Get this useless piece of shit out of here, now!" yelled Castillo as he motioned for his personal guards to take care of Raul.

Two guards manhandled Raul out of the hallway and onto the large patio area adjacent to the hacienda's lit parking lot. Incoherent cries for help and screams begging for mercy were heard around the hacienda compound from Raul. His cries for help provoked many work hands on the premises to look the other way. As usual, they did not see anything.

"Bien, mi amigos. In a day, McCord goes back to work," Castillo said before going to his office for a few shots of his private bourbon.

"Our DEA bitch is going to get her fill of dick in the next few days," muttered Castillo quietly as he quickly threw down one shot and poured another. "Then the gringos will find her dead in a cheap whorehouse in south Santa Cruz."

Almost to the point of being out of control with rage, Castillo could not wait to execute his vengeance on McCord for monitoring his business and for suckering him into rehabilitating her. He was a fool to think he could trade her for five imprisoned cartel members. Damn the Americans. He looked like a true sucker in the eyes of his cartel members and the other cartel kingpins in Mexico and South America. He knew that looking weak and being suckered by the gringos had deadly consequences. The other cartels would like nothing more than to take over his operations.

While Castillo smoked one of his premium cigars and savored his rare brand of bourbon, he looked out of his office window. Raul was dragged across the parking lot for his return trip to his apartment in La Paz—a nine-hour drive. The two cartel members escorting Raul would ensure he was alive and safe for his journey.

"Hola, Stephen," Castillo, now feeling the effects of the alcohol, yelled out into the hallway for his top lieutenant. Moments later, Stephen was found and directed to join Castillo in his office. Entering his boss' office, Stephen was sure his boss was drunk so he treaded lightly.

"Si jefe, a sus ordenes," Stephen politely stated while taking a seat at his usual place in front of Castillo's desk.

"Escúchame Stephen, I trust our old friend Raul will pay dearly for his part in trying to deceive us." Castillo took a puff on his cigar and admired the blue-gray smoke flowing out of his mouth. "Call our people taking Raul on their trip back to La Paz and inform them to find Raul's mother, Dr. Barbara Lopez. When our people say goodbye to Raul, they are to tell Raul that his mother will be told goodbye."

"Si mi jefe," Stephen replied, failing to understand the cruelty of such an action, but he followed orders or he would also die.

CHAPTER

23

The following day, the central dispatcher for the La Paz Police Department received an anonymous call, reporting what appeared to be a dead individual parked in a car at the Rendezvous Hostel. After much confusion and squabbling between the various municipal law enforcement agencies in La Paz, it was determined the Municipal Police would handle the investigation—it sounded like a typical cartel killing. However, the young detective assigned to investigate, painstakingly studied the crime scene and determined it was a suicide. The gunshot to the head with the Colt 45 pistol still in his hands had all the signs of a deliberate suicide. The detective determined there wasn't a need to search for fingerprints; however, he did search the car for personal items that would assist in identifying the victim. The body was sent to the La Paz Municipal Medical Center for cold storage while the family members were being notified.

Using one of the Hostel's conference rooms, the detective laid out the personal items found in the vehicle on a large, wooden conference table. Among the various personal belongings was a leather wallet. Inside, he found a common access card, linking him to the US Embassy. The name read: Raul Lopez, Administrative Assistant.

The detective reported the suspected suicide to his supervisor where the standard diplomatic protocols started notifying the US Bolivian Embassy, US State Department, and the Justice Department. Eventually, notification was made to the appropriate family members. In this case, Ambassador Burton and the embassy chaplain were the first to notify Barbara Lopez of the tragic death of her son. Understandably emotionally distraught, Ambassador Burton and the staff followed embassy protocol to comfort her. As sincerely as Burton could, considering his cold and indifferent attitude toward the embassy staff, he tried to comfort her and encouraged her to take all the time necessary to grieve Raul Lopez's passing

Barbara Lopez, working to temper her emotions, like the professional she was, began working with the human resources officer on the funeral arrangements, which included possible transportation to the United States. A makeshift, impromptu memorial ceremony was scheduled for the following day. Ambassador Burton would officiate the ceremony.

"Who the fuck is Raul Lopez, and why did the son of a bitch have to kill himself under my watch," said Burton as he returned to his office and slammed the door shut. He murmured to himself, "This could really make me look bad at State."

"Lisa," Burton pressed the intercom button to his executive support lead, "get going and write a draft memorial speech for me regarding this guy, Raul, and try to put a positive spin on it for me."

CHAPTER
24

"Roberta, it's urgent I speak with you immediately." Mercedes left a message on the contractor's cell phone. She was in Santa Cruz preparing for her role in the upcoming rescue attempt.

Mercedes waited on a small park bench near the embassy tapping his foot on the ground while he waited. He was sure his usual places were being monitored. A few minutes passed in restless anticipation. Finally, his phone buzzed, and he answered it before the second ring.

"Mercedes, this is Roberta." The woman's calm voice reassured him. "Yes, yes as we spoke earlier. I understand Raul Lopez most likely spilled his guts to his friends at the Sola Mesa Cartel prior to his suicide."

"I was hoping we could pull off this rescue mission prior to Castillo finding out about the bogus prisoner swap," Mercedes reasoned. "There is no doubt he had revealed our leadership and involvement in this scheme."

"OK, Mercedes. Poor McCord is supposedly going back to be raped repeatedly by the Sola Mesa Cartel members— if she is indeed still alive," Potter said. "They certainly will take out their vengeance with great enthusiasm on McCord, knowing they have been suckered. However, I am not sure how much information Raul told Castillo and his thugs about the possibility of a rescue mission. We can rest assured knowing they would not expect any type of rescue with the fake prisoner swap being discovered."

No words were spoken as Potter and Mercedes were faced with the critical and deadly decision of what to do next. Both were seasoned professional intelligence agents who would have a tough time living with themselves if they failed to try to save DEA Agent Bonnie McCord, who was one of their own.

It grated on Mercedes that McCord was being left behind with no urgency or help from the United States—except him and a few daring mercenaries and volunteers. Mercenaries who claimed they volunteered for this mission stating, "it was all about the money." The money motivation was a logical reason for mercenaries to volunteer; however, they all missed the danger and deadly risks of their current profession—they could never get it out of their system.

Without reservation, Mercedes moved to execute this high probability of failure and suicidal rescue mission. Any chance of success totally depended on Roberta Potter's ability to infiltrate the hacienda, find McCord, and protect her until the rescue team could get to them. Everything depended on Potter.

Potter made it clear, her motivation for working the mission was simple—big money for her unique services. However, unbeknownst to Mercedes and the other team members, Potter was livid and incensed that a woman federal agent was being used as a trophy fuck by a bunch of illiterate drug cartel members, and no one, including the President of the United States, was doing shit about it.

"What do you think, Roberta?" Mercedes hesitantly asked.

"I feel confident I can infiltrate the hacienda as an upscale call girl who lost her way from the ranch hand's living quarters to the hacienda," Potter said. "I'll seduce one of those drunk and horny ranch hands to show me around the place, and when we get close to the hacienda, I'll inject him with a strong sleeping drug.

"I'll park the truck near the secluded passageway leading into the hacienda with the ranch hand sleeping in the driver's seat," Potter added. "I'll find my way to McCord's room where we'll both, if she is alive, hunker down until your team arrives.

"Again, once I find her room, I'll give you call on the secure phone with our tactical radio as a backup with her location and health status—dead or alive," Potter said. "Do you have any issues?"

"No, Roberta. I have none." Mercedes wanted to relay to Potter that he understood the odds of her even making it to McCord's room were slim to none, and her escaping the hacienda would be a near impossible task. However, if anyone could pull it off, it would be Roberta Potter—she was known to be very tough to kill. Those poor bastards, if only they knew what they were about to be dealing with.

"OK, Mercedes, please reaffirm with me what happens after I contact you from McCord's room."

"Four Bolivian Federal Police SUVs will enter the hacienda's compound at the guarded entrance and make their way up to the security checkpoint manned by an assortment of contracted security men and woman—most, from what we understand, are retired local police officers," Mercedes relayed. "One of our DELTA volunteers will imitate a Federal Police commander, uniform and all, and demand to see Juan Castillo about one of his cartel members raping and molesting a teenage girl at a local bar near Santa Cruz."

"Once security guards have made the call to the hacienda regarding the police visit, they will storm it immediately."

"I am sure that Castillo will direct one of his lieutenants to meet with the police commander at the front entrance, invite him in, and try to 'make happy' with him. At that point, all of the uniformed Federal Police officers, which are really our rescue team members, will rush the opened front door and find their way to you in McCord's room.

"Oh, and, Roberta, please don't be looking for a fight—let us take care of it," Mercedes stressed. "Your number one priority is to protect McCord."

"Yes sir, understood!" replied Potter, knowing full well she was going to give as much shit and hellish payback as possible.

"Roberta, what time tomorrow night do you plan on being at the Ranch?" Mercedes asked, allowing her to make the call when the rescue operation would start since everything depended on her success.

"I have worked out the details and scenario a hundred different ways for timing and would like to plan on being at the hacienda alternate entrance at 11:00 PM," she said.

"Alright, the rescue team will plan on being at the hacienda security checkpoint at 11:15," Mercedes confirmed. "That will give you fifteen minutes inside the hacienda to find and secure McCord. Is that enough time for you?"

"If not, I'll give you a call with my status."

"One other item I need to remind you of." Mercedes was sorry he did not mention this to her earlier. "Members of the Nueva Confederación will be following the Federal police SUVs."

"What is their role again?" Potter didn't want to shoot the wrong people.

"Once our team storms the hacienda, the Confederación members will take over mopping up after the action while we're headed to the airport. Good luck, Potter. See you inside the hacienda," Mercedes concluded and ended the call.

Calling the team members, who were hunkered down at the La Vista Grande Ranch bunkhouse, Mercedes told Franklin that the rescue mission was a go for tomorrow evening with an execution time of 11:15 PM—go as planned.

CHAPTER
25

"I need a taxi," demanded the well-dressed attractive woman as she strode through the lobby of the Los Tajibas Hotel and Convention Center in downtown Santa Cruz. The rapid clicking of her heels echoed off the high ceilings.

"Right away, ma'am." The concierge waved to the next cab in line outside the hotel. He took a second look at the woman. She was different from the other high-end call girls that frequented the hotel and convention center.

Wearing a tight, slim black dress, traditional black stockings, and stiletto heels, she showed off plenty of shapely leg. Her expensive and fashionable black fur wrap drew the eye upward. She made exaggerated breaths that caused her generous breasts to rise and fall quickly beneath the low neck of the dress. Deep red lipstick emphasized an intriguing smile that said there was more than met the eye.

Here was a woman who knew her value and would settle for nothing less. Several men at the front reception desk failed to conceal their stares. Even the regular contingent of working girls at the hotel took notice. A few couldn't help their dismissive glances, glad to have her out of the hotel where they wouldn't have to compete with her.

"Señorita, your taxi." The young concierge swallowed nervously and ran to the taxi loading area to ensure all was set for her departure.

"Place this on the seat next to me." The woman handed the concierge a large and expensive suitcase. She pulled out one hundred dollars, stuffed them in the young man's shirt pocket, and gave him a quick kiss on the check. The exotic smell of the woman's perfume caused his heart to flutter. The lipstick mark would make him the envy of the staff tonight.

The taxi driver watched the alluring woman approach his cab. He immediately got out to assist her with the door and her luggage. The driver and the concierge jockeyed to assist her with the driver winning. He returned to his seat to watch the woman slowly slide across the back seat. Entering the cab with her legs apart, she revealed the mysteries under her tight dress. The taxi driver was mesmerized by what he saw. Smiling at the driver, the woman pulled down the short dress and crossed her legs.

"Wouldn't it be a good idea to keep our eyes on the road?" The woman winked.

"Si, señorita, where would you like to go?" The overly excited driver tried to avert his attention from the beautiful woman.

"Aquí!" She said as he handed him the directions to where she needed to go.

Turning on the taxi's overhead light, he put on his reading glasses and studied the address given to him. The address was that of one of the most notorious and ruthless drug cartel bosses in Bolivia, Juan Castillo. The driver had driven many, many women in the past few months to this address but had never carried a woman this sexy and alluring.

"Señorita, usted sabe que esta dirección esta muy lejos de aquí?" the driver added. "The fare will be very expensive—possibly over two hundred dollars."

"It is well worth it to me." She placed five one-hundred-dollar bills on the front seat of the cab. "Don't you think I am worth it, señor?" With a sly grin, she slightly opened her black fur wrap, intentionally showing the driver a little more of paradise.

"Por supuesto, señorita." The heavy-breathing driver tried to concentrate on getting out of the hotel's concourse. Soon they headed toward the Ranch on National Route 4 near the Rio

Grande O Guapay. "It'll be about an hour's drive."

"Señorita, I apologize for bothering you again," he politely said, "I need to know where on the Ranch you need to go. It is a very large complex with various security posts. Do you wish to go to the big house, the hacienda, or the bar and lounge?"

"Where do you think I need to go?" Her curious smile implied the driver should already know.

"I would guess you need to go to the small conference complex next to the Ranch employee's dormitory and lounge," answered the driver, knowing where the taxis usually dropped off their lady visitors.

"You are correct, my friend." She applauded the driver's correct answer and settled back with a thin wrap covering her legs. Pulling out what appeared to be a smartphone, she put in earphones and pretended to listen to music. In fact, she was monitoring the secure task force tactical radio frequency as they prepared for that night's raid. Everything sounded normal and on time as they conducted final briefings. Everyone was anxious to hear news from Roberta Potter. She acknowledged back by tapping on her phone's keypad, "No issues, on time."

CHAPTER
26

"Señorita, estamos aquí!" announced the driver as they approached a large cattle guard, leading onto the ranch property. The paved asphalt road had various side roads leading to the hacienda, airport, and ranch facilities.

Looking out the window, everything mirrored what she had expected. She had memorized the layout of the property with an emphasis on the hacienda, well-lit guard shack overlooking the parking lot, and the fence surrounding the premises.

The taxi continued on the paved ranch road toward the ranching complex when suddenly behind them, two large pickup trucks with police emergency lights and ultra-high beam headlights directed them to stop.

While the driver was pulling the taxi over to the side of the road, his passenger discreetly pulled out her loaded Beretta pistol hidden under the blanket. Potter readied herself for the coming reception by pulling up the hem of her dress and pulling the neckline lower. Her breasts were barely concealed beneath the fur wrap.

The men approached both sides of the taxi. She could hear their slurred speech, indicating they were possibly drunk. The beams of their flashlights flooded the taxicab with white light. Intentionally wanting the men to see her most attractive assets just for a second, she strategically dropped the wrap before slowly replacing it over her shoulders.

The security boss checked out the driver and his intentions. The other three men continued to point their flashlight beams on the woman in the backseat.

"I'd much rather fuck this bitch than that DEA gringo up at the hacienda," said one of the men who grabbed his crotch for further emphasis. The guards made harsh explicit sexual comments to Potter and what they would like to do with her. Potter thought quickly about how to take advantage of this situation—it only took her a minute. The security boss was still talking to the driver when Potter interrupted them.

"Perdón, jefe." Potter tried to get the attention of the guard boss.

"Si, señorita. Como puedo servirle?"

"Would it be too much to ask for one of your trucks to drive me to the bar and lounge?" asked Potter. The security boss was surprised to hear such a request, especially after what she had witnessed from their behavior. The two other security guards heard her request and enthusiastically agreed to help the lady.

"It is up to you, señorita. I have no problem with your request." She must be some kind of nymphomaniac or not easily satisfied. The men would take full advantage of the situation, but it was her call. "Damn, horny bitch," he murmured then turned off his flashlight and returned to his patrol truck.

The remaining guards assisted Potter and her luggage to the front seat of the second truck.

About one hundred yards away from the parking area of the lounge, the taxi driver turned his taxi around and headed for the exit. With his headlights on high beam, he could make out his passenger in the front seat of the security truck between two of the security guards who stopped and harassed her.

CHAPTER

27

"Aren't you going to take me to the bar and lounge so I can meet up with my john?" Potter pouted, pretending naivety. She sat between the two men who reeked of alcohol and unwashed bodies. The obnoxious odor of the men was stifling. "Can you roll down a window?"

"How much does a woman like you cost a night?" The guard in the passenger seat clumsily tried to lift up the hem of her dress.

"Oh, a couple thousand a night—depends on what the customer wants," Potter coolly replied as she attempted to fend off the guards groping. "Tell you what fellas, why don't we go somewhere a little more secluded where we can take care of business."

Both men were now breathing heavily with anticipation. The driver eagerly shifted the truck in drive and headed for a secluded spot near a small fishing lake a hundred yards down the road from the ranch complex. Parking the truck on a makeshift gravel parking area not visible from the service road they just came from, the driver turned off the engine. The pair quickly and excitedly began taking their clothes off. Pants and underwear came off first, thrown about the cab of the truck.

"Hey beautiful, ain't it time for you to take your clothes off?" demanded the passenger.

"Sin duda!" replied Potter. "But before I do, I want you boys ready to go."

Reaching for the passenger's hardened penis, she moved it up and down in her hand. He leaned back in the seat anticipating the ultimate pleasure of her mouth. Potter bent down toward his lap and suddenly thrust a medical injector syringe containing a strong sedative into his bare thigh. His screams of pain prompted Potter to push an old, dirty rag in his mouth. In a moment, he was in a deep sleep.

The driver watched the commotion with confusion. Alcohol dulled his reactions, leaving him questioning what he had witnessed.

"I gave your friend some medicine to take him to new highs during sex." Potter took a second injector syringe and rammed it in the driver's exposed thigh.

His loud screams interrupted the quiet night air. Like his partner, the driver fell silent as he slipped into unconsciousness.

Potter calmly sat between the two sleeping men to reflect on her incredible fortune. Having access to a ranch security vehicle and all the equipment that went along with it gave her confidence in the success of her mission. Plus, the guard's off-the-cuff comment told her that McCord was still alive.

Opening both doors, she easily pushed the drugged men out of the pickup and onto the gravel parking area. Grabbing a flashlight from the dash, she searched the interior of the cab for any items useful for the rescue effort when she heard radio traffic coming from the driver's lifeless body. She immediately jumped out of the cab and searched for the radio. Besides the security radio, she discovered a common access card and an employee identification card on the driver. Searching the passenger seat, she found a Colt 1911 pistol—a weapon of choice by various drug cartels. She had always found it to be a reliable weapon.

She placed her newfound treasures in the pickup, ensuring the radio was close by. Next, she pulled both men's bodies away from the small parking area and dumped them in a drainage ditch that ran next to the road they had just come from.

Returning to the pickup, she retrieved her suitcase from the cargo area and opened it. She pulled out a pair of worn jeans, a tight-fitting t-shirt, a long-sleeved blue denim work shirt, and other accessories that matched her new role as a ranch worker. Pulling her hair back, she put on a used plain black baseball cap.

Getting back on her secure tactical radio, she contacted Franklin and Mercedes to tell them about her good fortune. She began monitoring the rescue team's tactical frequencies and, just as important, the ranch's security radio network.

"I estimate I can be in the hacienda in thirty minutes—maybe sooner," Potter said over her cell phone. "What is your status?"

"Great news, Potter," Franklin answered. "We are all suited up and ready to roll out of the assembly area. We'll plan to be there in thirty—I am showing 2100 hours now, does that check with you?"

"Roger that."

"Just a reminder, Potter, we'll be arriving at the hacienda guard shack in Federal Police SUVs, wearing Federal Police uniforms," Franklin added. "When we hit the guard shack, we'll dismount and assault the front entrance to the hacienda so please be careful and don't confuse us with the cartel security guards—is that clear?

"Also, we have some friends from a rival cartel who have volunteered to back us up," informed Franklin. "They will be wearing green florescent vests, so be careful not to counter them if they come your way."

The "volunteers" were most likely members of the Nueva Confederación Cartel from the La Vista Grande Ranch. Potter had deep reservations of one cartel helping to destroy another, but it was not her call, thank goodness.

"Understand, but also please watch out for me also," Potter stressed. "I'll have a yellow florescent band around my ball cap."

"Anything else before we execute?' Franklin asked, allowing little time for her questions.

"Yes, I am not sure what your plans are after we breach the hacienda. Where do we find and secure McCord?" Potter asked. "I foresee numerous fire fights in the hacienda. How do you plan on getting McCord out safely without killing her?

"Thank you, Potter, and I apologize for not briefing you sooner on this," Franklin said. "Do you recall the briefing by Señor Mario Fernandez, the Brazilian drug czar, now in a Texas jail?"

"Yes, but please be quick," Potter warned, nervously looking at her watch. "I'm moving out in a couple of minutes."

"Do you recall the large aircraft hangared near the ranch's airstrip that is always fueled and ready to go? We are going to have our contract pilot, Ben Gray, check out the aircraft just prior to the raid. If he can accomplish a quick preflight inspection, open the hangar doors, start it, and taxi it to the runway, we'll have McCord and our team doc fly out of here," explained Mercedes calmly as if he was just going to a travel agent to buy a ticket.

"Where do these guys dream this shit up? What a fuckin' fairy tale," Potter thought to herself and tried to stay tempered.

"What about a fuckin' backup?" she yelled over the phone, frustrated that they had not talked about possible exits for McCord.

"Listen to me, Potter," Mercedes sternly stated. "Worse case is that we'll carry McCord out to one of the SUVs, with the doc, and drive back to our friends at the La Vista Grande Ranch—that is the best we can do!"

"All right," sighed Potter, resigned to the fact they were literally making the rescue plan up as they went.

"I'm heading up to the hacienda now, and I'll take a few minutes to run by the aircraft hangar and ensure it is still there," advised Potter. She paused to think for a minute. "I'll also check to ensure access to the hangar is not locked. If it is, I'll break the locks for easy access. If you don't hear from me, assume the aircraft is OK."

"Roger that," Franklin affirmed.

Getting off the phone, Potter gathered up all the equipment she would need going into the hacienda. The security radios were a real prize, giving her access to ranch security radio traffic during the raid. Her personal signature suitcase was filled with tactical pistols, ammunition, knives, smoke grenades, and Potter's weapon of choice, a garrote made of piano wire used for a close, quiet execution. She tucked her switchblade into the pocket of her pants.

Quickly, she transferred all the weapons and tactical equipment from the suitcase to a large, sturdy trash bag. If she was stopped or challenged inside the hacienda, she would say she was new and simply taking out the garbage. Once the inventory was complete, she double-checked her coordinates with the GPS and headed for the aircraft hangar. Taking a deep breath and saying a short prayer, she placed the pickup in drive.

Parking next to the hangar, she could see light shining through the large hangar doors. Someone was doing some work on the aircraft. He was probably a lone mechanic preparing the aircraft for a launch or performing routine maintenance. Looking like an attractive maid from the hacienda, Potter opened the side entrance and slowly walked onto the hangar floor. She glanced around, attempting to gain some situational awareness without attracting any attention.

"Who's there and what is your business?" yelled a man in dark overalls under the aircraft's wing. Quickly, he stood and grabbed a pistol from his toolbox and began searching the hangar for an intruder.

"Señor, I apologize if I startled you." Potter came forward to present herself openly to the mechanic.

Startled, the man quickly turned and aimed his pistol at her. "Stay where you are. What is your business here?"

Potter slowly came toward the man and stopped a few short feet away. The security radio hung on her belt and the stolen employee identification badge hung on a string in front of her breasts. To the mechanic, it appeared she was just another ranch employee—probably given a job because she screws the boss. The mechanic slowly let his guard down. His hand relaxed its hold on the pistol as he lowered it.

"Señor, the boss man wanted me to check with you to ensure the plane was all fueled and ready for his trip tomorrow morning," said Potter professionally.

"Bien, mi dolce. Please tell the boss that I fixed the minor write-ups from his last flight. She is all ready to go tomorrow."

The mechanic cleaned his hands with a white cotton work towel and took a moment to admire Potter's physical assets.

"Thank you, sir. I'll run up and tell them the status," Potter replied as the mechanic walked suspiciously closer and closer toward her—exactly what she wanted.

"Come on, sweetheart, don't you want to see what the inside of the aircraft looks like?"

"Whoo, you'll show me the inside of the plane?" She smiled slyly and teased the mechanic by revealing more of her breasts. "OK, show me."

The mechanic aggressively pulled Potter close and tried to take off her jeans. She kicked him in the groin. He backed off and held himself bent over, attempting to find relief from the pain. Potter pulled the garrote out of her back pocket. Quickly, she placed the garrote's loop around his neck and pulled tight. A foot on his back helped her tighten the loop further. He struggled hard for his life, but she finished her grim task. Emotionless, she dragged his , covered his body with a tarp she found, and closed the door.

She took a moment to clean the piss and vomit produced from her handy work.

Returning to the aircraft, she removed any sign of him working on the aircraft, praying to God it was just a routine equipment check. Quickly climbing into the cockpit, she ensured the keys were available and any locks were removed. The Beechcraft Super King Air appeared ready to fly.

Running down the aircraft stairs, she searched for the electric control box for the massive hangar doors and inspected to see if there was a computer. Jotting down a few notes about the hangar layout on a small notepad, she hurriedly walked to the entrance and searched for anything she might have left behind. Finding nothing, she ran to the truck.

"Franklin, I'll be quick," Potter called from the cab of the started truck. "Everything is OK at the hangar and the aircraft appears ready for immediate takeoff."

Potter quickly briefed Mercedes on the layout of the hangar and added that she killed the mechanic working on the aircraft and left his body in the parts room. She confirmed that the agency pilot was still on schedule to arrive at the aircraft just prior to the raid beginning.

"Good work, Potter," Franklin commended. "When do you believe you'll enter the hacienda?"

"Approximately fifteen minutes, with fifteen minutes to find McCord's room," Potter estimated. "Will you be at the guard shack in thirty minutes?"

"Yes," replied Franklin. "If we are delayed due to unforeseen circumstances, are your prepared to hold out in the hacienda?"

"Do I have a choice, Einstein?"

"Good luck, Potter."

CHAPTER
28

Monitoring the Ranch's security radio, she found no menacing radio traffic except for repeated attempts to contact the two drugged guards. The other two she had met joked about their good time with the prostitute they picked up earlier. Their disappearance had passed without concern. Good news.

Starting the security pickup, she reviewed a small map of the area again, confirming the roads leading to the back of the hacienda. She checked her Beretta and silencer and placed them on the seat next to her. A quick check in the rearview mirror told her she was ready to go.

She rammed the pickup into drive and drove behind the hacienda without incident. A couple of other vehicles passed her, but they didn't seem to take notice of her.

Arriving at the alternate entrance, she was surprised to see various types of vehicles parked in the makeshift parking lot. They were all older models that had seen better days. Many were rusted and needed repairs. The household staff couldn't afford the luxurious vehicles of those higher up in the cartel.

Knowing time was critical, she found an out-of-the-way obscure parking place twenty yards from the hacienda. She took a few precious moments to configure the pickup for a possible quick getaway. The keys beneath the driver's seat and a pistol in the glove box gave her a backup plan if shit hit the fan.

The team counted on her successful infiltration of the hacienda prior to their arrival. She checked her watch.

Ten minutes 'til go time.

CHAPTER
29

After a quick final check, she threw her garbage bag over her shoulder and headed for the service entrance. A lone guard in a broken wooden chair monitored the door. Smoke escaped the dimly lit entrance.

"Chiquita, come over here and give me a kiss." The drunk guard held his fleshy arms open.

Though repulsed by what she observed, she continued on. He would see soon enough that the common access card she possessed belonged to the indisposed security guard. Maybe she could seduce him to let her pass without incident.

"Bien, guapo." She gave him a kiss on the check and promised to meet him in the parking lot after her shift in the kitchen.

The guard was momentarily enchanted by Potter and allowed her entrance without requiring the swipe of her access card or checking her employee badge.

"See ya after work, papi chulo." With a small wave, she walked into the hacienda and into a large utility room, her large black plastic bag over her shoulder. The storage area wasn't the kitchen she was looking for. She'd have to keep looking.

"Hey, you! Stop where you are. Who are you?" came a loud voice behind Potter. "What are you doing here?"

The large, intoxicated man grabbed Potter by the arm and swung her around to face him. Using her theatrics and fake charm, she simpered like a frightened girl.

"Señor, I am the new kitchen assistant and have lost my way." With loud wailing, she took a moment to size him up. She even managed to produce a few tears while her free hand searched for her hidden switchblade.

"La pobrecita, I'll take you to the kitchen." He grabbed her by the arm and pulled her alongside him. As they approached a large set of utility stairs leading to the next floor, she could smell the distinct aroma of cigars. The man continued to hold her as he led her down the elaborate hallway. The delightful smells of picante de pollo and papas rellenas overpowered the stench of smoke the closer they got to the kitchen.

Potter was not worried about her safety. She was more concerned about the timing of the rescue team. Anxious to get to the kitchen fast, she pleaded with the man to hurry or she would be fired. The man appeared to take pity on her and took her directly to the kitchen director.

"Pedro, I found one of your lost sheep downstairs, confused and forgetting where the kitchen was." The man let go of her arm.

The kitchen director set down his pen and eyed her from his seat behind a desk cluttered with papers. It was obvious he did not recognize her but was unwilling to investigate further. He was in desperate need of a dishwasher. Yes, she would do just fine and for more than just kitchen work.

"What is your name again?" Pedro acted as if he had forgot, while focusing on the woman's full breasts.

The man who brought her, satisfied all was well, turned and left.

"Sir, my name is Barbara. I am very grateful for the job you provided me." Potter dropped her bag and leaned on the desk, pushing her breasts higher between her arms. "Is there a private place I can show my appreciation for allowing me to be late?"

Pedro began breathing heavy at the prospect. She gently ran a finger along his arm and grabbed his hand. With her free hand, she reached into her bag. His gaze never left her cleavage.

"Yes, yes." Pedro directed her into the private manager's office, quickly closed the door, and locked it.

The next thing he knew he was in a lock hold. The woman's shapely leg was wrapped around his neck. She immediately applied zip-type handcuffs around his hands and ankles. Pedro began struggling in a vain attempt to be free. A strip of duct tape across his lips put his screaming to a stop.

"Pedro, look at me." Potter spoke with a reassuring tone as she kneeled next to him on the floor. "I am not here to hurt you—you must understand that."

Pedro looked into Potter's eyes with confusion and fear.

"All I need from you now is the location of the DEA woman—nod your head if you understand," she ordered.

Pedro nodded his head.

"Very good." She could not believe her good luck. "I'm going to remove the tape from your mouth so you can help me with some questions. But if you scream or yell, I will put this knife into your heart." She pulled the sleek commando knife out and showed him. He stared at the deadly weapon and knew without a doubt she would kill him. He began crying quietly with fear as Potter drew the tape off his mouth.

"What do you want and why are you doing this? I had nothing to do with her. I swear."

Potter held a hand over his mouth as a warning. "I'll ask the questions." She punctuated the warning with a slap across the face, resulting in more crying and heavy breathing. Potter returned to her soft, reassuring tone. "Where in the hacienda is the DEA woman being held?"

"She is on the next floor up in a private bedroom, close to Mr. Castillo's office and a private conference room where the men wait for..."

"Wait for what?" she asked but unfortunately already knew the answer.

"Their turn with the DEA woman."

"Are there any committed guards stationed at the room?"

"Only roving security patrols that routinely walk around the hacienda," answered Pedro.

"Thank you. I'd advise you for your own safety to stay exactly where you are until your staff finds you and cuts you lose. Do you understand?"

"Yes ma'am," a relieved Pedro replied.

Placing the duct tape over his mouth, Potter looked at Pedro one last time and placed her finger to her lips and said, "Shh." She grabbed her bag and found her way to the massive food pantry in the kitchen where she quickly pulled out the tactical radio from her belt holder and called Mercedes and Franklin.

"This is Franklin."

"Everything is going as planned—better in fact," Potter quietly relayed. "I have the location of McCord and she is alive."

"What is the room location for McCord and is there anything else that we need to know?" Franklin asked.

"Her room is on the second floor of the hacienda and just down the hall from Castillo's private office and across from a large conference room. My source tells me there are no standing security guards, only roving patrols."

"We'll be at the guard checkpoint in ten minutes. Will that give you enough time to secure McCord and wait for our arrival?"

"Affirmative!" a relieved Potter replied.

"Potter, these men are itching for a fight so be prepared to hunker down when you hear the shooting start."

"Understand." Adrenaline pumped faster in her system in anticipation of the upcoming fight. "I'm on my way to McCord's room."

Double-checking that she looked like a poor peasant girl carrying out the trash, she quickly departed the kitchen and found the stairs leading up to the second floor.

CHAPTER

30

"Ricardo, whose turn is next with our DEA playgirl?" The voice came from the conference room to the left of the stairway Potter ascended.

"I believe Julio is screwing her now." Ricardo laughed. "Hope he does not get the bitch pregnant." Roars of laughter followed.

Potter slowly and quietly eased her way down the hall to the conference room. Light streamed from the cracked door, but thankfully, they couldn't see her move toward what she believed was McCord's room. Julio was going to have one big fucking surprise soon.

She put her head to the door. The distinct sounds of a man having his way with a defenseless woman confirmed that she had found McCord's room. Before making her entrance, Potter ensured she had her garrote and knife ready for immediate use. She braced herself for what she was sure was a tragic and sad sight.

Slowly turning the brass doorknob, she gently opened the unlocked door and quickly slid inside. With the same cautiousness, she closed the door with a soft snick. A horrified Potter was sick with disgust as a small nightstand light revealed a horrific sight. A large, fat man had sweat pouring down his fleshy body. The skeleton of a woman was barely visible beneath him. The only fight that seemed left in McCord were her agonizing cries. Bile rose in Potter's throat at the sight.

"Hey, Julio! How would you like to fuck me?" Potter's voice caused him to momentarily pause his thrusting. She rushed toward him and quickly placed the garrote noose around his neck and violently pulled. Using her foot on his body to add extra strength, she pulled with everything she had. Trying to grasp some air, he helplessly tried to pull the garrote off his neck. Knowing he was fading fast, she positioned his body to fall on the side of the bed away from the poor woman. He hit with a large thud.

"Julio must be having such a rough time with McCord that he fell off of her," a comment was heard from a cartel member waiting his turn in the nearby conference room. Lots of laughing and jokes about Julio's lovemaking could be heard from the others waiting in the conference room.

Dazed with an expressionless stare at Potter, McCord attempted to lift her hands up to shield herself from any further attacks. She tried to determine what had just happened while expecting more pain.

Potter checked Julio's pulse then pulled his heavy body over to the room's corner and found a filthy, stained blanket to cover him. A hard kick to his side released some pent-up frustration. She immediately returned to McCord's bedside and took stock of her condition. Tears ran down Potter's face. Wiping her eyes, she slowly sat next to McCord on the bed.

"Bonnie McCord," Potter whispered and held the limp hand sitting on the used coverlet. "I am Roberta Potter. I work for the CIA. Listen to me very carefully and do exactly as I say, and we'll get out of here."

McCord squeezed Potter's hand slightly. Encouraged, she gave the woman a bottle of water to drink and a can of mixed fruit, which she slowly ate, savoring every piece. McCord's survival instincts kicked in as she put water from the bottle in her hands and tried to clean her face. Tears left muddy streaks down her pale, sunken cheeks.

"We are going to be OK, Bonnie. You look like you are feeling better," Potter encouraged, knowing McCord did not have time for any extra attention—time was short.

Potter turned away to hide her emotions and reached for the radio. "Franklin, I am in McCord's room. She is alive. Get us out of here."

"We are approaching the guard post now. I suspect you'll be hearing shit in just a few minutes—hold on!" Franklin gave the signal for the team to move on the hacienda.

"Hurry!" Potter put the radio back and let out a relieved sigh.

"Is Robert with you?" a surprised and bewildered Potter turned and looked at McCord. She was attempting to sit up in the bed, still somewhat bewildered, and again stared at Potter with her angelic green eyes. "Robert promised me that he would come get me."

"Yes, Bonnie. Robert is on his way now with the rest of the rescue team." Potter wanted to reassure her though she didn't know if the Robert the woman wanted was even on the team.

However, they both were in extreme danger.

"Bonnie, I am going to pick you up and lay you down on the sofa." Potter carefully picked up McCord from the filthy bed and laid her on the small, worn sofa on some clean sheets she had found stacked in a closet.

"Are you comfortable, Bonnie?" Potter draped a clean blanket over the half-naked woman.

McCord gave a weak smile and asked for another bottle of water.

Potter began preparing the room and McCord for the inevitable deadly visitors that were sure to come and attempt to repeatedly rape and kill them, if the team did not arrive soon. No doubt, even while the rescue attempt was in progress, the cartel members would put a priority on killing McCord—she knew too much.

"Bonnie, Bonnie, stick with me, girl," Potter encouraged and held McCord's face firmly by the chin. "I need your help, Bonnie."

Bonnie looked at Potter and nodded her head.

Potter pulled a pistol out of her bag, ensured it was loaded and cocked, and slowly handed it to McCord. Potter positioned the pistol next to McCord's body for easy access if needed.

"Bonnie, this is a Beretta 92 FS service pistol." Potter attempted to have McCord feel the pistol in her hands. "I know through your DEA and military service record that you are an expert with this weapon."

McCord attempted to hold the pistol. Dawning recognition flashed across her mind the longer she held the weapon. She instinctively attempted to pull back the slide to chamber a bullet with no success. Potter was just pleased that she remembered to pull the slide back—some things one never forgets.

"Let me help you." She pulled the slide back and readied the pistol for semi-automatic firing. "The pistol has fifteen rounds."

McCord slightly nodded her head, understanding the instructions. She was becoming more animated under Roberta's care.

"If you need to defend yourself, you'll be ready." Potter ensured McCord kept the pistol next to her, ensuring she had an easy reach for the trigger. Potter was hoping that in the worst-case situation, McCord's pent-up anger could enable her to fire the pistol.

Reaching into her trash bag, Potter pulled out a small, sturdy carrying case and immediately opened it. Inside were various medicines and syringes. She ripped open a pack containing a wet wipe and cleaned McCord's butt. Then she filled three syringes with three different drugs and gave them to McCord.

"What are you doing?" McCord asked in a weak voice.

"I am giving you some drugs that will help you feel better—that is all you need to know for now." Potter smiled and McCord nodded.

After caring for McCord, Potter laid out the weapons she would need if anyone came in prior to the rescue team arriving. Completing her inventory, she pulled out a generic woman's nightshirt and put it on over her jeans and work shirt.

"Bonnie, I am going to take your place here in your bed." Potter did not look forward to lying down in the sewer McCord had been living in.

Bonnie gave her a curious look.

"If they come in here looking for you, they'll find me—what a big surprise for them. If they try to fuck me, they will be in for the ride of their lives." Potter tried to make light of the situation while she laid out her pistol, garrote, and commando knife.

"Franklin," in almost a whisper, Potter relayed, "McCord and I are good waiting your arrival. Please hurry."

"Potter, the Federal Police SUVs with the rescue team are approaching the guard shack now—hang tight. We'll be there soon."

CHAPTER
31

As the string of Federal Police SUVs approached the guard shack, the last one veered off on another road, heading for the hangar. The SUV stopped at the side of the hangar and Ben Gray got out of the vehicle. He carried his flight suitcase that contained a Beechcraft checklist, aviation maps, a possible flight plan, and a couple of Beretta pistols. More importantly, he found that the aircraft ramp area and runway still had their lights on.

"What an incredible break," Gray excitedly said to the other team members. "Having the lights on means our chances of getting out of here on the Beechcraft just became possible." Gray knew only too well that taking off at night with no runway lights was close to suicidal, but he smiled and thought of all the night takeoffs he'd done in Vietnam with no lights.

"Thanks, Mack, for the ride and tell Franklin about the runway lights," Ben Gray said to the SUV driver. "Let's see if we can make this bird fly." Gray waved as the SUV sped away to catch up with the others.

The hangar was blessedly deserted when he walked in the large double doors. It took him only a few strides to reach the stairs leading up to the cockpit.

He took a seat and immediately felt at home. Of all the aircraft he'd flown for the CIA, the Beechcraft King Air was his favorite.

In the captain's seat, he grabbed the aircraft's checklist out of his pilot's bag and began the preliminary checklist items. At the same time, he was monitoring the tactical radio to stay updated on the progress of the raid. He was relieved to hear that Agent McCord was alive.

"OK, let's kick the tires and light the fire." The old aviator was excited to be back in action.

CHAPTER

32

"What is your business here?" an approaching security guard demanded. He carried a flashlight and a drawn pistol as he approached the driver of the first SUV.

Franklin got out of the vehicle smoking a cigar. An official-looking portfolio completed his Bolivian Federal Police Captain's uniform. "Get that light out of my face or I'll take you in for obstructing justice. I need to speak with your boss, right now."

At this, the other officers began exiting the SUVs with their weapons drawn. They covered their faces with bandanas as was common practice for law enforcement officers. The covering protected their identity like the bulletproof vests protected their hearts. Franklin was the only one not wearing a bandana.

A security guard was immediately dispatched inside the hacienda to brief Juan Castillo of the arrival of the Federal Police. Castillo knew and employed most of the police officers in his area. He could not figure out what they might want, especially so late in the evening. In his office, he directed one of his lieutenants, Diego Sordo, to go to the guard shack a see what the police wanted.

Castillo had a sixth sense something was not as it appeared. He walked to his office window and looked at the guard post. He picked up his binoculars to get a better view of the dismounted police officers. The captain was not a police officer.

While Sordo was talking with the police captain, Castillo alerted his staff and area cartel members of a potential attack on the hacienda by rogue Federal Police officers. He tried to figure out who might be after him. There were a few large cartels that could challenge his cartel's power, but starting a war made no sense and would not benefit anyone in the drug world.

"Señor Castillo asks, what is the problem? Why are you here?" Sordo directly and firmly asked Franklin. "You tell me, and I will relay the information to Señor Castillo."

"I asked to speak with Señor Castillo not some errand boy." Theatrically acting as a true Federal Police captain would under the same situation, Franklin said, "If I don't see him soon, I'll put handcuffs on you and take you in."

Sordo laughed at the notion.

Whack! A sudden quick slap across the face forced Sordo to stumble back for a moment. He placed his hand over his stinging cheek and just stared at Franklin. Castillo's blood boiled as he watched the slapping incident wondering who would have the guts to personally strike one of his people so blatantly—especially on his property.

Embarrassed, Sordo pulled a concealed .44 Magnum from his waist and clumsily fired it at Franklin—slightly grazing him in the leg.

A stun grenade was thrown in the guard shack, disabling the remaining guards. The remainder of the rescue team immediately rushed the front entrance of the hacienda, throwing stun grenades and donning gas masks. They moved with speed through the building. In each room, they encountered dazed cartel members who clumsily fired their weapons at no particular target.

Mass confusion prevailed as cartel members ran out of the hacienda seeking some sort of refuge from the grenades and the team's relentless firepower. The rescue team attempted to detain as many members as possible using zip-tie handcuffs and holding them in one of the many conference rooms. Each passing moment, the captives grew in number. Some sporadic firing continued both inside and outside but was quickly subsiding.

Air Force Combat Controller and McCord's love, Rob Madden entered the hacienda finding the front conference room filled with half-dressed and hungover cartel members. He limped slightly thanks to a leg wound. Grabbing the first prisoner he came to, he demanded to know where the woman DEA agent was.

The prisoner shook with fright and pointed upstairs.

A dirty and irritable Madden was on his way upstairs when he was blown back by a tremendous explosion right above where he was going.

Explosions and gunfire reverberated off the walls in McCord's room. "Well, it appears the team is here." Gleeful, Potter wanted to join in the mayhem, but she was playing it safe by staying and protecting McCord.

Castillo was totally confused about what was happening at the guard shack and the sudden fighting in his hacienda. He was still in his office waiting for Sordo's report back from the Federal Police captain when a concussion grenade detonated just down from his office. He was shocked to see the police officers charging into the hacienda and quickly taking down his startled and confused cartel members.

"What happened to my security?" he yelled at the few cartel members still with him. "What do these assholes want? Get down there and try to find out who these fuckers are!"

Castillo ordered reinforcements from the ranch complex over their radio. He still couldn't understand why anyone would be attacking the Sola Mesa Cartel.

"McCord!" he thought to himself. "They are here for McCord." The other cartel members pleaded with Castillo to allow them to go to her room and finish her off—as a parting gift to the DEA.

"No, you stay here and hold back these people while I go take care of McCord," ordered Castillo. "We're going to give them their precious agent on a cross."

Running down the hallway, past the now shredded conference room because of one of Potter's grenades, he burst open McCord's room to find her still in bed. Two dead cartel members were lying on the floor naked with what appeared to be their necks cut. Stunned by what he was seeing, he did not see Potter slowly ease out of the bed with her garrote and come behind him, ready to wrap the deadly piano wire around his neck.

However, he sensed something was amiss in the room with the two dead bodies on the floor. In a split second, he was able to get his hands around his neck, limiting the garrote's impact and providing him the opportunity to throw Potter down on the floor. Hitting hard, she immediately lost her grip on her deadly hold. Instinctively throwing off the garrote from his neck, he pulled a hidden knife from the back of his pants and lunged at the woman, striking her in the upper thigh.

Potter instinctively reeled back, holding her bloody knife wound while trying to pull her concealed commando knife from her waist. Castillo lunged again and struck her in her lower abdomen. She laid in a fetal position, waiting for the final blow that would kill her and trying desperately to determine if she had any options left. Disoriented and in extreme pain, Potter searched in vain for a weapon, but was immediately kicked in the stomach.

"Listen up you fuckin' bitch," Castillo roared while searching frantically before finally finding the garrote. He lifted up the deadly wire for Potter to see.

Her life would be gone in a matter of seconds she had no doubt. Praying to God for strength, she prepared one last strike.

"With your garrote, I'm going over to our DEA bitch to finish her off in front of your eyes," Castillo screamed out of control. "I am going to be the last person to screw her prior to using your garrote to kill her."

Potter lay helpless, bleeding profusely and attempting to find some way to stop Castillo's move toward McCord. He pulled off the blanket. McCord attempted to scream but only struggled to make faint, lifeless sounds. Castillo hurriedly dropped his pants and underwear to the floor, grabbed the garrote, and roughly entered McCord while attempting to place the garrote around her neck. Agony twisted her features as his tempo increased ready to climax in McCord at the same time he would pull the garrote to its death hold. Potter could see the end was coming within a few seconds by observing Castillo's fatal and sadistic treatment of McCord.

"McCord, damn you. Use your weapon! Use your weapon!" Potter used every ounce of energy she had left to scream.

Castillo's rhythm became more frenzied as he neared his climax and began to pull the piano strings tighter. McCord knew the end was seconds away. Pain clouded her mind. Why was Potter yelling at her about a weapon?

Castillo was relishing using and killing McCord and was not distracted by Potter's screams. He was satisfied his death grip on McCord was nearly complete.

Boom. Boom. Boom. The loud, dull thuds of the pistol reverberated in the room. Castillo's body bounced three times slightly skyward and fell motionless on top of her. The only sounds now were coming from Castillo, moaning in incredible pain as a result of the three pistol shots fired into his stomach. He was confused about what had just happened. Attempting to roll off McCord, his body dropped to the floor with a loud thud.

Potter surveyed the cluttered bedroom floor and stumbled upon a dead cartel member holstering a .44 Magnum handgun. Barely able to crawl, she worked her way over to the now screaming Castillo and aimed the gun at his testicles.

"Oh please, God have mercy, please," he begged.

Potter, barely able to hold the gun, fired it. The bullets shredded Castillo's groin area. Cocking the powerful gun again, she managed to aim the gun at his chest. The screaming and begging stopped—he was lifeless.

"Bonnie, are you OK?" Potter painfully asked, seeing some signs of life in McCord's body as she let go of the now smoking pistol.

She was relieved to see a thumbs-up from McCord. With that, Potter painstakingly crawled around, trying to find some clothes and towels to apply to her wounds. In her first aid kit, she found morphine and antibiotics, which she quickly applied. She kept some vials attached to her clothes in the event medical care would be necessary thanks to her experience in the military. The doctor would know what medicines she had applied to herself.

CHAPTER

33

"They are in here," an excited team member announced over the radio. "Second floor across from a conference room. Bring the doc ASAP."

"What is their status?" Franklin asked while he searched for cartel survivors.

"Potter is in bad shape. Took a knife to the belly. McCord is alive, but bruised and weak."

"Hey, Doc. I'd like you and Madden to hustle up to the second floor to where McCord and Potter are located," Franklin ordered. "Do what you can but get them ready to move ASAP."

The DELTA physician's assistant and Madden raced up the stairs and down the hall. McCord's room had four naked dead cartel members and blood splattered on the walls and floors. The obnoxious smell was sickening to breathe. The two men immediately pulled the dead bodies out of the room and placed them in the shattered conference room.

The doctor immediately checked on both women. While both were in critical condition, Potter's wounds needed immediate attention if she had a chance of living. Madden saw McCord's thin and fragile body lying on a makeshift sofa bed. She still had a loose grip on a Beretta pistol. Madden cautiously picked up the pistol from McCord, emptied the magazine, and put the safety on.

"Oh, my poor sweet Bonnie," Madden kept repeating while holding her hand and lovingly stroking her caked and dirty hair.

He held her hand so tight while McCord just stared at Madden with a watery smile. Tears streamed down her face and her mouth quivered with joy and relief. She held Madden's hand firmer as both stared into each other's eyes. They wanted to hold each other tight and never let go. The doc worked extensively on Potter's wounds and immediately was able to stop the bleeding. He explained it could have been much worse, but felt she would be able to move because of the medical glue gun used to close her wounds.

"Robert, I knew you would come get me," McCord softly said, while reaching her hand up and stroking his face.

"Sweetheart, I am so, so sorry we could not get to you sooner." Madden tearfully answered while applying some cleaning cloths to her neck and chest. She continued to stare at him, holding him tight with her weak and shaking fingers.

"I want you to take care of me. I am so tired Rob, so very, very tired."

"I won't let you go, sweetheart," Madden assured her. "Bonnie, I want you to get some rest—we have a nice journey ahead of us.

She stared affectionately at Madden and touched his face with her grimy hands. Not wanting to let him go.

"Hey, Doc. Looks like we are finished here. How soon can we get McCord and Potter down here?" Franklin's voice rattled over the radio.

"We are going to need a stretcher for Potter," Doc answered and then yelled over to Madden, "Can you carry McCord downstairs?"

"Affirmative," a reluctant Madden answered not liking the answer. He'd much rather have her on a stretcher but would carry her to safety—regardless of the distance.

While the rest of the team and hired Nueva Confederación Cartel mercenaries stood guard outside the hacienda, two team members created a stretcher out of the heavy plantation blinds covering many of the windows. Rushing up the stairwell, the men passed Madden carrying a dirty, frail Bonnie McCord. They stopped, stunned at her appearance. They were glad they came all this way to save this brave woman who volunteered for a dangerous mission, was tortured and raped by the cartel, and was responsible for killing the top drug cartel boss in Bolivia. Everyone knew she was a hero.

"Doc, here is your stretcher, ready to go." The two men looked in a hurry to vacate the premises.

"Help me lift Potter here on the stretcher."

The three men slowly and carefully secured her to the makeshift stretcher. The doctor pulled the center pole off a set of blinds and attached an IV to it. The younger men picked up their ends and carried her down to the assembly area. They waited impatiently on the ground floor, ready to evacuate.

The members outside getting the SUVs ready were now setting their eyes on the lone large hangar that housed their getaway. There appeared to be no activity at the hangar, causing an enormous amount of anxiety amongst the rescue team members. It was their only way out.

CHAPTER
34

"Ben Gray, do you hear me? Over," Franklin called over his radio to the team pilot. "Gray, what is our status? Over." Franklin continued trying to contact Gray with no luck. Meanwhile, the team members gathered near the Federal Police SUVs for a possible race to the La Vista Grande Ranch if the aircraft could not be used.

"Fuck!" Franklin clinched his fist. "Get in the SUVs. Let's get out of here before the real Federal Police show up."

"Franklin, this is Gray. Franklin, this is Gray. Do you read me? Over."

"Fuck yes, I read you. When are you going to get that aircraft ready?"

"You did not tell me of all the shit that was wrong with it," Gray vented. "I simply put a Band-Aid on all the problems, but it'll fly."

"OK, start it up and let's get the fuck out of here," Franklin ordered. "When we see you started and leaving the hangar, we'll drive like hell over to meet you. We'll commence loading in the parking area directly in front of the hangar once you get the aircraft started and out of the hangar. Once those doors open, we are moving. Do you copy?"

"Copy that."

Watching from the hacienda parking lot, everyone on the team and the rival cartel members who joined in on the raid strained their eyes to watch the lone hangar a couple of hundred yards away. Suddenly, a sliver of light began growing as the immense hangar doors opened. The whining sounds of the aircraft's two Pratt & Whitney Twin-Turbo Propeller engines were loud enough to reach the group. Slowly the aircraft moved forward, lighting up the area with its ultra-bright lights.

"Let's go," Franklin roared as everyone loaded into the SUVs.

One SUV stayed behind while the others moved toward the hangar. Franklin stayed to thank the cartel members and warn them about the strategically placed explosives in the hacienda.

Felipe Formosa, the boss of the Nueva Confederación Cartel, had his driver take him to the parking lot where the rescue team was loading up to drive to the aircraft. One of his men found and escorted him to Franklin who was on the radio with the aircraft.

"Señor Franklin!" Formosa greeted a busy Franklin who in turn smiled and shook his hand. "Looks like you got your girl, and you certainly have destroyed the Sola Mesa Cartel. Will you be requiring any more of our services?"

"Felipe, if we cannot use that aircraft for escape, we'll make a dash to your ranch and go from there."

"One last thing," Formosa warned, grinning, "your success tonight has made us the top drug cartel in Bolivia. How will Mercedes reckon with that in Washington and the DEA?"

"Not my problem," answered a grinning Franklin. "I am just hear to get our girl out—nothing more. Who knows, we may be coming after you next, Felipe."

"Si, es possible!" Formosa replied. "However, amigo, I am not that stupid to take a DEA agent hostage where I am going to have the likes of you come after me."

"Just remember, Señor Franklin, no DEA agents are allowed in Bolivia." Formosa grinned. "So I guess I will not be seeing you!"

"Well, Felipe, you got me there." Franklin smiled and grabbed Felipe close for a few brief important comments.

"Highly recommend you get your people out of the hacienda immediately and get as far away as possible," Franklin warned. "When we leave, we are destroying the hacienda. There will be nothing left."

At Franklin's warning, Formosa rounded up his members. Men began streaming out of the hacienda, arms full of loot.

"Remember, Señor Franklin, no DEA agents in Bolivia, so don't be coming looking for us." Formosa smirked and headed down to the Ranch to pick up some vehicles for their new owners.

"What have we done?" Franklin thought to himself, shaking his head. "What have we done?"

CHAPTER

35

"Franklin, this is Gray. We are just about loaded up. You coming?"

"On my way." Franklin raised his hand forward and got into the SUV. The engines grew louder the closer they got to the hangar. The powerful propellers blew dirt and dust everywhere.

"Damn it, Gray, do you have to have all those lights on the aircraft," Franklin yelled over the radio. "There are still a ton of people shooting at us."

"Sorry, Franklin, force of habit," an embarrassed Gray replied, turning off all of the aircraft's taxi lights. Wild shots could be heard everywhere—especially from the ranch complex. Franklin could not determine if the gun shots were coming from the rival cartel they were working with, taking advantage of the disastrous situation with the Sola Mesa Cartel.

The driver parked on the side of the hangar. Franklin and the team exited and ran for the open passenger door of the plane. They covered themselves against the strong jet blast.

Inside the aircraft, Doc had prepared makeshift hospital beds for Potter and McCord. He gave McCord a series of shots and connected her to an IV. Doc did all he could to stabilize Potter until they got to a medical facility. Several painkillers helped alleviate her pain.

A few other team members had been slightly wounded during the engagement. However, they were all retired special forces types who were experienced in battlefield first aid—never requesting attention for themselves.

Franklin was the last to board the aircraft and immediately took a head count. Before finding his seat, he took a moment to receive an update on the two women.

"Franklin, I'm going to need Madden up here in the copilot's seat," Gray said.

Franklin knew Madden, with his Air Force Combat Controller experience, would be invaluable in supporting Gray in the cockpit, but also knew that McCord needed to have him with her.

"Madden!" Franklin disliked disturbing Madden's care for McCord but got his attention.

"Yes, sir!" Madden continued to lovingly clean McCord with alcohol pads.

"Gray needs you to copilot. I understand you are a certified air traffic controller and can help Gray get us into Argentina—you speak Spanish perfect and know how to speak with the various aircraft controllers."

"I love you," Madden whispered to McCord. He kissed her check and stood. She smiled and closed her eyes.

Finding his way to the cockpit, he took the copilot's seat and buckled in. Gray adjusted the engines and prepared for takeoff.

"Thanks for your help. I need you to monitor the instruments and work the radios and transponder. God knows what we are going to run into on the way to Argentina."

Madden immediately found and adjusted the copilot's radio headset then familiarized himself with the instrument panel.

"Do we have a map and flight plan?" Madden asked.

"No time to brief you, Rob. Here is the plan and the map." Gray handed the materials over then began taxing the Beechcraft onto the long taxiway that paralleled the active runway. The aircraft's ability to takeoff depended on using every inch of the optimum runway. With the wind conditions, it was imperative that Gray taxi the aircraft to the end of the runway, turn the aircraft around, and take off. Gray did not have a choice as he quickly taxied the aircraft down the taxiway and turned the Beechcraft onto the runway. He had spent a few precious minutes taxiing but did not have a choice.

"Shit!" Madden yelled.

Two trucks barreled down the runway aimed right at them. The members in the back of the aircraft were stunned to hear of this sudden disastrous development.

"Are you going to shut her down so we can get out and fight," a scared but calm Madden asked Gray.

"Hold on, Madden." Gray worked the aircraft's controls and taxied the aircraft back to the taxiway.

"What the fuck? Do you plan on taking us back to the hangar?"

"Have everyone strap into their seats," Gray ordered. He positioned the plane to look straight down the taxiway and turned off all of the exterior and interior lighting. "We are taking off on the taxiway," he shouted over the loud and piercing aircraft engines.

"Prepare for takeoff." Gray pushed the Beechcraft's engine throttles to full power. "Keep an eye on our speed. Let me know when we hit 120 knots."

Madden kept an eye on the aircraft instruments while Gray worked the aircraft's controls, with only the adjacent runway lights paralleling the unlit taxiway available to him.

Taking off on a taxiway vs. a runway was extremely dangerous even in perfect conditions during daylight hours, but in the middle of night with no lights, was considered suicidal.

"Eighty knots," Madden announced. The aircraft continued building speed down the bumpy taxiway.

Running down the taxiway unnoticed, the Beechcraft passed a caravan of lit up, what appeared to be police cars, going straight down the runway opposite their direction. The police cars now saw the Beechcraft speeding down the taxi way and immediately turned around racing to catchup with no possible way.

"One hundred knots," Madden announced. A pair of headlights at the far end of the taxiway were coming straight at them. "You see that?"

"Yeah, I see it." Gray knew he might have to unfortunately and dangerously takeoff earlier, way earlier, than considered possible.

"One hundred ten knots," Madden urgently yelled over the loud engines.

"Rotate." Gray pulled the aircraft control back to climb, knowing they were well below the minimum performance requirements. No other options were available. He had to take the risk.

Barely climbing, Gray had no choice but to level the aircraft a few feet above the taxiway—close to skirting it. The pickup lights were closing in on the aircraft's low nose. Playing a game of chicken, the driver of the oncoming vehicle continued his suicidal collision course with the aircraft. Both Gray and Madden remained poised and continued to fly the aircraft straight for the oncoming trucks. They knew there was nothing else to do and prepared for a catastrophic crash.

In the last second, the pickups veered violently to the right to avoid the inevitable collision. Gray continued to barely fly the aircraft down the taxiway, with no acknowledgment of the near tragedy. Speed was built up enough where Gray was able to trim the aircraft into a slow climb to gain altitude.

"Like being in Vietnam again," a grinning Gray commented, glancing at Madden who looked at him in awe.

Madden was shaken and immediately grabbed a bottle of water. The cool liquid helped calm his nerves. He chugged it down in a second and grabbed one for Gray who gratefully accepted.

"Gray, nice job!" Franklin said as he found himself in the observer seat in the cockpit. "We need to make a pass over the hacienda."

"What for?" a curious Gray asked while adjusting the aircraft engine throttles for optimum climb settings.

"Unfinished business." Franklin smirked. He gave a thumbs-up signal to a team member in the back of the aircraft. "Prepare for a firework show and some turbulence."

Two redundant electronic detonation signals, one on a mobile phone and one on a tactical radio, were established to set off the explosives in the hacienda. The explosion was configured to also ignite the natural gas lines running into the hacienda.

The Army DELTA team member returned the thumbs-up and immediately sent the signals for detonation.

The unexpected explosion created a bright fireball that slightly shook the aircraft. Below, the hacienda was no more than a burning pile of debris.

"I'm sure that will send a message to anyone planning to abduct and torture an American citizen, especially those in law enforcement," Franklin boasted then pulled out a couple of large folders from his Army-issued map case and reviewed a few documents.

CHAPTER
36

The Beechcraft continued its slow climb to ten thousand feet. Once there, Gray leveled off to ensure the aircraft's oxygen system was functioning properly prior to climbing to a higher altitude. As the only pilot on board, Gray found the pilot's oxygen mask and immediately began using it in the event the aircraft's cabin pressure function was malfunctioning.

Making a gradual turn to the right, Gray steered the aircraft in a southerly direction toward the Argentine border and directed Madden to put on his oxygen mask before giving him control of the aircraft.

"Madden, would you please monitor the plane while I have a short discussion with Franklin?" Gray requested. Madden nodded with the intent of trying to listen in on this discussion while also monitoring the plane's radios.

"OK, Mr. Franklin." Gray turned in his pilot's seat to have a discussion with Franklin. "We are in a confiscated, drug lord's aircraft with an illegal DEA rescue team who just obliterated the Sola Mesa Drug Cartel with the help of a rival cartel, and we are heading for, what I suspect is, a safe haven in Argentina."

"Pretty exciting, isn't it?" Franklin smiled and nodded his head.

Gray just shook his head.

"Here are the documents I just received from Mercedes." Franklin handed the pilots copies of flight plans and maps.

Gray turned on the cockpit lights to review the plans.

"Mercedes has been working with our embassy in Buenos Aires. We are set to arrive at the El Palomar Air Force Base," briefed Franklin. "Do we have enough fuel to get there?"

Immediately grabbing the aircraft performance manual from the side compartment, Gray double-checked the aircraft fuel gauges with the current estimated time of arrival at El Palomar. "Yes, we have enough fuel. But can the women make a five-hour flight?"

"Doc feels confident he has stabilized Potter's injuries but is anxious to get her to a medical facility soon," Franklin said. "McCord is doing fine but still has moments where she screams. The men are taking extremely good care of both of them."

"Alright then, we'll just hope Mercedes and our people at the embassy work their magic and give us permission to land," Gray said.

"Oh, one other thing," Franklin said, "when we get into Argentina, their air traffic controllers and military radar are going to go ape shit wondering who we are—suspecting we are unidentified drug runners. Given your background, Madden, I suspect you have worked with South American aircraft controllers and can speak their language."

Madden nodded.

"Our aircraft call sign will be Air Mobility Command 45, in short MAC 45, and you will display 4500 in the transponder," directed Franklin. Special operations frequently used safe, nonthreatening MAC call signs to mask their missions. Air Force MAC aircraft carried things around the world and nobody viewed them as a threat.

"What if they ask about the nature of our flight?" Madden asked.

"Tell them we are carrying Bolivian Embassy personnel for specialized medical training in Buenos Aires, and we are sorry for not making the appropriate notifications."

The aircraft glided into the dark Argentine night below a billion stars. The aircraft was performing well and meeting their fuel usage expectations. Suddenly, the radios came to life with urgent calls from the Argentine air traffic and military airspace controllers.

"Unidentified aircraft crossing the Argentine border on a magnetic heading of 170 degrees contact Santiago Center on channel 123.7 and squawk 3401 on your transponder. Over," came the order over the universal aircraft emergency frequency 121.5.

"Good morning, Santiago Center. This is MAC 45, frequency 123.7, squawking 3401, requesting flight level 250," Madden replied, nervously awaiting their reply.

"MAC 45 your request is denied. You are directed to land immediately at Salta Airport. Contact the Salta Airport control tower on frequency 122.4 and descend and maintain five thousand, heading 230. Over."

Gray began a slow decent to five thousand feet, while Madden attempted to explain to the aircraft controllers that they had authorization for a direct flight to El Palomar with no luck.

"If we land, we will most likely be arrested for various crimes, detained, and possibly imprisoned," Gray summarized while briefing Franklin on the situation.

Franklin agreed completely, knowing they had no friends to cover for them at the Salta Airport, and there would be too many questions asked by the local authorities.

In the event they were forced to land, Franklin immediately ordered all the weapons and ammunition jettisoned out of the aircraft immediately since they were at a safe altitude. With all that had happened, they were oblivious to their Bolivian Federal Police uniforms. Franklin ordered them to jettison those as well.

"Follow their instructions, however, be slow in your actions, very slow," Franklin instructed Gray. "Shit, I'll contact Mercedes and brief him on the situation."

The Santiago Center demanded an immediate landing, or the Argentine Air Force would shoot them down for noncompliance. They were unaware of the MAC 45 flight plan and assumed it was a drug cartel aircraft attempting to enter Argentina.

"MAC 45, this is the supervisor at the Santiago Center. How do you read me? Over."

"Santiago Center, this is MAC 45," Madden acknowledged. "Read you loud and clear, sir."

"MAC 45, you are cleared to proceed directly to El Palomar Air Force Base, climb and maintain twenty-five thousand feet. Maintain this radio frequency for further instructions."

"Roger, Santiago Center, proceeding directly to Palomar at twenty-five thousand feet. Over," Madden confirmed.

Pushing the throttles forward, Gray placed the Beechcraft back on its original heading. The aircraft climbed to its original flight level with an estimated time of arrival of four and a half hours.

"Sounds like Mercedes has some pull with someone in the Argentine military—thank God!" a relieved Gray said.

While the MAC 45 sped across the Argentine interior, Mercedes updated Franklin on the plans for their arrival at El Palomar AFB. John Gale, CIA Station Chief in Buenos Aires, had gained permission for Potter and McCord to be admitted to the Hospital Aeronáutico Central. Gale ensured Mercedes that an ambulance would be ready at the base to transport both women to the military hospital.

Franklin spent the next couple of hours in the aircraft conversing with Mercedes over the secure satellite communications system. Both believed, in all probability, the Bolivian government would, in their own best interest, not comment on the rescue mission. They would deny any culpability and would ignore the fact that the United States knowingly stationed a DEA undercover agent in Bolivia. The country's newly elected president thought it prudent not to cause any problems with the United States. The country was receiving an incredible amount of aid from the US to support the new democratic government.

The Bolivian response was easier to imagine than that of the US Justice Department. Hopefully, Bolivia would not request a formal report or issue a complaint and they could all pretend that it never happened. Thinking ahead, Mercedes and Franklin agreed the best course of action would be an internal investigation by the DEA's inspector general—the official responsible for independent and objective investigations in the DEA. Also, an investigation would officially document McCord's bravery and courage during her imprisonment with the Sola Mesa Cartel.

Mercedes was guardedly relieved that Franklin wanted a DOJ investigation. Since DEA was an agency under the Department of Justice, it certainly made sense that they would take the lead. Also, the CIA had no law enforcement powers with their primary job focusing on foreign intelligence. The CIA supported the DEA and the State Department with foreign intelligence and that is exactly what happened with the McCord rescue.

Mercedes and Franklin agreed that an internal DOJ investigation would be the best possible course of action for many reasons.

"There are many advantages for McCord. If she is medically retired due to her numerous injuries, she will be awarded a well-earned pension for the rest of her life," concluded Franklin. "If she is medically qualified to resume her duties, her accomplishments will be recognized with distinguished service awards and advancements with well-earned promotions."

"She was following orders, bottom line," they concluded.

"Potter is a contracted specialist who we hire for certain operations including this rescue mission. She reports directly to me," Mercedes explained. "I will emphatically ensure that she receives the lion's share of the credit of tonight's success and will be rewarded accordingly."

"Just curious, Mercedes, why isn't Potter a full-time General Service employee with your agency?" asked Franklin.

"Potter was one of our top hand-to-hand instructors at our training facility in Virginia, but she got tired of all the bullshit that went along with being a full-time government employee," recounted Mercedes. "We desperately needed her skills in the field, so we had her hired by one of our front companies—everyone won!"

"Before we both get totally engaged in writing our reports, do you have any details about what we can expect when we land?" Franklin asked.

"This is what I know from Gale," Mercedes said, "Your aircraft will be taxied to the Argentina Air Force complex near the civilian airport where our people will ensure your team members are offloaded and escorted to a nice secluded and secure hotel. A change of clothes and meals will be provided to you when you arrive."

"How long before we leave?" Franklin asked.

"Each team member will be given first-class American Airline tickets to the Dallas Fort Worth International Airport. Departure time is tomorrow afternoon 1745L. They will need the bogus passports we provided earlier."

"Understood," Franklin said. "Their immediate departure is a must. We don't need them getting in trouble here."

"Now regarding McCord and Potter, we have arranged for a military ambulance to transport them to the military hospital in Buenos Aires. They will immediately be admitted to the Emergency Services section."

"Are the doctors any good?" Franklin naturally cared for his team.

"John Gale has assured me that he has the best doctors and staff available," Mercedes added. "Argentinians regard working for a military hospital as reaching the top of their medical profession."

"One last request, would it be possible for Rob Madden to stay with McCord in Buenos Aires? There is a strong bond between the two."

"My God, if that is not already obvious," observed Mercedes, smiling. "Yes, of course, we'll ensure Madden can stay with her in her room. Also, sounds to me that having Madden with her will be the best kind of medicine for her."

"Before we get off, how did this agent of yours, John Gale, convince the Argentine Air Force to assist us?" Franklin asked. "I realize we are all friends and we do give them tons of money to fight drug cartels, but is there something else?"

"John Gale made a deal with the commanding officer at El Palomar Air Base: his assistance for the Beechcraft Super King Air."

CHAPTER
37

"MAC 45, this is El Palomar aircraft approach control, you are to land on runway twenty-three," the aircraft controller directed. "Contact ground control for taxi instructions on 121.9 when you land."

"Roger, El Palomar, copy all," Madden replied.

The Beechcraft taxied off the active runway and parked at the military installation's parking ramp in front of two huge aircraft hangars. Government vehicles with lights on met them at the aircraft parking area. Gray was directed to follow a lead vehicle into one of the open hangars. A tow truck appeared, attached a large tow bar to the front wheels, and towed the Beechcraft into the hangar. Uniformed men walked in front of the aircraft and directed it to the middle of the hangar.

Gray saw a hand signal, stopped the plane, and applied the brakes. He sat back for a moment of relief then completed the aircraft shutdown checklist. Gray opened the cockpit windows and released the rear passenger door for opening. A well-groomed, athletic built man wearing what appeared to be an expensive blue suit, climbed aboard the aircraft escorted by two Argentine Air Force security police. The team members remained quiet as the man looked them over. He had expected hearty-looking, dirty men in filthy, bloodstained commando-style clothes after what he had been briefed. Instead, he saw a bunch of worn-out cowboys that just escaped from a pretty rough rodeo, all wearing stained and battered Texas A&M t-shirts.

"What the fuck." CIA Agent John Gale could not believe his eyes.

"You must be John Gale. I'm John Franklin." The team leader walked over and shook hands with the agent.

"Good to meet you, Franklin, and good job to you and your team. Let's get your injured people in the ambulance immediately."

An Argentine Air Force ambulance was parked near the aircraft. A doctor jumped out and boarded the aircraft to make a quick examination of the injured members. The team doctor briefed the Argentinian doctor on Potter's vitals, condition, and treatment. She appeared to be stable, but the sedatives had made her drowsy.

"Good job," the doctor said then turned to two orderlies who had walked in behind him. "Let's get her in the ambulance."

The doctors moved out of the way so the emergency techs could move her to a stretcher. Potter muttered incoherent sentences as she fluttered in and out of consciousness. The men picked her up and carried her off the plane.

"She will be immediately prepared for surgery when we get to the hospital," the military doctor said.

"You'd better bring your lunch if you want to fuck Roberta Potter," she suddenly said to the surprised and stunned doctor escorting her. She was coming in and out of a trance as a result of the drugs she was taking.

The doctor heard it all before in his career and just smiled. "OK, I won't bring my lunch."

Potter was quickly placed in the ambulance where she received a new IV and was hooked up to some monitoring devices.

The military doctor then turned to Bonnie McCord. Rob Madden sat holding her in his arms, tears streaming down his face. The doctor hated to interrupt their time together, but for her sake, it was necessary.

"Excuse me," the doctor softly said while tapping Madden on the shoulder.

"Oh, of course, doctor." Madden let go of McCord and whispered to her, "Sweetheart, the doctor is going to talk with you and take good care of you."

McCord would not let go of Madden's hand. The doctor understood and moved forward with his examination, working around Madden the best he could. Orderlies boarded the aircraft and carefully carried McCord to the ambulance. The doctor followed behind the stretcher.

"Doctor, are you aware of what she has been through these past few weeks?" Madden stopped the doctor before he could leave the aircraft.

"I was given a short briefing by John Gale. My brief examination gave me an idea of the depth of her injuries." The doctor placed a comforting hand on the larger man's shoulder. "Our best medical staff will attend to her. She'll be OK, but it will take time and patience."

"Also, Madden, our staff has dealt with many raped and traumatized women. Rest assured, she is in the best hands."

"Come with me. We'll go to the hospital," the doctor suggested, patting Madden on the back.

Franklin heard the conversation and nodded his approval.

They quickly left the aircraft and settled into the waiting ambulance. Sitting in the back, Madden held McCord's hand. She kept her teary gaze on him.

Back on the plane, Franklin gathered the team around him. The remaining ten members moved into the seats closest to the team leader. More relaxed now that the mission was complete, he chuckled at the sight of his men in their cattle ranch attire.

"In a few minutes, you'll arrive at a hotel where you will find a clean set of clothes and toiletries. An early breakfast is also being arranged for you there. Tomorrow evening at 3:00 PM, a chartered bus will carry you to the nearby international airport for travel back to the US in first class. Make sure you make the bus and have your fake passport."

"How in the hell did we rate first-class tickets home?" asked a dirty, bloody, and sweating Navy SEAL. "We usually are given seats near the toilets."

The team chuckled at his remarks.

"Ok, I'll tell how," Franklin said. "Unbeknownst to you all, there is a well-known philanthropist in Nebraska who funded a large share of this mission."

This surprise announcement caught everyone's attention with much fanfare. "Do we get a large bonus out of this mission?" an Army DELTA member kidded.

"Settle down, fellas," Franklin directed. "Our benefactor asked that each of you be given a first-class ticket home—if you survived." He paused to make sure everyone understood his meaning. "I need not remind you that the mission is top secret. We'll meet up where we started at Webb Air Force Base in Big Springs, Texas, for the formal debriefing in a couple of weeks. Any questions?"

"What about McCord and Potter?" a burly Navy SEAL member asked. "Shouldn't we stay together so all of us return together?"

"I completely understand your sentiments; however, for their safety and yours, it is best you leave Argentina immediately. No use raising suspicion about our presence."

"Yes, sir. I understand," the frustrated SEAL replied.

"They'll stay here until they receive clearance to travel back to the US." Franklin held up his hands. "I know what you're thinking, but John Gale assures us that their military hospitals are the best. And he will have his private agency doctor checking in daily."

The men seemed satisfied with the care being given to the two women.

"Well, if there are no more questions, I look forward to seeing you in two weeks. You'll be advised of times and dates."

A nondescript tourist bus arrived. The friendly driver opened the door, and they began climbing aboard.

"Excuse me, señor," the inquisitive bus driver asked, looking at the strange assortment of ranch clothes. "May I ask what you do for a living?"

"Well, señor, we hate to brag but we are all university professors working with Argentine ranchers to breed healthier Zebu cattle," the team member said. The bus driver stared at them with awe. "And I'll tell you, señor, these Zebu cattle can be very tough to work with."

"It certainly appears so." The confused driver shut the bus door and headed for the team's contract hotel.

CHAPTER
38

"Both McCord and Potter have been admitted to the hospital's intensive care unit," Franklin updated Mercedes.

"Good work, Franklin." Mercedes praised his efforts. "I realize it is too soon to tell, but as soon as you can, find out when both women can travel. We'll get them home."

"Right, I'll contact Madden," Franklin added. "He's a retired Air Combat Controller. I am sure he has worked hundreds of medevac flights in his career and can possibly assist in requesting one."

"Good idea! Any words on McCord?" Mercedes hoped for the best.

"He's continually by her bedside, holding her hand and stroking her hair. Ah, love." Franklin paused for a moment. "Mercedes, one more thing, the chief resident says she was pregnant before her abduction. The beatings and horrific sex acts on McCord have taken their toll on her—mentally and physically. I'll get back to you with more updates as soon as I get them."

On both ends of the phone there was silence as the men grappled with their emotions; however, tears streamed down their faces.

"Did McCord know about this?" a teary-eyed Mercedes asked.

"I'm not sure, but do not believe it wise to mention this to her during her treatment here or even later back in the States."

"Let's keep it quiet for now, and if this question of pregnancy rises, we'll let our professionals work it," Mercedes recommended. Franklin concurred.

"Also, the rest of the team is heading back to Texas tomorrow evening," Franklin added. "Apparently, their work with breeding Zebu cattle in Bolivia was a huge success."

Mercedes laughed for the first time in weeks. "When are you departing, Franklin?"

"Just as soon as I feel confident that McCord and Potter are progressing well."

"Couple of quick updates for you, Franklin. John Gale is going to take the lead in their care while in Argentina. I believe he has his own security force of agents in the hospital now."

"Very good!" a relieved Franklin sighed.

"Word is going to get out on the street soon about McCord's rescue." Franklin was beginning to be concerned about the repercussions of the rescue and the efforts leading up to it.

"Franklin," a now stern Mercedes requested, "we will need to talk at length this afternoon to coordinate our after-action reports. There is a lot that will be happening that you need to be aware of and might even surprise you."

"All of it is classified top secret," Mercedes warned.

"Right!" was the only answer Franklin dared give, knowing Mercedes was up to something.

CHAPTER

39

"I'll be darned," mumbled Jose Mercedes as he read the headline from the USA Today newspaper.

American Law Enforcement Agent Rescued by Bolivian Federal Police Raid.

"In an early morning raid lead by the Bolivian Federal Police, the abducted DEA Special Agent Bonnie McCord was rescued from her abductors at the hacienda that was the headquarters for the Sola Mesa Drug Cartel. Reports indicate that McCord was tortured and raped repeatedly by cartel members in retaliation for her undercover work reporting on cartel operations. McCord was barely alive and was initially cared for by Bolivian care providers before boarding a US Air Force Critical Care Air Transport for the trip back to the US."

"Inquiries into the raid with the Bolivian government and Bolivian Federal Police have gone unanswered, explaining that much of the planning and execution of the raid was highly classified. The raid resulted in the deaths of several cartel members and the total destruction of the cartel's hacienda near Santa Cruz. Surviving Sola Mesa Cartel members reported that the raid was led by the Bolivian Federal Police. No further details are known at this time."

"Doctor Mercedes," came the call on his intercom.

"Yes," Mercedes slowly answered, smiling as he put down the paper.

"Sir, the ambassador would like to see you in his office immediately," came the urgent call from the ambassador's executive officer.

Anticipating such a call, Mercedes grabbed a thick folder of documents and proceeded to the ambassador's office. Mercedes sat quietly in the outer office, reviewing one of his many memos and reports he was responsible for reviewing. The ambassador's door opened, and Mercedes was escorted in by an administrative clerk. Ambassador Burton sat silently as he came in. Usually when guests entered the office, the ambassador stood and offered them a seat, but not on this occasion. Ambassador Burton was beet red and nervously twitching. Mercedes took a seat in front of Burton's desk.

"Doctor Mercedes, I just received a phone call from the Secretary of State wanting to know more about the rescue of DEA Agent McCord by the Bolivian Federal Police." The ambassador slammed a file full of papers on his desk. "Did you have anything to do with this? What part did you and your agency play in this?" He pointed a finger in Mercedes' face. "I know you had something to do with this. Don't deny it."

Not waiting for Mercedes to respond, his voice raised as he continued. "Half the world is sending congratulations to the President of Bolivia, who has yet to disclose any details of the raid. Other than taking credit for it, of course. Damn it, man! He expects a little reciprocity in the way of cash and resources."

"I'll be darned." Mercedes had a concerned look on his face but was laughing within. "Do you think they will go after other cartels like they did the Sola Mesa?" He smiled at the angry ambassador. "At least we didn't have to trade five Bolivian cartel members in our prisons for McCord."

"Get out of my office now, you son of a bitch!" Burton yelled.

Mercedes rose and made it to the office door where he stopped and faced Burton. "Oh, all those little secrets about your personal life are safe with me, ambassador. I'd like to keep it that way."

Mercedes smiled then went back to his office to drop off the reports. An espresso at his favorite coffee bar was in order. He made the short walk, enjoying the beautiful weather.

"Who knows what today may bring," he said to Manuel Vargas, the owner. Mercedes sat at his favorite table under the line of trees on the boulevard. He took a drink of the espresso and listened to the birds chirping.

Mercedes had just pulled off one of the most incredible and dramatic CIA operations in South America. And he managed to end the control wielded by the Sola Mesa Cartel.

He soaked up the sun, enjoying a moment of peace and reading various international newspapers. A sixth sense told Mercedes there was something wrong. Two well-dressed men walked up the avenue's sidewalk toward him. Instinctively, he pulled his pistol out of the holster under his coat jacket. The men made a beeline for him while pulling their weapons out. They fired shots directly at him before he had a chance to aim his pistol. Two hit their mark. Mercedes reeled while attempting to shoot. Luckily, he hit one of his attackers. The surviving assassin jumped into a waiting car and flew down the avenue.

"Dios mío." Manuel Vargas witnessed the shooting and had his cashier immediately call for an ambulance and the police. Vargas raced to his friend's side on the sidewalk and quickly judged that he was still alive.

The man Mercedes hit slowly rose from the ground and came toward them with his pistol raised. He was going to finish the job.

"A little payback from the Sola Mesa Cartel, bastardo." The now lone assassin aimed his pistol at the lifeless Mercedes.

Boom.

Vargas had picked up Mercedes' pistol and shot the assassin before he could fire. The assassin fell to the ground. Several medical professionals, also enjoying their morning espresso at the Caffettino, rushed forward to give assistance to the hurt agent.

CHAPTER
40

Special DEA Agent Bonnie McCord and CIA Contractor Roberta Potter landed at Joint Base Andrews on the US Air Force Medical Transport aircraft and were immediately transferred to an awaiting US Marine Medical Evacuation helicopter that flew them to Walter Reed National Military Medical Center. A specialized team of doctors and medical staff met the two women at the helicopter landing pad and rushed them to ICU. Rob Madden remained by McCord's side during her treatment, holding her hand and speaking softly to her.

A knock on the door to McCord's room startled Madden and McCord.

"May I come in?" asked a pleasant looking woman wearing a white doctor's lab coat with "Colonel Maggie Nordland MD" stitched above the coat's pocket.

Madden rose to meet the visitor while still holding McCord's hand. It was obvious McCord did not want to let go of him. The doctor understood.

"Good morning, Bonnie, and I suspect you are Chief Master Sergeant Rob Madden," she greeted them. "I am Doctor Maggie Nordland. Welcome to Walter Reed. I am a resident physician here and look forward to being part of the team caring for you."

Nordland was the hospital's resident psychologist whose specialty was women with Post Traumatic Stress Disorder as a result of sexual assault. She made her way to McCord's bedside, smiling.

"You make a lovely couple." Nordland stood near the bed on the opposite side from Madden. His hawkish gaze analyzed her every move.

"Thank you." Madden squeezed McCord's hand. He glanced quickly at her to ensure she was OK before returning his gaze to the doctor.

"Bonnie, do you mind if I take a seat here next to you for a few minutes?" Nordland patiently asked.

"Please, doctor." McCord gave a faint smile and nodded her head.

Slowly taking her seat, Nordland never took her eyes off McCord. "Bonnie how are you feeling today?"

"I am very grateful to be here." Tears swam in McCord's eyes.

The doctor noticed the tears unsure if they were from relief or if this was a bad time to discuss her recent trauma. Her years of experience told her to proceed with some basic questions.

"Is there anything we can do for you right now? Perhaps a drink?" Nordland asked.

"Gosh, a diet coke would be great," McCord replied.

"Absolutely, Bonnie. Do you mind if I have one also?" Nordland thought sharing a drink together would provide an opportunity to get McCord to open up. They spent a few minutes talking about benign topics.

"Doctor, can I talk to you about some things that I went through?" McCord asked while avoiding eye contact.

Sweat broke out on Madden's forehead. He had no desire to listen to her ordeal. He asked Bonnie if he could excuse himself for a short while.

"I'll be here for you, sweetheart." Madden bent over and kissed her forehead.

It appeared to Madden that Doctor Nordland was a seasoned professional. He felt confident she would place McCord on the road to recovery.

After a while, he returned to McCord's room and found her asleep. It was quiet in her room except for a young nursing assistant who startled him.

"Are you Chief Master Sergeant Madden?" the nursing assistant asked while checking the IV.

"Yes, I am."

"Doctor Nordland asked that you receive this." She handed him an envelope with a note in it. He opened and read the note asking him to meet with her in the hospital office—if it was before 8:00 PM. Madden left quietly and walked to her office. After going through the maze of departments and offices, he found hers and politely knocked on her door.

"Just a moment please," Nordland replied. "Who is it?"

"Doctor, I'm Rob Madden. You requested to see me, ma'am."

"Please come in," Nordland replied.

He looked around her spacious office. Framed degrees and certifications surrounded the walls as an "I love me wall." In his past life in the military, many high ranking officers placed and framed all of their decorations, diplomas, letters, etc. on a wall in their office. The intent of the wall was to impress visitors coming into their offices. The term was a joke directed toward officers who thought too much of themselves. Ironically, most service members had equivalent items to place on a wall, but elected not to, not wanting to be show-offs.

"Please have a seat, Rob. May I call you Rob?"

"Of course, Colonel," Madden said.

"Call me, Maggie."

Looking at Nordland, Madden could tell that she had been crying. Her eyes were red, and tears had ruined her makeup.

"Rob, I'll cut to the chase regarding Bonnie's condition and be advised, she has given me authorization to speak with you about her health." Nordland showed him McCord's authorization to brief him. "There are several issues about Bonnie. I'll lay it to you straight—but definitely not to her now. There eventually will be a time and place to tell her once she has recovered.

"From what she has said, it is obvious that you and Bonnie have a trusting and therapeutic relationship. Each of you believes in and wants to help the other.

"After reviewing her service record with the DEA, I found her to be an independent, competitive, and tough woman who wanted to be recognized for her work and achievements. Am I reading this correct?"

"Yes, your observations are correct," he confirmed.

"I believe because of her character and determination, and with you by her side, after our treatment and rehabilitation, Bonnie will probably slow down a little and appreciate her love and companionship with you.

"However, Rob, there are no guarantees that Bonnie will not develop mental health disorders as a result of her experience. Be aware, studies have indicated that the majority of women who have experienced intense sexual violations, also had histories of depression, bipolar disorder, post-traumatic stress, substance use, and various forms of anxiety.

"You'll receive more intense briefings on these issues, but for now, we are working to get her vitals under control and rid her of any sexually transmitted diseases she may have been contracted."

"I understand." Madden had a sense there was something else she wanted to discuss. It was obvious she was getting emotional with tears coming from her eyes. There had to be a reason a box of tissues was sitting next to the visitor's chairs.

"Rob, did you know Bonnie was pregnant when she was in Bolivia?" Nordland came right to the point.

Madden could not answer. He was totally surprised and stunned. They had wanted to raise a family together and planned to actively try when her assignment was completed in Bolivia.

"With all the horrific abuse she endured in Bolivia, I am sure it was aborted."

"Oh my God, oh my God." The tissues next to Madden's chair were useful as streams of tears flowed down his face.

Nordland got up from her desk and sat next to him, not saying a word. It took some time for Madden to regain his composure.

"I should not have let her go to Bolivia. I should have been their sooner." He dropped his face into his hands. "I should have married her and kept her home."

The blame went on for several minutes. Nordland gave him the time he needed to vent and release his emotions.

"Will she be able to have children in the future?" Madden asked but didn't have much hope.

"Probably not," replied Nordland. "Rob, she is going to get through this with her health, and frankly, she is lucky to be alive."

"Did she even know she was pregnant?"

"She might have had her suspicions as early as it was," Nordland answered. "But with all she has gone through, who knows."

For the next hour, Nordland and Madden talked about McCord's future care.

She stood and escorted Madden to her office door.

"Rob, go back to Bonnie's room and be with her. She's waiting for you." Nordland laid a hand on his shoulder as a gesture of comfort. "I'll be in to check on her this evening. Right now, you are the best medicine we can give her."

Madden nodded his head and found his way back to McCord, focused on getting her well. They had a future together and much to share.

CHAPTER
41

A knock sounded on McCord's hospital door. "May I come in?"

It had been one week since their arrival to Walter Reed, but visitors continued to come by. Madden stood to see who the visitor was while the nurse replaced the medication in Bonnie's IV.

"Can I help you, sir? Madden asked the well-dressed and groomed man wearing a DEA Agent lapel pin on his suit collar. "You do realize this is a restricted area?"

"Yes, Chief Madden. I'm Doctor Fred Tafoya. I am the Administrator for the Drug Enforcement Administration," Tafoya introduced himself and directed his attention to McCord who was now sitting up in her hospital bed.

Madden was in no mood to play nice with the DEA leadership after their screw-ups in Bolivia. Tafoya could sense Madden's ill feelings toward him but understood.

"Good Morning, Special Agent McCord. It is an honor to finally meet you." McCord just stared at Tafoya with no emotion but remembered she was still a DEA agent and would act accordingly. Colonel Nordland quietly entered the room and stood in the background. She didn't want Tafoya's visit to upset her patient.

"Bonnie, may I have a seat?" Tafoya asked. With her approval, he sat in the chair next to the hospital bed. McCord noticed Tafoya had tears coming down his face and drew a handkerchief from his back pocket. McCord didn't know what to make of it and was somewhat confused that one of the most powerful government leaders in America was at her bedside crying. All was silent in the room, except for the vital monitors reporting McCord's health.

"Bonnie, I am so very sorry about what happened to you in Bolivia and consider the incident to be all my fault," Tafoya confessed. "I failed to adequately oversee the special mission our people placed you on."

"The preliminary Department of Justice Inspector General's report showed your performance was stellar—above and beyond that normally expected of a DEA agent. You are now promoted to your next highest pay grade. You have your choice of assignments if you wish to remain with the DEA." Tafoya glanced at the psychologist who nodded her head in encouragement. "Of course, if you wish, a medical retirement would be more than possible."

McCord and Madden were unprepared for the administrator's visit and subsequent promotion. They were surprised to hear that she had the option of another assignment or medical retirement. They looked questioningly at each other, trying to comprehend what she was just offered.

Tafoya leaned in his chair toward McCord.

"Bonnie, we cannot make up for the mistakes we have made, but we are doing our best to make it right for you now. That is all we can do." Tafoya placed a DEA Purple Heart medal on McCord's bedside. "This is in honor of the trauma you suffered at the hands of the Sola Mesa Cartel."

A few tears of joy trickled down her cheeks. She reached out to shake Tafoya's hand. He carefully took her hand to avoid causing further pain.

"Doctor Tafoya, sir," McCord slowly and softly asked. "What about the men on the rescue team and Roberta Potter?"

"They are being recognized and handsomely rewarded for their courageous and selfless acts in freeing you."

"What about Roberta Potter? Is she doing OK after her injuries from the fight with Castillo?" McCord asked.

"I'm surprised a thug like Castillo got the best of her knowing her reputation. In fact, the hospital staff has advised me she needs to calm down and allow her injuries to heal." Tafoya grinned. "She needs to stop picking fights with the Marines on her floor."

Rising, Tafoya extended his hand to Madden, and they shook hands.

"I understand you were enrolled in a doctoral program in education at Stanford University in California before McCord's abduction in Bolivia. Is this correct?" Tafoya asked.

"Yes, sir. That is correct," Madden said. "But Bonnie is my only priority now."

"Well, I took the liberty of contacting Stanford's president and he advised me that you will be welcome to continue your pursuit of the doctorate degree at any time." Tafoya pulled a business card out of his pocket and handed it to the other man. "Here is my personal contact information. If I can assist you and Bonnie in any way, contact me immediately."

With a quick pat on Madden's back, Tafoya left with Nordland following behind him.

With the DEA director's departure, Madden moved over to the chair next to McCord, leaned over, and gave her a big kiss while she found his hand and held it. Their eyes locked.

CHAPTER
42

Months passed while DEA Special Agent McCord continued her treatment for PTSD and other serious injuries that resulted from her abduction and torturous treatment by the Sola Mesa Drug Cartel. Further treatment was provided by various government medical facilities around the Washington D.C. area. As her condition improved, she was invited to speak at several DEA functions, including new employee orientations, special agent graduations, and course presentations at the DEA Academy at Quantico, Virginia. The medical professionals believed her participation in such functions improved her morale and were useful to other DEA members.

Madden escorted McCord to all her medical appointments and DEA functions. Standard University granted his request for a leave of absence from his pursuit of a doctoral degree in education. Stanford education professors provided Madden with courses and required readings he could accomplish away from the university—until he returned. He greatly appreciated their efforts so he could continue his studies while also caring for McCord.

McCord and Madden could be seen walking hand-in-hand through the various parks and monuments of the capital. At night, they counted their blessings and saving grace for their second chance in life. They remembered the brave woman and men that volunteered to rescue her.

"Rob," McCord announced one night while Madden was making dinner for them. "It is time for us to decide when we are going to marry and where we are going to live."

Madden stared at her for moment, took off his apron, and walked over to McCord. He hugged and kissed her like never before.

"You are a part of me, Rob."

"OK, Bonnie, we have so many wonderful options ahead of us." Madden picked her up and carried her to the bedroom. "What do you think, where are we going to start?"

"The first thing we are going to do is get married," McCord ordered.

CHAPTER
43

"Good morning, ladies and gentlemen," the tall, attractive, and professionally dressed flight attendant announced over the aircraft's intercom system. "Could I please have your attention?" The announcement woke the tired passengers on Avianca Airlines flight 283.

"We are a few minutes away from landing at Dulles International Airport. Please ensure all your personal items are stowed away, and you have your seatbelt fastened," the flight attendant instructed. The flight attendants made a routine inspection to ensure everything was ready for landing.

"Excuse me, sir," the first-class flight attendant Carol Stotts approached a passenger with a long black ponytail and expensive gold rings who had not fastened his seatbelt. A half-finished shot of vodka sat on the tray while he worked on his laptop. "Please put on your seatbelt and put away your computer for landing."

The passenger's deadly stare matched his lack of facial expression. A few moments lapsed as he focused on the attractive face and well-proportioned breasts of the flight attendant.

She had asked thousands of passengers in her career to use their seatbelts and discontinue using electronic devices, but she could tell by his deadly stare he would be trouble. The man seemed used to having his own way. "Sir, I am sorry for the inconvenience, but we do need you to fasten your seatbelt and turn off your electronic device prior to landing," she asked politely again.

The athletically built man grudgingly followed her instructions as if he was doing her a big favor by complying. The passenger had made several unwanted advances to her for most of the eleven-hour flight from La Paz, Bolivia. He slowly reached in his tailored suit pocket for his business card and several hundred-dollar bills. The well-known womanizer had connections with the largest drug cartels in Bolivia.

Roberto Castillo was the son of the late Juan Castillo— former head of the infamous and notorious Sola Mesa Drug Cartel in Bolivia. Despite his elite education complete with a law degree, he enjoyed being the rich boss' son. No actual responsibilities meant he had more time for women, parties, and fútbol.

His father decided that Roberto would not be involved with the family's drug operations. The legitimacy and popularity of his son's soccer career added to the Castillo family reputation. More importantly, Juan didn't want his son involved in the dangerous and illegal business that had sent many other family and cartel members to jail or the morgue.

Traveling to Washington DC this hot summer day, Roberto represented the Castillo family and the Bolivian Zebu Cattle Owners Club in lobbying congress regarding the economic benefits of producing Zebu cattle in the United States. Besides his family's reputation as a powerful drug cartel, the Castillos were well-known and respected cattle ranchers. Roberto was planning on making his pitch to the representatives of the United States Congress and then flying on to Denver for the Western National Stock Show, where the Club had many cattle entries.

"Sir," the flight attendant said while bending down in the aircraft aisle getting close to the passenger. He paid more attention to the mysteries up her revealing skirt. "I am flattered you gave me your business card; however, airline regulations prevent me from taking such a gift." She intentionally moved her hand, so he noticed the large diamond wedding ring on her finger, which, as she well knew, meant nothing to him. She pressed the card and money back in his hand, stood, and continued through the cabin.

"Fuckin' bitch," Roberto mumbled and showed a devilishly sly grin as he continued eying her movements. The flight attendant took her seat for landing, giving him a nice view of toned, shapely legs under her form-fitting skirt. He caught many passengers also eyeing the woman appreciatively as the aircraft landed and taxied to its assigned parking area.

"Ladies and gentlemen, welcome to Dulles International Airport," the flight attendant announced. "Please remain in your seats until the aircraft has come to a complete stop at the terminal. Airline representatives will greet you upon leaving the aircraft and guide you to customs and the baggage claim area. Please have your Custom Declarations forms completed prior to entering the custom's area and have your passports ready."

"On behalf of the Avianca flight crew, it has been a pleasure flying with you today, and we look forward to flying with you again soon." The charismatic flight attendant hoped the obnoxiously friendly passenger in first class left quickly without incident.

As the passengers began flowing through the aisle and exiting the aircraft, she noticed one first-class passenger still in his seat on the phone. The last of the passengers was about to exit when the passenger got up, grabbed his carry-on, and slowly made his way toward the flight attendant.

"I want to know you better, mi dulce," he whispered near her ear while thrusting his business card and a wad of one-hundred-dollar bills in her uniform pocket. With his free hand, he grabbed her bottom and gave a squeeze.

The flight attendant immediately pushed him away. The captain had witnessed the sexual harassment and intervened, immediately positioning himself between her and the passenger. With a stern warning, the captain discreetly pressed the passenger off the plane. The taller man laughed and threw down a few hundred-dollar bills on the exit ramp, then headed for baggage claim and customs.

Roberto Castillo was written on a sign held by what appeared to be a chauffeur inside the baggage claim area. The professionally dressed man spotted Roberto at the arrival lobby, quickly made a beeline for him, and immediately picked up his luggage.

"Señor Castillo," the man affectionately addressed Roberto, "it is good to see you again. I have taken care of everything for your stay here in Washington."

"George, very good to see you again, and thank you for meeting me here," Roberto sincerely said.

"Señor, please follow me to the limo, and we can discuss your trip."

After ensuring the luggage was placed in the limo with care, George opened the rear passenger door for Roberto, closed it after him, and quickly jumped in the driver's seat. It would take at least an hour to get to the hotel.

"Señor, we have you staying at the Willard Hotel on Pennsylvania Avenue as you requested." The historic hotel was close to the White House and known for its luxurious suites and important guests.

"Perfecto, George. I'll plan on making my congressional visits tomorrow morning and head out to Denver in the evening for the Western National Stock Show."

"Señor, I'll ensure all is ready for tomorrow's schedule. Will you be needing anything else for today?" George asked.

"Thank you, George, but no. I have some people I need to meet this evening near the capital," Roberto said. "The walk will do me good."

"Very good, señor," George confirmed. "We'll be ready tomorrow morning for your capital visits."

After checking in to the Willard Hotel in early afternoon, Roberto exchanged his expensive Alexander Amosu Vanquish II Bespoke business suit for a pair of Levi jeans, polo shirt, and a pair of Asics walking shoes. He was looking forward to walking around the National Mall and Ellipse as he had done many times in the past. However, besides the pleasure of a walk, he had another, more sinister purpose. He made the easy walk from the Willard to the Ellipse. He found a private, secluded set of park chairs under a huge Sycamore tree where he sat and reflected on the past year.

A year where the DEA and CIA destroyed the family's hacienda and many of their employees, a year where Bolivian Federal Police assisted the US Feds in bringing down the Sola Mesa Cartel, and a year where an undercover DEA agent murdered his father in his own hacienda. So went the legend as described by the sole survivors of the "Hacienda massacre," as it was now known.

"Excuse me, sir."

The male voice startled Roberto. He blinked rapidly, trying to bring his mind back to the present.

"Sir, excuse us, but may we share these chairs with you?" the unexpected visitor asked.

Roberto, half awake, looked up to see two men pleasantly looking down on him napping. After a few moments, he recalled the men working for his late father. These loyal associates had managed various banking and business ventures, growing the cartel's accounts. They could be trusted.

Carlos Castro and James Rodriquez wore casual yet expensive business suits commonly worn by Washington high rollers—especially investment bankers and influence peddlers. Both grew up in elite families in La Paz, Bolivia, and were educated at the finest educational institutions in Bolivia and the United States. Juan Castillo used his power and influence to ensure Castro and Rodriquez were positioned in areas most beneficial to his cartel. Both owed their rise and success to Juan Castillo.

"Roberto, it has been a long time since we have seen you." Castro smiled. "Last time I saw you, you were playing fútbol in Santa Cruz."

"Yes, those were good days, my old friend," Roberto replied. "Good and happier days."

"We are all saddened at the passing of your most beloved father, who we owe our lives," Rodriquez said, a hint of emotion entering his normally monotone voice. "I still cannot wrap my head around what actually happened at the hacienda."

Roberto stood and stretched for a minute to collect his thoughts. He sat and briefed the two men on what he knew about the raid on the hacienda gathered from cartel eyewitnesses who survived that night. "According to unsubstantiated reports, the undercover DEA agent held at the hacienda killed my father with numerous pistol shots. The Bolivian State Police and a DEA rescue team rescued her and arranged for her safe passage to the United States."

"She recently was released from the Walter Reed Medical Center for various serious injuries," Roberto explained. "McCord is currently going through rehabilitation in the DC area."

"What is the agent's name?" Castro asked sternly, while typing notes into his smartphone.

"Bonnie McCord," replied Roberto.

"Roberto, you recall that American saying, 'paybacks are bitches?'" Castro said with a smirk on his face.

ACKNOWLEDGMENTS

I would like to acknowledge the support and professional efforts of Cynthia Croon (artist), the City of La Vista Public Library, along with Concierge Publishing Services, and editor, Misti Moyer. Your guidance and support of *Saving Bonnie* made the book possible.

www.ingramcontent.com/pod-product-compliance
Lightning Source LLC
Chambersburg PA
CBHW020640260626
47157CB00008B/2836